They... ...ever die...

like...
in...
fing...
eye...
ma...
hac...

Ho...
wa...

His...
eig...

Im...
tim...
yo...
his...

Ma...
ma...
bu...

BEVERLY
BARTON
worth dying for

HQN™

ISBN 0-373-77012-X

WORTH DYING FOR

This edition published by arrangement with Harlequin Books S.A.

® and TM are trademarks of the publisher. Trademarks indicated with ® are registered in the United States Patent and Trademark Office, the Canadian Trade Marks Office and in other countries.

www.HQNBooks.com

Printed in U.S.A.

In memory of my parents,
Doris and Dee Jr.,
young lovers, tragically parted too soon.
His heart went with her long ago and
now his soul has joined hers forever.

PROLOGUE

I hold it true, whate'er befall;
I feel it, when I sorrow most;
'Tis better to have loved and lost
Than never to have loved at all.
—Lord Alfred Tennyson

WHERE IS HE? Amy wondered. It wasn't like Dante to keep her waiting. During the ten months they'd been dating, he had proven himself to be trustworthy and reliable. Wary of people in general, she had made him earn her trust. She hadn't even let him kiss her until they'd been going out for nearly two months.

He would be here soon. Whenever she had to work late, as she had tonight, he made a point of being there when she got off so he could drive her home. Tapping her foot nervously, Amy checked her watch. He was already ten minutes late.

The November wind picked up, seeping through her thin sweater. She should have brought a jacket.

Of course hindsight was twenty-twenty. A piece of paper whirled through the air and floated down the sidewalk, then landed on the curb. Maybe she should go wait back inside where it was warm.

Just as she turned to open the door of the Dairy Dip, where she worked after school three evenings a week and all day on Saturdays, Jerry Vinson came outside and locked the door behind him. Jerry was part owner and full-time manager of Colby, Texas's only local fast-food restaurant.

"Dante still hasn't shown up?" Jerry asked. "This is the first time he hasn't been here waiting on you at quitting time."

"I know." Amy rubbed her palms up and down her arms in an effort to warm herself. "Something must be wrong. He probably had car trouble. He has to work on that old Mustang all the time just to keep it going."

"Want me to wait with you until he shows up?"

Jerry and his wife, Lorna, were new parents, and Amy understood how eager Jerry was to go home to Lorna and their six-week-old son.

"No, you go home," she told him. "I'm sure Dante will be here soon. Besides, this isn't Dallas or Houston. This is Colby. It's not as if I won't be safe on a downtown street at ten o'clock."

Jerry chuckled. "Yeah, you're right. But if Dante doesn't show soon, go to the corner pay phone and call me. Or if you don't want to wait, you can go with me now and I'll run you over to the Morrisons on my way home."

She shook her head. "I'll wait for Dante. If I'm gone when he gets here, he'll worry. And if he shows up at the Morrisons to check on me, they won't like it. They're good people and they've been kind to me, but they think I'm too young to be serious about any guy, especially a guy like Dante."

"It's your life, kid," Jerry said, a concerned frown on his round, rosy face. "But your foster folks have a point, you know. Dante's pretty rough around the edges and you're a sweet and innocent seventeen-year-old."

"Dante's only nineteen."

"Yeah, nineteen going on thirty-five."

Amy sighed. She'd heard it all before—from the Morrisons, from Jerry and even from a couple of her teachers. How could she make anyone else understand what she knew in her heart—that Dante Moran was a good man? The man she loved. The man she wanted to spend the rest of her life with.

"Go home. I'll be fine." Amy smiled warmly at Jerry. "Stop playing big brother."

She knew he meant well, just as everyone else did when they doled out advice. But no one could imagine what it was like to be her. To have lost both parents when she was in first grade. To have spent the past eleven years being shuffled from one foster home to another. More than anything she wanted a family of her own. With Dante, she could have that family.

"Call me if he doesn't show."

"He'll be here soon. Don't worry."

Nodding, Jerry grinned at her and then headed off around the building and into the alley behind the Dairy Dip where his car was parked.

Huddling in the doorway, seeking protection from the wind, Amy hugged herself as she looked up the street, hoping for a glimpse of Dante's car. *Please, hurry up.* If he didn't pick her up soon, they wouldn't have any time together tonight. The Morrisons expected her to be at home no later than ten-thirty on weeknights, which usually gave her only thirty minutes with Dante. She lived for those precious minutes when he held her in his arms and kissed her and told her how much he loved her.

One day soon, she and Dante would be together all the time, without having to follow other people's rules and meet her foster parents' strict curfews. Dante and she had a secret, one they couldn't share with anyone else. They were engaged and planned to marry when she turned eighteen next May and graduated from high school. Two weeks ago they had exchanged rings—symbols of their commitment to each other. He'd given her a half-carat diamond, which he jokingly said he would be paying for until he was on social security. She had given him her father's diamond and onyx ring. She had worn that ring around her neck on a chain ever since she was six and the social worker had given her a small bag containing several personal items that had belonged to her parents.

Now she kept her engagement ring on the chain around her neck and always made sure it was well hidden beneath her clothes. But in seven and a half months, she could proudly wear her engagement ring, along with a wedding band. She longed for that day. There was nothing she wanted more than to be Dante's wife. She loved him so much, more than anything, more than life itself. No matter what anybody said, what she felt was true love, the kind that would last a lifetime. In her heart of hearts, she knew that Dante and she would love each other forever.

As she waited impatiently, several cars passed by, but she didn't see anyone on the streets. Colby's Main Street wasn't very crowded after dark and was all but deserted after ten o'clock. The Dairy Dip stayed open until ten, which was a good hour after most other places had closed.

Amy heard rather than saw the stranger as he approached. Soft footsteps, the kind made by athletic shoes on the pavement. Probably just a jogger, out for an evening run, she thought as the man approached her. She looked at him, a smile on her face. Folks in Colby tended to be friendly, even to people they didn't know, and she didn't recognize the man who paused when he drew near.

"Evening," he said, his voice husky and quiet.

"Evening," Amy replied.

She realized he wasn't dressed for jogging in his faded jeans and bulky knit sweater. A trickle of uneasiness danced up her spine. Don't be silly, she told herself. This man doesn't look dangerous. His brown hair was cut conservatively short, with just a hint of curliness. His hazel brown eyes, clean-shaven face and average features broadcast Ordinary Joe to Amy. Just an average-looking guy, not some freaky character she should fear.

"Are you waiting for someone?" he asked.

"Yes, my boyfriend is picking me up."

"He shouldn't keep a pretty girl like you waiting."

"He usually doesn't. I figure he had car trouble."

The man moved closer. Amy's heartbeat accelerated. A foreboding sense of doom tightened her stomach muscles.

He smiled. She didn't like his smile. There was something sinister about the way he looked at her, as if he knew something she didn't know. Amy shrank away from him, her back pressing against the locked front door of the Dairy Dip.

I can scream, she told herself. *Someone will hear me.*

She opened her mouth, intending to tell him to leave her alone or she would scream, but before she could utter one word, he whipped a handkerchief out of his pocket, grabbed her and shoved the foul-smelling handkerchief over her nose and mouth.

Oh, God! Help me!

She struggled against his superior strength, but within moments she realized she was going to pass out.

Dante! Dante, where are you?

DANTE DROVE at breakneck speed, all the way from the junior college campus into town. He'd already kept Amy waiting nearly twenty-five minutes. By now she was probably chilled to the bone and worried sick. When he'd come out of his night class, which had run late by fifteen minutes, and saw the right front tire on the old Mustang was flat, he'd used a nearby pay phone to call the Dairy Dip. Apparently, Jerry had already locked up and left for the night because no one had answered.

Maybe Amy had caught a ride home with Jerry. No, she would wait, he told himself. He picked her up every night that she worked so they could have a few stolen moments together. Thirty damn minutes. Crazy how his whole life revolved around the time he spent with her. Amy's foster parents, the Morrisons, were nice people, but they didn't approve of her dating him. They had a problem with him being a couple of years older and a lot more experienced. When he'd first met Amy, the only thing he'd had on his mind was how long it would take him to get in her pants. Hell, that's all he'd ever wanted from a girl. Sex. And God knew Amy was the kind of girl who made a guy hard just looking at her. Blue-eyed, blond-haired and built like the proverbial brick shit-house.

But Amy Smith hadn't fallen into his arms the way most girls did. From the time he'd been fourteen, girls had been chasing him. Was it his fault that they found him irresistible? Dante chuckled softly to himself.

When he'd met Amy ten months ago, he'd already left behind a string of broken hearts and had intended to make Amy one more notch on his bedpost. But Amy hadn't even let him kiss her for a couple of months. At first when she'd been so reluctant for them to even hold hands, he'd told himself to walk away and find a more willing playmate. But heaven help him, he'd been a goner from the very beginning. He'd never been in love before and falling hard and fast for sweet, innocent Amy had taken him by surprise. Although they'd dated eight months before he'd been able to talk her into making love, he'd figured that once he'd had her, he wouldn't want her so badly. Boy, had he been wrong. He couldn't get enough of her. The more they made love, the more he wanted her. Now all that mattered to him was making her his wife, binding her to him for the rest of their lives. Other girls still came on to him. He practically had to beat them off with a stick. But he didn't give any of them the time of day. All he wanted was his Amy. Now and forever.

Dante pulled the Mustang into a parking spot directly in front of the Dairy Dip. Main Street was all but deserted. He didn't see a soul. Where was Amy? He flung open the door and jumped out. As the night wind whipped around him, he zipped up his leather jacket and turned up the collar around his neck. Cupping his hands to either side of his eyes, he peered inside the Dairy Dip, thinking maybe she was waiting where it was warm. The place was empty. Walking up the block and then retracing his steps, he searched for her. When he headed to the opposite end of the block, he stepped on something that crunched under his feet. Pausing, he lifted his foot and looked down at a shiny object on the sidewalk.

Dante's heart skipped a beat. He leaned down and picked up a thin gold chain. The chain was broken. Had he broken it when he stepped on it? No, he didn't think so. The catch had been stretched apart, as if someone had snatched it off and tossed it aside.

A small diamond ring was still attached to the chain. The engagement ring he'd given Amy. The one she wore around her neck and hid beneath her clothes.

"Amy!" Dante cried. "Amy!"

He ran up the street and into the alley behind the Dairy Dip. Frantic, fear eating away at his insides like acid, he kept calling her name, hoping beyond hope that she would answer him. But in the deepest recesses of his consciousness, he knew she wouldn't reply, that she couldn't reply.

Don't assume the worst, he told himself. *Call the*

Morrisons. Call Jerry. And if they don't know where she is, call the police. You'll find her. No matter what's happened to her, you'll find her.

"If anyone has hurt her, I'll kill them," he shouted aloud as he stood in the middle of Main Street. "I'll find you, Amy. I swear to God, I'll find you."

CHAPTER ONE

Seventeen years later

DANTE MORAN got off the private elevator on the sixth floor and entered the Dundee Agency. As the newest employee of the private security and investigation firm, he'd decided to make a good impression by showing up early his first official day on the job. The agency's suite of offices took up the entire floor, with each agent having his own small office. He'd been in and out of this place several times over the years, in his capacity as an FBI agent, so he was familiar with his surroundings. Having seen the way a former federal agent and now Dundee CEO, Sawyer McNamara, ran this organization, Dante had realized that he, too, was better suited for private security than the government job he'd held for the past twelve years. He'd always felt restricted as a federal agent; and God knew he'd alienated his superiors with his rebellious, maverick mentality. Realizing he wasn't in line for any major promotions, that he'd gone as far as he could with the bureau, he'd decided the smart thing to do was cut his losses and move on.

"Good morning, Mr. Moran," Daisy Holbrook, the office manager, welcomed him.

He'd heard the other agents refer to her as Ms. Efficiency. She looked every inch the young professional in her tan dress slacks and matching jacket. Being a connoisseur of women, he wouldn't assess Daisy as a beauty by any means. Pretty, yes, in a fresh, youthful way, with her light brown hair, honey-brown eyes and dimpled cheeks. Unfortunately she was a bit too plump to fit the beauty standards of today's society. A hundred years ago, her hourglass figure would have been the ideal.

"Good morning," he replied. "You're looking very pretty today, Ms. Holbrook."

"Please, call me Daisy." Her dimples deepened when she offered him a warm smile. "And if you need anything, just let me know."

"I think I'll get a cup of coffee from the employees' lounge, then head to my office and settle in."

"You might want to take your coffee straight to Mr. McNamara's office," Daisy said, and when he looked at her inquisitively, she continued, "He came in nearly an hour ago and had me start rounding up every available agent for a big powwow this morning."

Interesting, Dante thought. Something important must be in the works. "Do you happen to know what's going on?"

"All I know is that he's already been on the phone with the governor of Mississippi and both state senators this morning." She lowered her voice. "Three agents are in there with him, and we're expecting two more to arrive anytime now."

Dante nodded. "I think I'll skip the coffee and go straight to Sawyer's office."

"Good idea."

When Dante reached the CEO's office, he found the door closed. McNamara's private secretary wasn't at her desk, so he assumed she hadn't yet arrived for work. After all, it was barely eight-thirty. He paused, knocked on the door and waited.

Vic Noble, a tall, lanky former CIA operative opened the door. "Come on in."

Dante nodded, then entered McNamara's large, professionally decorated office, the area as elegant and sophisticated as the man who occupied it. Behind his back, the other agents referred to their boss as Beau Brummell because the guy always looked as if he'd just stepped out of a *GQ* ad. But looks could be deceptive and that was particularly true in McNamara's case. Those who didn't know him by reputation might pass him off as nothing more than a highly intelligent pretty boy. But there was a lot more to the man than brains and good looks. Beneath that deceptive facade beat the heart of a deadly warrior.

"Join us, Moran." Sawyer McNamara motioned him over and pointed to an empty chair. "We'll get started as soon as Dom and Lucie arrive. I couldn't reach her by phone this morning, so I sent Dom by to pick her up."

Dante noted the frown on Sawyer's face and suspected that Lucie Evans was the cause. Before joining the Dundee agency, he'd heard about the ongoing feud between Sawyer and Lucie, both former FBI agents. And since he'd come on board and gone through several weeks of orientation, he'd seen the two of them in action. Whenever those two occupied the same space, sparks flew. The words "dynamite" and "lit match" instantly came to mind.

After sitting, Dante glanced around the room, nodded cordially to the other two agents and settled comfortably into his chair. His gaze kept wandering in J. J. Blair's direction and when she caught him staring, she smiled and winked. Grinning, he winked back at her. Now, there was one good-looking woman. Petite and curvy, with jet-black hair and big, dark eyes that appeared black, but were, on closer inspection, a deep bluish purple. Judging her by using his vast experience with the ladies, he figured Ms. Blair was one tough cookie, the type of woman who could easily devour a man in one bite and then spit him out in little pieces.

"I don't think we've met." A burly guy, with a rough face, military-short blond hair and friendly smile offered Dante one of his big hands. "I'm Geoff Monday. I've been on assignment in London for the past month." The man's accent was decidedly British, with just a hint of something else. Scottish?

Dante stood and shook hands with Monday. "Dante Moran. I'm the new guy."

"Yeah, you were a fed, weren't you?"

The office door flew open and Lucie Evans stormed in, her long, curly red hair hanging wildly around her shoulders and her green eyes shooting fire in Sawyer's direction. Domingo Shea came in behind her and paused in the doorway, as if he wanted to distance himself from any fallout that might occur.

"What do you mean sending Dom to fetch me?" Lucie planted her palms down atop Sawyer's desk and glowered at him. "I just got in from D.C. last night and I'm supposed to be starting a five-day vacation."

"Your vacation has been canceled," Sawyer said.

"The hell it has!"

"Sit down and shut up." Standing, Sawyer faced Lucie, who rose to her full six-foot height. Their gazes locked in mortal combat. "We have a special case on our hands and I need every available agent here so we can decide who's the best qualified to take on the assignment and to head up the team I'll be sending to Mississippi this morning. With your background in psychology and your stint as a profiler with the bureau, it's possible you'll be the best agent for the job."

Breaking eye contact first, Lucie gritted her teeth, then turned around and sat in the chair that was farther away from Sawyer's desk than the other two empty chairs. "If it turns out this isn't my assignment, I'm taking those five days off."

Sawyer didn't reply, instead he turned to Dom Shea. "Close the door and take a seat so we can get started."

Dom followed instructions and within minutes Sawyer patted a stack of file folders on his desk. Files containing information on what Dante assumed was a high-profile case.

There was a good chance that since he was the new man at the agency and low on the totem poll, so to speak, he would be sent in as backup for the agent chosen to head up the assignment. And that suited him just fine. He had to get his feet wet sooner or later. So why not the first day on the job?

"This is a special case," Sawyer McNamara told them. "Both Mississippi state senators and the governor himself put in calls to Sam Dundee early this morning to let him know they'd take it as personal favors if we accepted this assignment."

Lucie Evans let out a long, low whistle. "Who's involved? Must be somebody pretty important."

"G. W. Westbrook is one of wealthiest businessmen in the South and his family is one of the most prominent in Mississippi." Sawyer lifted the stack of thin file folders and passed them around the room, one for each agent. "His granddaughter has run away from home. She's sixteen. Not wild. Not into drugs. No special boyfriend. From all accounts, a good kid."

"What would make a good kid run away from home?" Vic Noble asked.

"That's an excellent question," Sawyer replied. "It's one her grandfather and her mother want answered. But first and foremost, they want Ms. Leslie Anne Westbrook found and returned home. She's an only child and the apple of Grandpa G.W.'s eye."

"Do they know for sure she ran away?" Dante Moran flipped open the file folder and quickly scanned the information condensed into a couple of paragraphs by the ever efficient Dundee office manager, Daisy. "Since Westbrook is a multimillionaire, can we be certain the girl wasn't kidnapped for ransom?"

"The girl's been missing for over twenty-four hours and no one has contacted the family with a ransom request," Sawyer said. "The mother is out of her mind with worry and old G.W. is ready to offer a quarter mil reward for information on the girl's whereabouts. Sam told me to get somebody to Fairport, Mississippi, ASAP and to send them on the Dundee jet."

"Are the feds involved?" Domingo Shea asked.

Sawyer shook his head. "There's no evidence of a kidnapping and the family says that they're certain the girl simply ran away. They don't want the feds. The local police and sheriff's departments are handling the case. But Sam suggested one of our former FBI agents might be the best choice to head up this assignment." He glanced from Lucie to Dante.

"Want to flip a coin?" Lucie smiled at Dante.

"Works for me," he replied, absently twisting the onyx and diamond ring on his finger.

"Read over the information we have and take a look at the girl's picture her grandfather faxed us." Sawyer spread apart his file and lifted the eight-by-ten photo. "She's a pretty girl. I'd hate to think of what might happen to her if she fell in with the wrong crowd or got picked up by the wrong person."

Dante's last case for the FBI had been to oversee an operation that busted apart a decade-old infant abduction ring. He supposed because of his background, he was now the Dundee expert on missing children and this case was perfect for his first assignment. He'd been with Dundee only a few weeks, undergoing their strict orientation, and was chomping at the bit to see some action.

Lucie looked at the photograph. "Oh, she is a pretty thing, isn't she? All blond and delicate. God, what a white slave ring would pay for a girl like this."

Dante pulled out the picture intending to give it a quick glance, but the moment he gazed at the girl's familiar face, he couldn't look away. His gut tightened painfully as he stared at what was obviously a studio photograph of a breathtakingly lovely girl.

"What the hell's wrong with you?" Dom Shea punched Dante's shoulder. "You look as if you've seen a ghost."

Yeah, he'd seen a ghost. That's exactly what it felt

like. Unconsciously Dante lifted his hand and ran the tip of his index finger tenderly over the girl's cheek and across her jawline. He closed his eyes, waited a minute and reopened them, thinking maybe his imagination was working overtime, that it had played a trick on him. He glanced back at the photograph. Damn! How was it possible that this sixteen-year-old girl was the spitting image of Amy? His Amy. His first and only love, who had died at seventeen. Died a lifetime ago.

"Are you all right?" Lucie asked.

"I'm fine," Dante said. "And I'll take this assignment."

"Good." Sawyer closed his file folder. "I'd hoped you'd take it. Despite this being your first job for us, I believe you're the best qualified, but I wanted to give you the chance to volunteer."

Lucie shrugged. "I guess that settles that. Will you need me to go along as backup?"

Sawyer's gaze narrowed on Lucie. "It's probably a good idea for you to go with him. You can keep the mother calm while Dante deals with the situation."

Dante nodded in agreement, but didn't take his eyes off Leslie Anne Westbrook's photo. Her resemblance to Amy was uncanny.

And impossible. Amy was gone. It had taken him a long time to accept the loss, and yet something about this young girl made him want to believe that somehow his true love still existed. That Amy was still alive.

Maybe it was the hope that still burned in his gut that had made him take the assignment. Though Dante had all but given up hope…

What the hell are you doing to yourself? Amy is dead. She's been dead for seventeen years. Just because her body was never found, just because you've hung on way too long to a hopeless dream doesn't mean Amy is alive, that this girl—he stared at the photograph—could be Amy's daughter.

"Go home, pack for a week's stay and go straight to the airport. The Dundee jet is ready and waiting," Sawyer said. "Moran will head up this assignment. Lucie, you'll be strictly panic control. You keep the mother and old G.W. in line, smooth their ruffled feathers and calm their fears. Dom, you and Vic go in as his backup and do the leg work. We'll coordinate everything from here."

"When I get back, I want ten days off," Lucie said.

"We'll discuss that later," Sawyer replied.

"There won't be any discussion. I'm taking ten days off and that's that."

Sawyer's nostrils flared. He deliberately didn't look directly at Lucie or respond to her.

"I want two reports every day. Morning and evening. I'll be reporting in directly to the governor and to Sam Dundee."

Dante glanced through the thin file folder he held, searching for more information about the Westbrook family, about Leslie Anne's mother in particular. All he found were the basic facts. Tessa Westbrook was G.W.'s only child. At thirty-five, she was single, the mother of one child and— She was thirty-five. A year older than Amy would be if she'd lived.

Every possible scenario he could think of that could explain Leslie Anne Westbrook's remarkable resemblance to Amy Smith flooded his mind, sending his thought processes into overdrive. Maybe Leslie Anne was adopted and she really was Amy's child. But did that mean Amy was alive now? Maybe Tessa Westbrook was a long-lost relative of Amy's and that's the reason her daughter looked like Amy. Maybe Tessa was Amy. Too far-fetched. And totally impossible. Or maybe in person Leslie Anne's resemblance to Amy wouldn't be as strong. Maybe...

Maybe I'm nuts!

"Is something wrong?" Dom clamped his hand down on Dante's shoulder.

Dante shook his head. "Nothing's wrong. I was just lost in thought there for a couple of minutes." If he told anyone what was going on inside his head, they would think he was crazy. And with good reason. How could he expect anyone to understand that the past haunted him. A part of him still blamed himself for what had happened to Amy. If only he hadn't been late that night. If only...

LESLIE ANNE kept wiping the tears away so she could see the road ahead. When she'd left home before daylight yesterday morning, she'd had no idea where she was going. All she knew was that she had to get away. She'd slipped into her mother's room and stolen three hundred dollars from her purse and her ATM card, which she'd used to get two thousand dollars before she'd left Fairport. She'd been twenty miles outside of town before it struck her that once her mother and grandfather realized she was missing, they would call the police. Her black Jaguar, which Granddaddy had given her on her sixteenth birthday, was easily recognizable and it would be a cinch to ID the car tag. She'd backtracked, called her friend Hannah, whose parents were in Europe for the summer, and asked to swap cars with her for a few days.

"Just keep my Jag parked in your garage and don't tell anyone that you've seen me," Leslie Anne had said.

"What's wrong? Why are you running off like this?"

"I can't tell you. I can't tell anyone." She'd grabbed Hannah's hands and pleaded with the girl who'd been one of her best buddies since they were toddlers. "Trust me. I've got to get away and think."

"Think about what? If you'd tell me, maybe I could help."

"No one can help." How could she explain that her whole world had just fallen apart, that everything she believed in, believed to be true, was a lie? Her entire life was just one big fat lie.

"What about your mom? You two share everything. She's the best. Nothing like—"

"No, I can't talk to Mom. Not yet. Maybe not ever." Hannah had always envied Leslie Anne's great relationship with her mom, so she could hardly tell her that she now hated her mother, hated her for lying to her all these years.

That had been yesterday, which seemed weeks ago instead of only twenty-four hours. She'd driven as far away as she could before nightfall, which didn't come until after seven. Thank goodness for daylight savings time. It had been a new and unnerving experience for her to stay at a motel. When she'd paid in cash, the clerk hadn't ask her any questions. He'd simply given her a key and told her that checkout was at eleven. Alone in a strange place, she hadn't slept for more than a few hours, waking over and over again when nightmares threatened her. Her mind kept replaying that horrible moment the day before when she'd opened the package addressed to her and read the letter that explained the enclosed newspaper clippings.

Leslie Anne's stomach growled, reminding her that she hadn't eaten breakfast or lunch, and it was now nearly two o'clock. She hadn't realized there would be so few places along Interstate 59 where she could find a decent restaurant. According to the last road sign she'd seen, she would be passing through Meridian in about fifteen minutes and there were all kinds of fast-food places where she could grab a burger and fries.

As hard as she tried not to think about the letter she'd received and the newspaper clippings about a serial killer who'd been executed in Texas ten years ago, she could think of little else. When she'd first read the letter, she hadn't wanted to believe it. She'd even gone straight to her mother, carrying the package with her, intending to give her mom a chance to deny everything. But the moment her mother smiled at her, she'd frozen, becoming mute and motionless.

"What is it, honey?" her mother had asked. "You look upset."

She'd shook her head and managed to utter a succinct lie. "I've just got a headache, so I'd like Eustacia to bring a supper tray to my room."

Maybe I should have told Mom about the contents of the package. Maybe I shouldn't have run off the way I did.

Her doubts and indecision had been the very reason she'd left Fairport. She couldn't confront her mother and grandfather with such damning accusations—not until she'd had time to sort through the information and come to terms with her own feelings. Even if every word was true, how likely was it that her mother would admit the truth? If it was the truth.

She would have lied to you. You know she would have. It's not as if she hasn't lied to you before.

When she'd been a preschooler and asked why she didn't have a father like everyone else, her mother had told her that her father was dead. That had been enough to satisfy a four-year-old. And later on at ten, when she'd become more inquisitive, her grandfather had explained that her parents had been unmarried teenage sweethearts and her father had been tragically killed in an automobile accident before Leslie Anne was born. Her father's name, he'd told her, was John Allen. It wasn't until she was fourteen and got hold of a copy of her birth certificate that she'd learned the truth. In the slot for father's name, the word "unknown" screamed the truth loud and clear. At the time she'd wondered several different things. Had there actually been a boy named John Allen? Or had he been a figment of her grandfather's imagination? Had her mother been with several young men and didn't know which one had fathered her child? Was her real father out there somewhere, and didn't even know he had a daughter? Although her mother and grandfather had stuck to their story of a boy named John Allen being her father, Leslie Anne had known they were lying. But not until she received the package from hell the day before yesterday had she understood why they had lied.

When the truth is too horrible to utter, too torturously painful to remember, only lies can protect you and those you love from the ugliness of reality.

CHAPTER TWO

THE WESTBROOK ESTATE consisted of five hundred acres and an antebellum mansion that had been in G.W.'s wife's family for five generations. John Leslie settled in Mississippi before it became a state. Prior to the Civil War, his son built the home in which members of that family had resided ever since. Located in the country, six miles outside the Mississippi River town of Fairport, the old Leslie Plantation lay claim to its own legends and folklore, some stories dating back to the early eighteen hundreds. Not as well-known as her nearby sister-city of Natchez, but equally rich in history, Fairport's economy now depended on two things—the tourist trade, which spilled over from Natchez, and the ten-year-old industrial park, comprised almost entirely of small businesses either owned by or invested in by G. W. Westbrook.

As Dante drove their rental car out of the sleepy little town, which hadn't seen many changes since the sixties, Lucie Evans hummed along to the upbeat tune playing on the radio. She appeared to be totally absorbed in the files containing info on the Westbrook family. Usually Lucie tended to be vivacious and talkative, but she'd remained fairly quiet since they'd left the Natchez-Adams County airport where the Dundee jet had landed. Although there was no commercial service into the airport, the facility boasted a runway large enough to land a Boeing 737.

They'd just dropped off Dom and Vic at the sheriff's department in Fairport, where they would obtain any updates on Leslie Anne Westbrook's disappearance and coordinate their efforts with the various branches of city, county and state law enforcement. Dante had every intention of joining them as soon as he met with G.W. and stationed Lucie at the mansion to control the old man and soothe his daughter. From what Dante had read in the updated files Daisy Holbrook had hand-delivered to the agents shortly before takeoff from Atlanta, G.W. would pose a problem for Lucie. Headstrong, tenacious and accustomed to using his power and money to get whatever he wanted whenever he wanted it, G.W. seldom listened to advice. It looked as if Lucie would have her hands full keeping him in check. His guess was that Lucie's only hope of controlling G.W. would be Tessa Westbrook. Ms. Westbrook, with a reputation for being as coolheaded as her father was hotheaded, should be able to exert enough influence over the old man to rein him in a little.

"What's so interesting in those files?" Dante asked, wondering if he'd missed something when he'd gone through the information while in flight. Admittedly, his interest in thoroughly studying those files had come as much, if not more, from his curiosity about the Westbrook girl's resemblance to Amy than to the case at hand.

"I'm not sure," Lucie admitted. "It's just reading these—" she waved the pages she held in her hand "—is like reading the script for a nighttime soap opera. I suppose the lives of all super-rich people have a tendency to seem melodramatic."

"What's melodramatic about the Westbrooks?"

"Are you kidding? G.W. came from fairly humble beginnings, married into money and more than tripled the family fortune. When she was eighteen, his beloved only child, Tessa, nearly died in a horrific car crash that killed her boyfriend, who was supposedly Leslie Anne's father. Then four years later his beautiful socialite wife died after battling cancer for years. G.W. supports his younger sister, his wife's sister, his niece, his current girlfriend and her son and—"

"Enough." Dante cut his eyes toward Lucie and grinned.

"Okay, but you see what I mean, don't you? We're walking into a scene straight out of that old TV show *Dallas*."

"This is a simple case of a runaway teen." Dante

wanted to convince himself of that fact, wanted to prove to himself beyond a shadow of a doubt that Ms. Leslie Anne Westbrook had no connection whatsoever to Amy Smith.

"Don't kid yourself. Nothing is ever simple with the ultrarich. I'll bet you a week's salary that there's some deliciously scandalous reason the Westbrook kid ran off." Lucie tucked the file pages back into the folder on her lap. "From all reports, this girl is squeaky-clean. A real straight arrow. A well-adjusted, happy teenager who adores her family."

"So maybe the report is wrong. Or it could be a matter of not having all the facts."

"My point exactly. We don't have all the facts. And what do you want to bet that we aren't going to get them from G.W. or Tessa."

Dante slowed the car when he saw the massive black wrought-iron gates up ahead on the right. Impressive. Damn impressive.

"Would you look at that!" Lucie let out a long, low whistle. "Southfork, here we come."

"My bet is the Leslie mansion will look a lot more like the plantation houses in *Gone with the Wind* than J. R. Ewing's humble abode."

"Hmm. Wonder if Tessa Westbrook has anything in common with Scarlett O'Hara."

Dante chuckled as he pulled the car up to the massive gates, then responded to the electronic guard, using the verbal code he'd been given by Sawyer

McNamara. The iron gates opened to reveal a long, narrow paved driveway. Half a mile later, the Leslie home came into view. He'd been right—the huge house boasted a series of massive white columns that wrapped around the front and sides of the well-maintained mansion. He'd no sooner pulled to a stop in front of the house than the double front doors opened and a tall, lanky man with a shock of steel-gray hair appeared on the veranda. The guy wore a plain black suit, white shirt and black bow tie. Although there was an air of confidence in the way the sixty-something man approached them, Dante instinctively knew this wasn't G. W. Westbrook. Dante's guess was this distinguished gentleman was a loyal assistant or servant.

The man rushed forward when Lucie opened the car door. "Good afternoon, ma'am," he said in a deep voice, dripping with a South Mississippi molasses, slow and sweet accent. "I assume you're Ms. Evans—" he glanced across the car's hood at Dante "—and you're Mr. Moran." He held out his hand to assist Lucie.

"That's right," Dante said. "And you're—"

"Hal Carpenter, sir. The family's chauffeur-cum-butler."

"Double duty, huh?" Lucie said.

"Yes, ma'am. Mr. Westbrook doesn't relegate his household staff to only one position."

"Saves on salaries that way, I suppose," Dante said.

Hal's back stiffened. "Would you come with me, please? Mr. G.W. and Miss Tessa are waiting in the library and are quite anxious to meet y'all."

With her eyes widened in a guess-he-put-you-in-your-place expression, Lucie grinned at Dante. They quickly fell into step behind Mr. Carpenter. Just as they entered the three-story foyer, Lucie managed not to gasp at the opulence. Instead she took the opportunity—since her mouth was already open—to ask the family chauffeur-cum-butler a question.

"Mr. Carpenter, do you have any idea why Leslie Anne ran away?"

He paused for a split second, then replied, "I'm afraid not, ma'am. We're all at a loss as to why Miss Leslie Anne would just up and leave the way she did."

"You don't think there's any chance she was kidnapped?" Dante asked.

"No, sir." Mr. Carpenter paused at the closed pocket doors outside what Dante assumed was the library. "When you meet Mr. G.W., please take into consideration the circumstances. He and Miss Tessa are terribly concerned—"

Lucie patted Mr. Carpenter on the back. "We understand."

Yeah, they understood, Dante thought. Mr. Carpenter had just warned them to go easy on the old man, to not ask upsetting questions and if Mr. G.W. acted like a crazed lunatic, they should forgive him because he was so concerned about his granddaughter.

The butler nodded, then knocked on the door softly. Without waiting for a response, he slid open the pocket doors and announced, "Ms. Evans and Mr. Moran from the Dundee agency."

A tall, robust man, with a receding hairline partially disguised by having his snow-white hair cut extremely short, stood in front of the six-foot-high fireplace flanked by bookcases. His keen brown eyes surveyed Dante and Lucie, studying them quickly but intensely.

"Come in, come in." G.W.'s words were a command, not an invitation.

Lucie entered first, a tentative smile on her face and her hand halfway extended, apparently prepared to withdraw if she met any hostility. Dante stepped over the threshold, but paused there and searched the room for any other occupants. His gaze settled on the woman rising from a leather wing chair to the left of the fireplace. For a moment his heart stopped. The woman whose gaze met his possessed Amy's brilliant blue eyes. The blue of a summer sky. But the moment passed and he took a really good look at Tessa Westbrook. She was approximately the same height as Amy, but her blond hair was darker and she was a good fifteen pounds thinner. He tried not to stare at her face, but he couldn't help studying each feature. There was a vague similarity in the features, but this woman was not Amy Smith.

Not my Amy.

"Well, man, don't just stand there staring at my daughter, come on in and let's get down to business." G.W. skewered Dante with his surly glare.

"Thank y'all so much for getting here so quickly." Tessa broke eye contact with Dante, then walked toward Lucie. The two exchanged a cordial handshake. "We're absolutely frantic about Leslie Anne."

"I can imagine," Lucie said. "Rest assured the Dundee agency will do everything possible to find your daughter and bring her home safely."

Tessa glanced at Dante. "Please excuse my father's rudeness, but he tends to be rather blunt, especially when he's upset."

Polite but not friendly, Dante thought. Tessa Westbrook possessed the type of cool, elegant beauty that made a man wonder if there were wanton fires hidden beneath the poised, chic veneer. Despite a few basic physical similarities between the two women, Tessa was as different from Amy as night is from day. Tessa appeared to be exactly what anyone would expect from the daughter of a multimillionaire. Dressed in expensive, tailored suede slacks, matching ankle boots and an oversize turtleneck cashmere sweater, the woman all but screamed *m-o-n-e-y.*

"No need to apologize for me, missy. I expect Mr. Moran has dealt with a lot worse than me in his time. Isn't that right, Moran?"

"Yes, sir, in my capacity as a federal agent, I've dealt with all kinds, even a few high-powered moguls with god complexes."

Absolute silence prevailed. Then G.W. let out a loud belly laugh and walked straight toward Dante. "Well said, young man, well said." G.W. extended his hand, which Dante accepted and the two exchanged a man-to-man shake.

"Won't y'all sit down." Tessa invited them with a mannerly sweep of her arm, her wide gold bracelet sliding just below her wrist. "Would either of you care for coffee or tea or—"

"If you don't mind, Ms. Westbrook, I'd like to get down to business," Dante said. "As soon as we finish this interview, I'll be joining our other two Dundee agents in the search for your daughter. Ms. Evans will remain here with the family to handle things on this end."

"Then let's get on with it," G.W. said. "What do you need from us?"

"Any information that might help us locate Leslie Anne," Lucie replied.

"We've done everything Mr. McNamara instructed us to do," Tessa said. "Starting with compiling a list of all her close friends."

G.W. picked up a sheet of paper from the mahogany desk and handed it to Dante. "We've spoken to everyone on the list and no one knows—"

"Sometimes kids won't tell parents things they'll

feel compelled to tell a private investigator," Dante explained.

Lucie glanced from Tessa to G.W. "If we knew why Leslie Anne ran away, it might help us—"

"We have no idea," G.W. said. Quickly. Much too quickly.

Dante figured if the old man didn't know why his granddaughter ran away, he had his suspicions. "What about you, Ms. Westbrook?" Dante turned to Tessa. "What would prompt your daughter to run away?"

"I told you that we have no idea." G.W. put his arm around his daughter's slender shoulders.

"Is that right?" Dante stared directly at Tessa.

Tessa nervously rubbed her neck, unintentionally bringing attention not only to the large diamond studs in her earlobes, but the tendril of golden blond hair that curled waywardly against the high plush collar of her red sweater. "Leslie Anne has no reason to leave home," Tessa replied. "She has an almost-perfect life."

Dante kept his gaze connected to Tessa's. Something inside him wanted to undo the loose bun of thick hair secured at the back of her head. Would her hair be as long and silky as Amy's had been? Even now, after seventeen years, he could still remember the feel of Amy's hair stroking his chest when she took the dominant position as they made love.

She's not Amy, he reminded himself. Amy is dead.

"If that's the case and her life is almost perfect,

then why are y'all so sure she hasn't been abducted?" Dante asked.

Tessa replied, "Because she—"

"Why is this information important?" G.W. demanded. "What difference does it make why she ran off?"

Tessa reached out and squeezed her father's hand. "Please, Daddy, if telling these people about Leslie Anne's note—"

"What note?" Lucie asked.

Tessa looked to her father, as if asking permission. He nodded. She squeezed his hand again, then glanced from Lucie to Dante. "Leslie Anne left a note for me." Tessa reached inside the pocket of her suede slacks and pulled out a piece of hot pink paper.

As if they were the only two people in the room, Tessa walked directly to Dante and handed him the paper. When he took the note from her, their hands brushed. They stared at each other and a crazy kind of sensation tightened Dante's gut.

Forcing himself to break the electrically charged link between them, Dante unfolded the small piece of paper and read the message Leslie Anne had written to her mother.

Mom, you've lied to me again, haven't you? I know the truth now. At least I think it's the truth. Why couldn't you have been honest with me? Right now I hate you and I hate Granddaddy. And I'm confused. I've got to figure out what the truth is, what I

*can and can't believe about myself. Don't try to find
me because I won't come home until I'm good and
ready. If ever!*

Dante lifted his gaze. Tessa stood only a couple
of feet away, her body tense, a fine mist of tears in
her blue eyes. "What did you lie to your daughter
about? What truth has she found out?"

"Hell, Moran, this is all nonsense," G.W. said.
"The child is sixteen. She's confused about everything. That's only natural for someone her age, isn't
it? Why she's gotten some cock-and-bull notion in
her head that we've lied to her, I don't know. It really doesn't matter, does it? What does matter is finding her as soon as possible before she gets into
trouble."

"Daddy, please." Tessa looked pleadingly at
Dante. The muscles in his belly tightened. "We
have…I have lied to my daughter all her life, but only
in an effort to protect her."

"Protect her from what?" Dante asked.

"From my past."

He couldn't breathe. *Hell, man, don't do this to
yourself. Tessa Westbrook's past has nothing to do
with Amy Smith's past and you damn well know it.*

"Tessa, don't—" G.W. barely got the two words out
before his daughter turned sharply and glared at him.

Returning her attention to Dante, she sighed
deeply. "I lied to Leslie Anne about her true parentage. We— I allowed her believe that she was the re-

sult of a teenage affair I had with a young man named John Allen. There is no John Allen."

He had to ask Tessa the one question that had been tormenting him from the moment he saw Leslie Anne's photograph. "Who are Leslie Anne's biological parents?"

"Are you asking if my daughter is adopted?" Tessa stared at him inquisitively.

Dante nodded.

"No, Mr. Moran, she is not adopted. I'm Leslie Anne's biological mother."

"And her father?"

An expression of unbearable pain, of a soul-deep agony appeared on Tessa's face. "Leslie Anne's biological father was the monster who raped me."

LESLIE ANNE pulled off the road at the first rest stop she found on Interstate 59 after crossing the state line into Alabama. She'd drunk a large Diet Coke at lunch and was about to pee in her pants. Three eighteen-wheelers lined one parking lot while an assortment of vehicles took up half the other parking spaces. With a crowd of people entering and leaving the rest rooms, she felt relatively safe to leave the car. The attendant greeted her when she entered the facility. She smiled and nodded, then rushed into the bathroom. After using the first available toilet, she washed and dried her hands. Her mouth and lips felt dry, so she rummaged around in her purse until she found her lip gloss. When she lifted the wand to her lips as she stared into the mirror over the row of sinks, her hand paused in midair. She stared at the face looking back at her.

She had her mother's blond hair and slender figure, although at sixteen, she was already three inches taller. But her nose, mouth and facial structure didn't resemble her mom's.

Leslie Anne's heartbeat accelerated.

Did she have his nose? His mouth? Was her face shaped like his?

It was possible, wasn't it? After all, if the information she'd received was the truth—and why would anyone tell her such a horrific lie?—then *he* was her father. His evil blood flowed through her veins. Had he passed down his malevolent genes to her?

The lip gloss wand fell from Leslie's Anne's fingers and hit the sink with a distinctive clink. As she swallowed her tears, she picked up the wand and stuffed it back into her purse.

"Honey, are you all right?" a kind voice asked.

Leslie Anne swatted away her tears. A sweet-faced grandmother with her two preschool grandchildren in tow looked at Leslie Anne with motherly concern.

"Oh, yes, ma'am, I'm fine. I think I've got an eyelash in my eye, that's all."

Leslie Anne rushed out of the bathroom and back to her friend Hannah's car. After locking the doors, she flipped open the glove compartment and yanked out a tissue from the dispenser inside, then wiped away her tears and blew her nose. She dumped the used tissue in the empty ashtray, then lifted the large manilla envelope from the floorboard on the passenger's side. Her hands trembled as she opened the package and removed the newspaper clippings. Sorting through the ones with photos, she searched for one that showed the man's face. Several had no accompanying photo and several that did showed the man from the side or with his hand up over his face. Just as she'd given up hope of finding one that gave a view of his face, Leslie's Anne's hand trembled.

There's one!

A photo taken outside the courtroom the day he'd been found guilty and sentenced to death in Texas showed the face of an angry man. She studied that face, searching for any resemblance to her own and found none. Was she seeing the truth or was she seeing what she wanted to see? She didn't want this man to be her father. But if he was, she certainly didn't want to look like him.

Please, God, please. Don't let him be my father. I can't bear it if he is.

MY PLAN WORKED even better than I thought it would. Leslie Anne must have believed everything I told her in my letter; otherwise, why would she have run away? If I'm lucky, maybe she'll disappear off the face of the earth. Maybe someone else will dispose of her and save me the trouble. That little brat's very existence is an offense to good, decent people everywhere. She should have been drowned at birth. With her out of the way, there's nothing to stop me from getting what I want, what I've always wanted.

And what I deserve.

Yes, of course, it's what I deserve.

But what if those Dundee agents G.W. hired find her and bring her home? What will I do then?

I'll have no other choice. I'll have to kill her. I've known this day would come. It's not as if I'll be doing anything wrong. By destroying the spawn of the devil, I'll be doing God's work. And if I benefit from her death, all the better.

CHAPTER THREE

TESSA BREATHED A sigh of relief when Lucie Evans asked if she'd take her upstairs to see Leslie Anne's room. She had desperately wanted to escape from the pained expression on Dante Moran's face. He'd looked as if someone had landed a fatal blow and he'd suddenly realized he was going to die. Odd that she should have felt his reaction so strongly. She seldom related to men on a personal level and what she'd sensed from Mr. Moran had been extremely personal. He might as well have shouted to the world, "I'll kill the son of a bitch who hurt you." Now, with several minutes and a good sixty feet separating them, Tessa wondered if she'd simply imagined the passionate anger she'd seen in Mr. Moran's sable-brown eyes.

"Are you all right?" Lucie asked as they neared the front staircase.

Tessa paused. "Only a handful of people know the truth about what happened to me—that I was raped and…"

"It's all right," Lucie told her. "You don't have to explain."

"I hope Mr. Moran will be all right with Daddy." Tessa took the opportunity she'd been given to change the subject. "I suspect they're going to lock horns."

"And you're concerned about Dante?" Smiling, Lucie eyed her quizzically. "Don't be. Dante could hold his own against the devil himself."

"Do you know him well?" Tessa started up the stairs, Lucie Evans at her side.

"We're friendly acquaintances and business associates. But I used to be an FBI agent and so did he. The guy had quite a reputation. Everybody at the bureau knew you didn't mess with Dante Moran. He was a bit of a maverick, liked to do things his own way. That's why he left the bureau and joined Dundee. We're allowed the freedom to use our individual skills as long as we don't blatantly break the law in accomplishing our goals."

When they reached the landing, Tessa turned right. "Leslie Anne's room is this way. Her suite is across the hall from mine."

"Suite?"

Tessa managed a weak smile. "Bedroom, sitting room and bath."

"Hmm."

"How long have you worked with Mr. Moran at the Dundee agency?"

"May I ask why you're so interested in Dante?"

Tessa stopped dead still, turned and stared at Lucie. "Did I give the impression that my curiosity was personal?"

"Do you want the truth, Ms. Westbrook?"

Tessa nodded, but her stomach did a nervous flip-flop.

"I have a rather keen intuition," Lucie said. "I seem to have a gift for reading people. I suppose that's why I wanted to work as a profiler for the bureau."

Tessa nodded again, suspecting what Lucie was going to say.

"You and Dante were sizing each other up down there. Checking each other out. I doubt your father noticed anything more than Dante staring at you, but I picked up on the tension between you two almost immediately." Lucie held up a restraining hand. "And before you deny it, let me say that these things happen and often under the oddest circumstances. We can't choose who we're sexually attracted to or when it'll happen."

Tessa wanted to adamantly refute what Lucie had said. She wanted to deny that her reaction to Dante had been based on sexual attraction. But she couldn't. "Actually I don't know how to respond to what you said."

"The only reason I brought it up was to warn you."

"Warn me?"

"Look, Ms. Westbrook, Dante's a good guy, but he's got a rep as a real womanizer. You seem like the one-man-woman type, so if that's the case, steer clear of Dante."

"I can assure you that—"

"Just take the advice."

Tessa let the subject drop. There was no need for Lucie Evans to give her any advice about Dante Moran because she had no intention of acting on the totally unwanted attraction she felt for the man.

After opening the door to Leslie Anne's suite, Tessa ushered Lucie inside and then closed the door behind them. "Everything is just as she left it."

The bedroom was decorated in varying shades of pink, white and cream, with a mahogany canopy bed that reached almost to the top of the ten-foot ceiling. Lucie figured all the furniture was antique, probably possessions of the Leslie family dating back well over a century, if not a century and a half.

"Wow! What young girl wouldn't love this. It looks like something out of a fairy tale. A room fit for a true princess."

"That's the way Daddy thinks of Leslie Anne," Tessa admitted. "And me, too. He's spoiled us both terribly."

"You're lucky to have a father who loves you so much."

"Yes, I am. He—he's been the most wonderful father any girl could ask for." Tessa didn't often allow herself to remember those endless months she'd spent in the hospital after her "accident." She'd suf-

fered unbearable pain and yet somehow she had
borne it, mostly due to the fact that her father had
been not only her loving support system, but her encouraging cheerleader. When time and again she'd
given up, wanting to die, her daddy had been her
strength and her courage.

"Does Leslie Anne keep a diary?" Lucie asked.

"Not that I know of," Tessa replied. "And, yes, I've
searched her room thoroughly and found absolutely
nothing."

"Do you think that somehow Leslie Anne found
out that you were raped and she is the…that her birth
was a result of that rape?"

"I don't know. I pray to God not." Tessa picked up
a framed photograph off her daughter's dressing
table. "Here we are on her sixteenth birthday this past
summer." She handed Lucie the photo.

"You both look very happy." Lucie gave the
framed picture back to Tessa.

"We were." Tessa set the photo on the dressing
table. "If she found out, I can't imagine how or who
might have told her. Only a handful of people know
the truth—" She couldn't bring herself to say the
words aloud again. *My daughter's biological father
is the monster who raped me.*

"Exactly who knows?"

Tessa took a deep breath. "I suppose the police
who were involved at the time know, but you'd have
to ask Daddy about that. He protected me from the

legal aspects of what happened." She'd never been interrogated by the police and had only a vague memory of being told what had happened to her. Later on, she'd been grateful to her father, grateful that G. W. Westbrook was so powerful and influential that he could manipulate the law to protect his only child. "Daddy knows, of course. And Aunt Sharon knows. Daddy confided in his sister because he couldn't burden my mother with the truth. Mother was battling cancer at the time and—" Tessa swallowed her tears as memories of her mother enveloped her. Those memories were so very bittersweet. "As far as I'm aware, no one else knows that I was raped."

"What's your relationship with your aunt?" Lucie asked.

"I beg your pardon?"

"Is there any reason your aunt would tell Leslie Anne about—"

"Certainly not! Aunt Sharon would never do anything to hurt Leslie Anne or me."

"I'm sorry. I had to ask."

"Yes, I suppose you did, but even implying that Aunt Sharon would tell someone is ludicrous. After Mother died, she became a second mother to me. And she adores Leslie Anne."

"I need to ask you another question."

Dreading the question, but understanding that Lucie was simply doing her job, Tessa nodded.

"If you intended to never tell your daughter the

truth about her father, why didn't you put this fictitious John Allen's name on her birth certificate?"

"Because at the time, neither Daddy nor I was
thinking straight," Tessa said. "It wasn't until Leslie
Anne was a preschooler and started asking about her
father that Daddy came up with a name to go with
the tale about my boyfriend dying in the fictitious car
crash."

"Oh, I see."

"We agreed that a lie—any lie—was better than
the truth."

"What did you tell her when she saw her birth
certificate?"

"I almost caved in, but Daddy rescued me. He
swore to Leslie Anne that John Allen was her father.
He even made up some elaborate tale about how
John was this brilliant orphan Daddy brought in to
work for him and when this John and I met, we fell
in love and—" Tessa heaved a deep sigh. "Of course,
Daddy and I and Aunt Sharon weren't the only ones
who knew John Allen was a figment of Daddy's
imagination. The whole family knew I hadn't been
seeing a young man named John Allen, not when I
was practically engaged to Daddy's godson, Charlie
Sentell, and Daddy just let Mother believe the baby
was Charlie's. And dear Charlie willingly played
along. Thankfully, Mother died not ever knowing the
truth."

"I'm surprised you were engaged at eighteen."

"I wasn't really engaged. Let's just say that Daddy had chosen Charlie for me."

"Why didn't you marry Charlie?"

"That wasn't possible."

"May I ask why not?"

"I made it impossible," Tessa admitted. "Charlie offered. Daddy pleaded with me. But I refused. I suppose my refusal had something to do with the rape and with the endless therapy I endured afterward. I'm not sure. Looking back, I realize marrying Charlie probably would have been the wisest course of action."

"Hindsight and all."

"Right." Tessa smiled. "Is there anything else?"

"I suppose not."

"Then shouldn't we go back downstairs and see if either Daddy or Mr. Moran is mortally wounded?"

When they left Leslie Anne's suite, Tessa closed the door and turned to go down the hall. Lucie reached out and grasped her arm.

"Yes?" Tessa asked.

"I want you to know that I think you're an amazing lady and your daughter is lucky to have you as her mother." Lucie released her hold on Tessa. "We'll find Leslie Anne and bring her home to you. Safe and sound."

Emotion lodged in Tessa's throat. "You must know what my greatest fear is."

"We'll find her. You have four of Dundee's finest on the job."

Tessa prayed that Dundee's finest would prove to be her child's salvation. The thought of her precious little girl enduring the same hell that she herself had lived through was Tessa's worst nightmare.

A HALF HOUR LATER, Lucie walked Dante to the rental car still parked at the front of the mansion. To Tessa's apparent surprise, when they'd come downstairs earlier they'd found Dante and G.W. sitting in front of the fireplace sipping G.W.'s best bourbon and talking as if they were old friends.

"Keep a tight rein on G.W.," Dante said. "You might have to remind him again of all the reasons offering a half-mil reward for info about his granddaughter is a bad idea."

"Check in often, will you?" Lucie told him. "Tessa Westbrook isn't as tough as she appears to be. Any news, even if it's that there is no news, will help her. She's terrified that Leslie Anne might wind up in the hands of a rapist."

"Even without her past history, her concern is a legitimate one."

"Find that kid, will you?"

"You like Ms. Westbrook, don't you?"

"Yes, I like her." Lucie eyed him speculatively. "Do me a favor, will you—pass on this one, okay?"

"What do you mean—"

"Don't pretend you aren't personally interested in her. All I'm saying is find Tessa's daughter, then move on. Your next conquest shouldn't be this woman."

All right, so he'd enjoyed his fair share of the ladies over the years and had acquired a reputation for breaking hearts, but surely Lucie knew he would never take advantage of a lady such as Tessa Westbrook. She might appear to have it altogether, but what if she didn't? He certainly didn't want to be the man to shatter her protective shield. After all, that shield might be all that was holding her together emotionally.

"I promise that I won't do anything to hurt Tessa Westbrook. Good enough?"

"Good enough."

Dante slid behind the wheel of the rented Chevy and started the engine. Why he glanced back at the front door, he didn't know, but when he did, he saw Tessa standing there, about ten feet behind Lucie. At this distance, with the bright afternoon sun shimmering all around her, Tessa looked breathtakingly beautiful.

Aggravated at himself for his unprofessional behavior, Dante shifted gears into Drive and headed for the main road leading back into town. Within twenty minutes, he'd picked up Dom and Vic, gone over the info they'd gotten from the local sheriff and told the other Dundee agents that they'd start by questioning the eight names on the list of Leslie Anne's closest friends. They split the list G.W. had given Dante, rented two more cars and moved forward with their official investigation.

"I HAVEN'T SEEN Leslie Anne in over a week," Hannah Wright said.

"When's the last time you talked to her?" Dante asked, convinced that the young woman was lying. His gut instincts told him that this cute little brunette, with the big chocolate-brown eyes of a puppy dog and the pole thin body of a boy, knew something about Leslie Anne's disappearance.

"Uh, you mean, like talked on the phone?" Hannah kept avoiding direct eye contact with Dante.

"Yes, I mean like talked on the phone with her. Or exchanged an e-mail. Or communicated in any way."

"Well, sure. We talk on the phone all the time. Like every day." Realizing she'd slipped up and confessed to daily contact with her friend, Hannah gasped, then laughed. "Well, at least usually. But I haven't talked her in…oh, at least four days."

Dante crossed his arms over his chest and gave the teenager his most deadly, fear-inspiring glare. Her face paled. Her eyes widened and she took a step backward, away from him.

"This isn't a game we're playing, Hannah," Dante told her, his tone harsh. "Whatever reason Leslie Anne ran away, she could be in serious trouble. A pretty young girl on the run all alone often winds up murdered or raped or—"

"That won't happen to Leslie Anne."

"Why won't it?"

"Because she's smart. And it's not as if she's hitching rides or anything."

"By that, I assume you mean she took her own car."

"I—I didn't say that. I told you I haven't—"

"Talked to her in four days. Yeah, I know what you said. But knowing Leslie Anne the way you do, you assume she drove her own car. Right?"

Hannah nodded nervously, then twisted a lock of her curly brown hair around her index finger. It was only a matter of time before the girl broke down and told him what he needed to know.

"The Mississippi state troopers and every law enforcement agency in the state have a description of Leslie Anne's Jaguar and the license plate number, yet no one has reported seeing her car. Why is that?"

"How would I know?"

"Do you have a car, Ms. Wright?"

"Me?"

"Yes, you."

"Uh-huh." She nodded.

"Where is your car?"

"Where do you think—it's parked in the garage, of course."

"Would you mind if I take a look at your car?"

"What for?"

"I'd really rather not involve your parents," Dante said, using the most threatening tone possible. "But unless you show me your car, I'll have to put in a call to them."

"You can't. They're in Europe."

"I should imagine one of the servants has their itinerary, so it's only a matter of—"

"How'd you figure it out? I mean, was it anything I said that tipped you off?" Hannah wrung her hands, the dark purple nail polish on her fingertips a vivid contrast to her light, freckled skin.

"Just an educated guess," Dante admitted. "It's a logical thing to do—switch cars with a friend so that when the police search for a black Jaguar with a certain license plate number, they won't be looking for a—?"

"She's going to kill me if I tell you." Hannah lifted her shoulders and hung her head as if she were trying to disappear like a turtle into its shell.

"And I might be forced to take drastic measures if you don't tell me."

Gasping, Hannah looked up at Dante, real fear in her eyes. If the situation wasn't so damn serious, he would laugh. And he would apologize to Hannah for scaring her half to death.

"Leslie Anne's Jag is in the garage," Hannah confessed, her voice trembling. "I let her take my red BMW."

"Make and model?" Dante asked.

"It's a convertible. A BMW Z4."

"Thanks, Hannah. You did the right thing, and I

promise I'll do my best to square things for you with Leslie Anne."

"You will?"

He grinned at her. "Yeah, I will." Without hesitation, with Hannah sighing and all but melting in front of him, Dante whipped out his cell phone and called Dom. "Contact Vic and tell him to meet us back at the sheriff's department in Fairport. We need to run a check on a BMW owned by—" Dante looked to Hannah for the info he needed.

"Anson Wright," Hannah said. "Technically, the car belongs to Daddy."

"The owner is Anson Wright. It seems Leslie Anne swapped cars with a friend of hers. The police have been searching for a car that's been parked in the Wrights' garage for the past thirty-six hours."

HE'D WATCHED the girl at the motel's restaurant and wondered what a kid her age was doing alone. All during her meal, he'd expected to see either a boyfriend or a parent join her, but she'd paid for her meal in cash and left by herself. Following her hadn't been a problem. She'd seemed oblivious to everything and everyone around her. He stopped down the hallway and watched as she inserted her card key into the lock and then went into her room. Glancing around to make sure no one was aware of him, he grinned when he realized the coast was clear. Whistling softly to himself, he nonchalantly meandered down the hall until he reached her door. Room 215.

He straightened his tie, put a friendly, trustworthy smile on his face and knocked on the pretty, sexy little blonde's door.

"Yes? What do you want?" she asked through the closed door.

She was probably staring at him through the peephole.

"Hello, miss. I'm sorry to bother you. I'm Joe Thompson, the assistant manger of Motel Bama. I'm afraid someone posing as motel security has stolen several of our keys, including the one to your room. For your safety, we'd like to move you to another room, one that's completely secure."

"Oh, my God," the girl whimpered.

He had her. It was as easy as that. She'd fallen for his line of bull—hook, line and sinker. All he had to do now was reel her in. "Please, don't be alarmed. You're perfectly safe. I'll be happy to personally escort you to a new room."

The door opened slowly and the girl peered out at him. Be charming, he told himself, and don't rush her. Show her you're a good guy, somebody she can trust as easily as she trusts her dad.

"I'll be glad to carry your suitcase for you, young lady." He stayed right where he was, patiently waiting for her to make the next move, not risking scaring her off. "You know, you remind me of my niece,

Cathy Jo. My sister named her Jo after me. Cathy's a cheerleader. You don't happen to be a cheerleader, do you?"

She shook her head, then opened the door completely. He took that as an invitation. He could keep her here in her room until he'd finished with her, but on the off chance that someone might know where she was and show up unexpectedly, he knew it would be safer to take her to his room.

After all, he had a nice little surprise waiting there for her.

CHAPTER FOUR

TESSA JERKED involuntarily when Lucie Evans's cell phone rang. Since Dante Moran had left over three hours ago, they hadn't heard a word from him. Her father had become so restless and agitated, that she and Lucie had finally managed to persuade him to take his Irish setters, Jefferson and Davis, out for a long walk. Lucky for her, Tessa had not inherited her father's high-strung, superaggressive personality. Her mother, Anne, had been easygoing, with a somewhat passive quality that, when she became ill, turned into a possessive, clinging, dependency. Time and again she'd seen her mother manipulate her father with no more than a sigh or a few tears. Tessa supposed she had inherited traits from both parents. Although she was, by nature, easygoing, she possessed an independent streak that occasionally set her at odds against her father. Often they disagreed about the best way to raise Leslie Anne.

"I see," Lucie said into the phone. "Well, that's good news."

"What news?" Tessa asked.

Ignoring Tessa's question, Lucie said, "Yes, she's right here. No, he's out walking his dogs." Then Lucie turned to Tessa. "It's Dante. He has some news about Leslie Anne, and he needs to ask you a few questions."

Tessa grabbed the phone. "Have you found my daughter?" *Please, God, please.*

"No, I'm sorry, we haven't. Not yet. But we will."

For a moment, the disappointment claimed Tessa totally, but when she heard Dante call her name, she snapped out of it immediately. "Yes, Mr. Moran, what can I do to help you?"

"We've found out that Leslie Anne swapped cars with her friend Hannah Wright so the authorities have been searching for the wrong vehicle."

"Hannah swore to me that she hadn't—of course, she'd lie to me if Leslie Anne had asked her to." Tessa paused long enough to regroup her thoughts. "So, the police are now looking for the right car."

"There's an all-points bulletin out for a red BMW Z4, and already we've had three reports of a law enforcement officer having seen that type of car. A car of that description was found abandoned and stripped, with no car tag, over in Louisiana. Vic flew over to check things out."

Tessa gasped.

"I just heard back from him a couple of minutes ago. It wasn't Hannah Wright's car."

Tessa expelled a whoosh of pure relief. "Oh, thank God."

"Hannah's car—the license plate definitely identified it—was found parked at the Bama Motel in Tuscaloosa, Alabama. The local police are on their way to the motel as we speak."

Tears pooled in Tessa's eyes. "And Leslie Anne?"

"We don't know. But Dom and I just landed by helicopter here in Tuscaloosa. We're on our way to the motel now. I'll call you as soon as we know something."

"Thank you."

"Tessa?"

"Yes?"

"Keep believing your daughter is all right. Keep telling yourself that we're going to bring her home very soon. Can you do that for me?"

"Yes, I—I can do that."

"Good."

Tessa held the cell phone out to Lucie. Amazingly Tessa's hand wasn't trembling. Outwardly she was in complete control. Inwardly, she was a shattered mess.

"Did he tell you everything before he spoke to me?" Tessa asked.

Lucie nodded as she closed her phone and returned it to her belt clip. "All we can do is wait and that isn't easy. Dante will get in touch the minute—"

"Leslie Anne is all right and he's going to bring her home very soon."

Lucie smiled. "You're absolutely right. Just hang on to that positive thought."

Yes, she would. She had to believe her child was safe because the alternative was too horrible to bear. If anything happened to Leslie Anne, what would she do? Her daughter was her life.

All during her pregnancy, she'd wondered if she could care about the child of her rapist or if the moment she saw the baby, she would hate it. When her father had suggested she have an abortion, she had seriously considered it. But her mother had inadvertently learned that Tessa was pregnant—she'd overheard two nurses talking about Tessa's condition. Anne Westbrook, who hadn't known her daughter had been raped, had pleaded with Tessa not to abort the child. How could she have refused her terminally ill mother's heartfelt plea?

Oddly enough, when Tessa first held Leslie Anne in her arms, it had been love at first sight. Something inside her—maternal instinct?—dictated her emotions and her actions, then as well as now. She had felt an overwhelming sense of love and protectiveness toward her newborn. But since at the time of her daughter's birth, she was still recovering from the "accident," she'd had to depend on her parents to look after Leslie Anne. On the day of her child's birth, she'd sworn she would recover fully, that no matter how long it took, the day would come when she would be whole again.

She had recovered fully from the devastating physical injuries she'd incurred, but even now, nearly seventeen years later, she was still emotionally incomplete.

"HERE'S YOUR NEW ROOM," the assistant manager told Leslie Anne as he inserted the key and then opened the door. "I'll bring your suitcase in for you and then be on my way."

Although she felt a certain sense of uneasiness—call it her self-survival instinct—Leslie Anne kept telling herself that this was a nice man who was simply doing his job.

She reached out for her suitcase. "That's all right. I can take it from here. Thank you."

He smiled at her and she thought how stupid she was for having any doubts about this man—Mr. Joe Thompson. Bad guys didn't identify themselves by name, did they?

"Certainly." He handed the suitcase to her. "Oh, by the way, you'll find a complimentary fruit basket in your new room. It's just the motel's way of saying thank-you for your cooperation and understanding."

"Oh. Yes, well…thank you."

"If there's anything we can do for you, don't hesitate to contact me in the manager's office."

Joe Thompson turned around and walked away. Leslie Anne let out a sigh of relief.

See, I told you that you were being silly to suspect that guy was up to no good.

THE TRAFFIC in Tuscaloosa was horrific. But this was a college town with thousands of students out and about at all hours. Dante tapped his fingers on the steering wheel as they waited at yet one more red light.

"Change already, will you," Dante grumbled under his breath.

"Calm down," Dom told him. "The police are at the motel, and they're going from door to door. If Leslie Anne Westbrook is there, they'll find her."

"Yeah, I know, but I'm telling you I've got this bad feeling in the pit of my stomach. And when my gut instincts tell me something's wrong, it usually is."

"Can't take your own advice, can you?"

"Huh?"

The red light changed. Dante wanted nothing more than to fly down the road, but with heavy traffic like this, he couldn't even make the speed limit.

"You told Ms. Westbrook to keep believing her daughter is all right."

"Yeah, well, what else would I tell the girl's mother?" Especially a mother who'd been raped when she was a teenager herself. Tessa must be going through a living hell right about now, worrying herself sick that what happened to her might be happening to her daughter.

"May I make an observation?" Dom asked.

"What the hell are you talking about?"

"You. Everyone at Dundee's knows your reputation. Mr. Do-things-my-own-way. But we were told that you are always able to remain objective, to stay personally uninvolved, which are two trademarks of a good agent."

"So?"

"So why do I get the feeling there's something personal going on with you in this case?"

"How could there be anything personal? I don't know the Westbrooks."

Dom shrugged. "Like I said, just an observation."

"An incorrect observation," Dante lied. Despite the fact that he kept telling himself Tessa Westbrook and her runaway daughter had no connection whatsoever to Amy, the same gut instincts that warned him Leslie Anne was in trouble, told him that there was some kind of connection. What, he didn't know. But he intended to find out.

"MY DEAR GIRL, why on earth didn't you let us know what was happening?" Myrle Poole swept into the library like a puff of lavender air, her chin-length, platinum blond hair bouncing against her rouged cheeks. Her ring-adorned left hand stroked the lavender silk scarf draped around her neck, which coordinated perfectly with her purple wool suit.

Hal Carpenter stood outside in the hall, his gaze apologizing to Tessa for the intrusion he'd been unable to halt. "Mrs. Poole is here," he said belatedly.

"And Miss Celia is waiting in the foyer for Mr. Sentell while he parks the car."

Tessa groaned inwardly. The horde was descending on them. She'd known it was bound to happen sooner or later, even though her father and she had decided not to share the news of Leslie Anne's abrupt departure with other members of the family. Her mother's sister, Myrle, and her daughter, Celia, had joined forces with her father's godson, Charlie, to form the first wave of the invasion. If these three had somehow learned that Leslie Anne had run away, then the others were bound to find out soon, if they didn't already know.

Myrle grabbed Tessa's shoulder, planted a light kiss on her cheek and then hugged her fiercely. "I'm sure G.W. didn't want to worry us, but he should have phoned me immediately. After all, precious little Leslie Anne is my only sister's only grandchild."

Aunt Myrle tended to be a tad melodramatic. A trait that seemed to run in the Leslie family, but one Tessa had not inherited.

Tessa returned her aunt's hug, but somewhat less passionately. "Daddy and I thought Leslie Anne would come home on her own and there would be no need to worry anyone else."

"Is there still no word? Oh, mercy, mercy. There's no telling what's happened to that poor child."

"I'm sure Leslie Anne is just fine," Lucie Evans said.

Myrle focused her blue eyes on Lucie, narrowing her gaze as she inspected the stranger. "And who are you?"

"Aunt Myrle, this is Lucie Evans, a Dundee agent. Daddy hired the agency she works for to help the police in their search for Leslie Anne. Lucie, may I introduce my aunt, Mrs. Myrle Leslie Poole."

"What on earth is the Dundee agency?" Myrle asked.

"And if she's supposed to be out hunting for Leslie Anne, what's she doing here?" Celia Poole asked as she entered the library.

Forcing a pleasant expression, Tessa turned to face her cousin Celia and the slender, elegantly dressed man at her side. Charles Sentell, who was her father's godson, still looked at her now as he had all the years she'd known him—with love in his eyes. If only she could have returned his feelings, everything might be different now.

"Lucie is one of four agents from the Dundee Private Security and Investigation Agency. The other three are working in the field and Lucie is posted here, with me." Tessa glanced from Lucie to the others. "Lucie, this is my cousin, Celia Poole." After each of her two divorces, Celia had resumed using her maiden name. "And this—" she looked right at Charlie "—is Charles Sentell, a family friend and my father's godson."

"Where's G.W.?" Charlie asked abruptly, effectively dismissing Lucie as nothing more than the hired help. One of Charlie's few flaws was his air of superiority. He considered three quarters of the people in the world to be his underlings.

For at least the millionth time in the past seventeen years, Tessa asked herself why on earth her father had ever thought she would actually want to marry this man. He was attractive enough, slender and physically fit, with light brown hair and gray eyes. Not tall, but not short, either. Medium. That one word described Charlie better than any other. Except for his impeccable taste in clothes and other material items, he had little to distinguish himself. Charlie had been working for her father since he'd graduated from college and most people whispered behind his back that if he wasn't G.W.'s godson, he wouldn't have climbed the ladder of success so quickly, if at all.

"Daddy's out walking Jefferson and Davis," Tessa replied.

"Charlie, perhaps you should go find Uncle G.W. and tell him that Aunt Sharon is flying back from Key West first thing in the morning." Celia rubbed her hand up and down Charlie's arm. Celia was simply a younger version of Aunt Myrle. A platinum blonde—both of them bleached blondes—with a flair for the dramatic. Snooty to the nth degree. Although she and Celia had been playmates and best friends as children, after her "accident," Tessa hadn't been able to reconnect with her cousin.

Charlie and Celia had been dating for the past year, shortly after Celia's second divorce, and everyone expected an announcement at any time. Tessa wished them well and felt a great sense of relief that Charlie had finally given up pursuing her. Over the years, he'd done everything in his power to persuade her to marry him. But as fond of him as she was, Tessa couldn't imagine Charlie being her husband. Truth be told, she couldn't imagine being married to anyone. She knew that nothing would have pleased her father more than her marrying Charlie years ago, but G.W. had finally reconciled himself to her remaining unmarried the rest of her life.

"Leave Daddy alone," Tessa said, her voice more commanding and harsh than she'd intended. "Please. He's a bundle of nerves, and it took a great deal of persuading on my part—and Lucie's—to get him out of the house for a little while."

"Well, of course, he's a bundle of nerves. He adores Leslie Anne. And with her missing, he's bound to be worried sick." Myrle looked past the others and zeroed in on Hal, who waited in the hall. "Hal, do be a dear and have Eustacia prepare some fresh coffee and perhaps some sandwiches. And in the meantime, bring me a glass of sherry. I'm simply overwrought and need a little something to calm me."

Hal looked to Tessa. She nodded. "Yes, please, bring Aunt Myrle some sherry and ask Eustacia to prepare coffee and sandwiches." Remembering her hostess duties and despite wishing she could tell everyone to leave, Tessa glanced around the room and asked, "Would anyone else care for a drink?"

"I'll take a sherry, too," Celia said.

"Bourbon. Straight," Charlie said.

"Lucie?" Tessa asked.

"I'll just wait for the coffee."

"Very well, that will be all, Hal." Tessa walked over to Lucie, looked up at her and said quietly, "It's going to become a three-ring circus around here and if you notice that I'm on the verge of losing it and telling everyone to go to hell, please stop me."

"Okay, I'll do my best." Lucie's lips twitched with a hint of a smile.

"What are you two whispering about?" Myrle frowned, the action deepening the wrinkles in her forehead and between her eyes. Undoubtedly Aunt Myrle was overdue for another Botox injection. "Goodness, Tessa, you know how unmannerly it is to whisper."

"I apologize," Tessa said, then deliberately changed the subject. "On second thought, Charlie, why don't you go find Daddy. It'll be dark soon and I'm sure it's getting cooler outside. I don't believe he took a jacket with him."

"Yes, certainly," Charlie replied. "Do you know in which direction he went?"

"Probably down around the river and the path through the woods near where the old grist mill used to be. It's a favorite walk of his and the dogs love it."

Celia grasped Charlie's arm. "Be sure to put your overcoat back on. We can't have you taking a chill, can we?"

When Charlie kissed Celia on the cheek, he cut his eyes in Tessa's direction, apparently checking for a reaction. Tessa hurriedly glanced away.

Myrle settled herself in G.W.'s chair beside the fireplace. "You should get Hal to replenish the firewood. It looks a bit low. And you should alert Eustacia that there will be guests for dinner this evening. I expect Olivia and Tad will be here soon."

"Olivia and Tad!" Oh, God, just what she needed. Just what her father needed. That femme fatale sycophant had been chasing her father for nearly three years now and Tessa feared the woman was actually wearing him down, inch by inch. After all, G.W. was only human, only a man. Being flattered by the attentions of a woman fifteen years his junior would be hard for any man to resist. But the most powerful weapon in Olivia's arsenal was sex, which she used quite expertly.

"Of course, I telephoned Olivia immediately," Myrle said. "After all, she loves your father and I knew he'd need her. I mean, she's practically G.W.'s fiancée, isn't she?"

Yes, of course. G.W. needed Olivia Sizemore and that worthless son of hers the way he needed another hole in his head. But because Olivia and Myrle had been friends since their days as sorority sisters, her aunt not only had been supporting Olivia's pursuit, but took every opportunity possible to point out to G.W. what a marvelous wife Olivia would make.

Tessa clenched her teeth, then looked at Lucie, a plea for help in her eyes.

"I'm sure Tessa appreciates your taking the initiative to let Mr. Westbrook's lady friend know about the situation with his granddaughter," Lucie said.

Tessa mouthed the words "thank you," then excused herself on the pretense of needing to take something for her headache. Instead she escaped to the powder room, dropped the commode seat and plopped down as the tears she'd barely been controlling broke free and ran down her cheeks.

"Please, Dante, call soon with good news," she whispered, as if saying the words aloud gave them more power.

LESLIE ANNE washed her face, brushed her teeth and put on her pajamas, then she eyed the fruit basket the motel had provided. She wasn't hungry, but she was thirsty and the small bottle of grape juice in the basket looked inviting. After all, she didn't want to get out and go down the hall to the cola machine. After turning on the TV, she lifted the bottle from the basket. Wonder why the basket isn't wrapped? She undid the cap on the bottle, pleased that it opened so easily. Often getting caps off could be a major hassle. She sat on the bed, lifted the bottle to her lips and sipped the juice. It was a little warm, but sweet and wet. It would do.

She pulled both pillows out from beneath the spread and propped them against the headboard, then settled in and channel surfed, searching for something of interest. She needed a silly, mindless program to help take her mind off her problems. And she had major problems.

God, I'm so miserable. What am I doing here in a motel room, all alone? I wish I were home in my own bed.

She could go home, couldn't she? First thing in the morning, she should call her mother and tell her she was coming home. She was an idiot for running off the way she had. What did running away solve? Nothing. If her biological father was a serial murderer, she could run to the ends of the earth and that fact wouldn't change.

But what if it wasn't true? What if whoever sent her the package had lied to her? She should go home, show the letter and newspaper clippings to her mother and grandfather, then demand the truth from them.

Leslie Anne finished off the small bottle of juice, then dropped the empty bottle on the floor. The channels were limited on the motel TV, so she decided to stop searching for something to watch. She yawned. Suddenly she felt very drowsy. Maybe the long hours behind the wheel and all the stress she was under had caught up with her.

She yawned again. The room began to spin around and around. What was wrong with her? Unable to sit up any longer, she fell across the bed sideways. When she tried to lift her hand, it seemed to weigh a ton. Her eyelids flickered open and closed of their own accord, as if she had no control over them.

Something was wrong with her. Terribly wrong.

WHEN DANTE and Dom arrived at the motel, he met up with the police lieutenant in charge of the search and pulled the man aside.

"Have you searched the entire hotel?" Dante asked.

"We've checked every room on the ground floor and have started on the second floor," Lieutenant Nesbitt said. "The management isn't happy that we're disturbing their guests and at first we weren't getting much cooperation."

"Screw the management. We've got a sixteen-year-old girl who could be in trouble."

"I realize the seriousness of this matter, but I don't have an army at my disposal. Just me and two officers. This is a big motel, in case that fact escaped you."

"Well, you now have two more men to help knock on doors," Dante said. "Let's stop wasting time and get upstairs."

"Hold on, Mr. Moran," Nesbitt said. "You should let us handle this."

"Look, Lieutenant, I'm heading upstairs to search

for Leslie Anne Westbrook and the only way you're going to stop me is to arrest me."

The policeman grimaced. "Just act official, will you?" Nesbitt told Dante.

"No problem."

Dante and Dom took the other side of the building from the lieutenant and his two officers. Dom went right and Dante left. First they knocked on the door, then waited for a response. If they didn't get someone to the door, they'd knock again and inform the guest that this was official police business. One by one the doors either opened or Dante and Dom used the keys, reluctantly provided by the manager, to unlock each door.

Dante knocked on the door to Room 231. No response. He knocked again. "Please open up," Dante said. "This is official police business. We're searching for a missing girl whom we believe is in this motel."

Silence. Dante knocked again, then inserted the key and unlocked the door. The room lay in darkness except for the faint shimmer of artificial light shining through the closed window blinds. At first he thought the room was empty, then he heard a muffled whimper. He felt along the wall for the switch, flicked it on and flooded the room with light. A naked middle-aged man jumped to his feet, his eyes wide with fear. Lying on the bed, naked and obviously drugged, lay a young girl. A young girl who was the spitting image of Amy Smith.

"Hey, it's okay. She's my girlfriend," the naked man said as he started to reach for his pants on the floor.

Dante pulled his Smith & Wesson from his hip holster and aimed it directly at the man's exposed privates. "You make one move and I'll blow your balls off. You understand me?"

The guy's erection went limp. He nodded. "I'm telling you, she's my girlfriend. Candy. Her name's Candy."

"Dom!" Dante shouted. Had they arrived in time to save Leslie Anne from being raped? He sure as hell hoped so.

Dom Shea flew into the room, then skidded to a halt behind Dante. "What have we here?"

"Take care of this pervert, will you?" Dante's trigger finger itched. God, how he wanted to castrate this slimy bastard. "If he tries anything…"

Dom glanced at the girl lying helplessly on the bed. "Damn!" He walked over to the trembling naked man, jerked his hands behind him and marched him out of the room. "Come on. The police are dying to meet you."

Dante walked across the room to the bed. He reached down and pulled the sheet over the girl lying there. She looked up at him, her eyes wide with terror. She opened her mouth. "Help me." Her words were a shaky, pitiful plea.

Wrapping the sheet securely around her, Dante lifted her up and into his arms. "It's okay, honey.

You're safe. Nobody's going to hurt you. I'm working with the local police. My name is Dante Moran. I'm with the FBI." He told a little white lie to soothe the young woman's fears.

"That man…he—he tried…he was going to…"

"Hush, honey. Don't try to talk. I'm going to take you to a hospital."

"I want my mama." Tears filled the girl's dark brown eyes.

"Sure thing, Leslie Anne. We'll get your mama here just as quick as we can."

CHAPTER FIVE

TESSA RACED into the emergency room, Lucie Evans at her side. On the flight from Fairport to Tuscaloosa, she'd heard Dante's words repeating again and again inside her mind and heart. *She's all right. Do you hear me, Tessa? Leslie Anne is okay.*

The Dundee agency had arranged for Tessa and Lucie to be transported by helicopter, and it had been all Tessa could do to persuade her father to let her go alone. She'd convinced him that at a time such as this Leslie Anne wanted and needed only her mother. That was true, of course, but she was also worried about her father's health. At sixty-eight, with high blood pressure and high cholesterol, plus a Type A personality, he was a prime candidate for a heart attack or a stroke. Leslie Anne's disappearance had put her father in a major tailspin.

"You take care of things here," she'd told G.W. "Get her room ready and see if you can't clear everyone else out before I bring her home. She doesn't need a houseful of family and friends. At least not for a while."

As they entered the E.R., Lucie lifted her hand and waved at a tall, broad-shouldered man with overly long black hair that curled around his collar. "There's Dom." Lucie practically dragged Tessa toward the Dundee agent. "He'll know where Leslie Anne is."

The man Lucie had called Dom made his way through the crowded waiting room and came straight toward them. "You made it in record time," he said.

"Dante told me to get here as quickly as possible," Lucie replied.

"Where's Leslie Anne?" Tessa asked.

"Oh, I should have introduced you two," Lucie said. "Tessa, this is Domingo Shea. Dom, this is our client, Ms. Tessa Westbrook."

"Ma'am." He nodded.

She offered him a fragile smile. "Please tell me where my daughter is."

"She's in there—" He nodded toward the closed double doors that led to the emergency room's private cubicles. "Tell the receptionist at the desk over there that you're Leslie Anne's mother and they'll let you go on back."

From his dark, Latin good looks, Tessa had halfway expected Dom Shea to speak with a Spanish accent, but his voice was pure Southern drawl. A Texas drawl if she didn't miss her guess, similar to Dante Moran's.

"Where's Dante…Mr. Moran?" Tessa asked.

"He's back there with your daughter," Dom told

her. "Ever since he rescued her, she won't let him out of her sight."

"What do you mean rescued?" Tessa's heartbeat drummed in her ears. "All Dante said when he called was that she's all right. Was she in an accident?"

"Big mouth." Lucie elbowed Dom in the ribs.

"Sorry." He gave Tessa a sympathetic look.

"What happened to my daughter?"

"Dante will explain everything." Lucie glanced around the waiting room. "No use sharing your personal business with a bunch of strangers, and in a place like this, you never know who's eavesdropping."

Tessa nodded, then turned and headed toward the receptionist's desk. The woman behind the glass-enclosed unit, looked up when Tessa approached.

"Yes, ma'am, may I help you?"

"My daughter, Leslie Anne Westbrook, was brought in earlier tonight. I'd like to see her, please."

"Yes, ma'am. Go right on back. She's in examining room number three."

"Thank you."

"We allowed her bodyguard to go back with her," the receptionist said. "I hope that was all right. She was terribly upset when the nurses asked him to leave, so they thought it best to let him stay with her."

"Yes, that's perfectly all right."

Tessa swallowed the tears threatening to choke her. Now was not the time to lose control. She had to be strong. Once beyond the entry doors, she hurried past rooms one and two. Then she saw him. Dante Moran stood outside room number three, his arms crossed over his chest, one foot propped behind the other. The instant he saw her, he came forward, halting when only inches separated them.

"I want to see her," Tessa said.

"You will. In a couple of minutes. The doctor is completing her examination."

"What happened to my little girl? And don't even think about trying to protect me from the truth. Was she in a car wreck?"

Dante shook his head, then clutched Tessa's shoulders and said, "Let's take a walk down the hall."

Instinctively trusting him, she went with him down to the end of the hallway, where they were completely alone. "What is it?" *Oh, God, please, please don't let it be what I've feared the most.*

"She wasn't raped," Dante said.

Tessa let out a loud, semihysterical cry.

Dante put his arm around her shoulders and spoke to her quietly. "The doctor told me that there is no physical evidence of rape, but she went ahead and called for a rape kit and that's what they're doing now." Tessa tensed. Dante stroked her back. "Leslie Anne told me that he didn't rape her."

"Tell me everything. I have to know."

"She had checked into the Bama Motel and according to what she's told me, some man passed himself off as the motel's assistant manager, got her to change rooms and left her a fruit basket with what we suspect contained a bottle of grape juice that he'd drugged."

"He drugged her?"

Is that what my rapist did? Tessa wondered. *Did he drug me first, then kidnap and rape me?* A part of her was thankful that she could not remember what had happened, that it would forever be a complete blank in her mind. But another part of her wondered how she had wound up the victim of a monstrous serial killer, whose M.O. included rape and torture.

"When I burst into the room, the son of a bitch was on top of her." Dante tightened his hold around Tessa's shoulders. "They were both naked, and since Leslie Anne had been drugged, she didn't have the ability to fight him."

Unbearable emotional pain ripped through Tessa, a pain so fierce that it exceeded all the physical pain she had endured during her months of recovery after her "accident." "No…no…no!" There was no agony on earth more brutal than the one felt by a parent on behalf of his or her child. And no love so unconditional as that of a mother and father.

Like a mother tigress, aggressively protective, Tessa wanted to rip apart the person responsible for hurting her baby.

She understood now, as she'd never understood before, how her father must have felt all those years ago when he'd sworn he would move heaven and earth to see her rapist captured and put to death.

Dante turned Tessa straight into his arms and held her protectively against his big body. She allowed herself to yield completely, to give herself over to his care. She couldn't remember ever instinctively trusting another human being, other than her father, the way she did Dante Moran. And why, she didn't know. This instant trust and physical attraction puzzled her, even made her question her usual sound judgment. But God, it felt so good to have him here to lean on.

"We'll take her home to Fairport tonight. I've already cleared it with the Tuscaloosa police." Dante eased Tessa out of his arms. He whipped out a white handkerchief, grasped her chin with one hand and then reached up to dab the tears from the corners of her eyes.

She hadn't even realized she was crying.

Tessa gazed up into Dante's eyes, so dark a brown they appeared almost black. What she saw in his intense gaze unnerved her. Longing. That was the only word to describe it. A soul-deep longing. Part sexual, but equally pure, raw emotion. Was what she saw, what she sensed, coming from Dante alone or was it also a reflection of what he was seeing in her eyes?

Forcing herself to break eye contact with him, Tessa cleared her throat, turned around and glanced down the hallway toward room number three. "Mr.

Shea told Lucie and me that Leslie Anne wouldn't let you out of her sight. I want to thank you for not only rescuing my daughter, but for making her feel safe." And that was the way he made Tessa feel, too. Safe. As if he could protect her from all harm.

Dante clamped his hand down on her shoulder. "She's one scared young lady. She's going to need you now more than she ever has in her life."

"I know."

"Yes, I suppose you do." His voice went deep and whisper soft. "Only too well."

Clenching her teeth, Tessa swallowed. "I don't suppose she told you why she ran away from home, did she?"

"No, she didn't."

"My greatest fear has always been that someday she'd find out the truth."

"Did you ever plan to tell her?"

"No."

Dante's grip tightened. "My mama used to say that the truth always has a way of coming out."

"If Leslie Anne found out about— I can't imagine how it could have happened. At the time, Daddy did everything in his power to keep things hush-hush. He—we didn't even tell my mother what had really happened."

"If Leslie Anne did find out that her biological father was—"

Tessa whipped around and glared at Dante. "An

inhuman monster. That's what he was. How could she ever cope with that knowledge?"

"With a great deal of love and understanding. You'll have to find a way to convince her that she didn't inherit any dangerously negative traits, that she doesn't have to worry that the day will come when she'll become her father's daughter."

Tessa gasped. Hearing her own fears voiced aloud shocked her. Somewhere in the back of her mind, all these years, she had wondered if it was possible to inherit criminal tendencies. But Leslie Anne's gentle, loving personality had allayed those concerns. For the most part. If those hideously ugly concerns existed in the remote corners of Tessa's heart, how much more prevalent would they be inside Leslie Anne's heart and mind? Inside her very soul?

"I love my daughter more than anything on earth," Tessa said. "I'd do anything for her. Anything. I'd lay down and die for her. Can you understand loving someone that much?"

"Yes."

"Do you have a child? Children?"

"No."

"Then—

"There was someone once, a long time ago." He spoke as if the words hurt him. "She was someone worth dying for."

A strange sensation wafted through Tessa, like a

very slow-acting narcotic that gradually induced a light-headed feeling. This man had loved a woman so completely that he would have been willing to die for her, as Tessa would for her child. Love that strong took on a life of its own, existing beyond the grave.

Love never dies.

Before Tessa could think of what to say to Dante, she noticed a slender brunette wearing a white jacket emerge from room number three.

"That's Dr. Ellison," Dante said.

Tessa hurried up the hallway, Dante directly behind her. The middle-aged doctor turned immediately and glanced up from the chart she held in her hand. She looked straight at Dante.

"Dr. Ellison, this is Tessa Westbrook, Leslie Anne's mother," Dante said.

The doctor nodded cordially to Tessa.

"How is my daughter?"

"Physically, she'll be fine," Dr. Ellison said. "I found no evidence of rape, no signs of penetration or bruising. But Leslie Anne has gone through an emotionally harrowing ordeal. I suggest that you see to it that she receives therapy to help her deal with what happened to her tonight."

"Yes, of course," Tessa replied. She'd undergone years of therapy and understood the profound way professional help could complement the love and support of a person's family. "May I see my daughter now?"

"Yes, of course. And as soon as she's dressed, you may take her home." Dr. Ellison glanced at Dante. "She's been asking for you, Mr. Moran."

Tessa rushed to the door of room three, then hesitated. Dante came up behind her, reached around and opened the door. The nurse was helping Leslie Anne into her jeans and blouse.

Tessa sucked in a deep breath, then entered. "Leslie Anne?"

Her daughter whirled around and stared at her. Tears pooled in her dark brown eyes. Tessa took a tentative step forward and held open her arms.

"Baby..."

"Mama!" Leslie Anne flew into her mother's arms.

"Shh—" Tessa stroked and caressed and murmured soothingly. "It's all right. I'm here. You're safe. Oh, sweet baby, I love you so much."

Leslie Anne lifted her head and looked right at her mother. "How can you love me? If—if it's true that I'm..." She gulped down her tears.

"Shush, baby, shush." Tessa hugged her daughter close.

"Am I?" Leslie Anne asked, her eyes closed, her head resting on Tessa's shoulder. "Am I the result of your...your being..."

"We'll talk about it later, when we're home." *Oh, God, she knows. Somehow Leslie Anne has found out the truth. That's why she ran away.* "Granddaddy's terribly worried. He'll be so happy to see you." Tessa knew she had to stay strong and not fall apart…for her daughter's sake.

The nurse handed Dante a black leather coat, then left the room without saying anything. He exchanged a quick glance with Tessa, then nodded toward the closed door. She understood he was telling her that it was time to leave.

After draping the coat across one arm, he walked over, placed his hand in the center of Leslie Anne's back and said, "Are you ready to go home?"

Leslie Anne lifted her head and looked back at him. "You're going with us, aren't you?"

"You bet I am."

"Thank you for everything." Leslie Anne turned all the way around to face Dante.

He lifted the black leather coat, whipped it around Leslie Anne's shoulders and pulled the lapels together. "It's chilly outside. You'd better wear this until we're on the helicopter."

Leslie Anne crossed her arms over her waist and hugged the supple leather jacket as if simply touching it somehow comforted her. It was then that Tessa realized Dante must have wrapped his coat around Leslie Anne before taking her out of the motel earlier tonight.

They were both naked. Dante's words rang out in Tessa's mind. Had Dante wrapped her daughter in a sheet to cover her nakedness and then given her his own coat to protect her from the nighttime chill?

"What about my car?" Leslie Anne asked. "I mean Hannah's car." She hung her head. "Mama, I'm sorry I ran away. I just didn't know what else to do."

"It's all right," Tessa said. "We'll have all the time in the world to talk things over once I get you home safe and sound."

"We'll have Lucie drive Hannah's car back to Fairport," Dante said. "She can exchange cars with Hannah in the morning." He opened the door and stepped aside. "We've got a helicopter waiting on us. Are you ladies ready?"

Tessa looked to her daughter, who nodded. "Yes, we're ready," Tessa said. "We're ready to go home."

CHAPTER SIX

DANTE EXITED the helicopter first when it landed at the Fairport airstrip a couple of miles outside town. The town was too small to support an airport, but the old airstrip, used now mostly by crop dusters and some small aircraft owned by local residents, was the ideal place to land a helicopter. Once on the ground, Dante assisted Leslie Anne and then Tessa out of the whirlybird. Seeing them standing side by side, he noted once again that the daughter stood several inches taller than the mother. They were both slender, blond beauties and except for being taller, Leslie Anne's figure, walk and mannerisms mimicked Tessa's. No one seeing them together would ever doubt they were mother and daughter.

So there's no way Leslie Anne could be Amy's child.

He had to keep reminding himself of that fact because Leslie Anne's resemblance to Amy Smith had been neither a trick of his imagination nor wishful thinking. Not only did she look just like Amy—except she was taller and her eyes were brown—but her voice even sounded like Amy's. But then, Tessa's voice reminded him of Amy's.

Once he was no longer assigned to this case, which should be within twenty-four hours, he intended to check into the possibility that Tessa Westbrook was related to Amy. There had to be an explanation for why Tessa's daughter could almost pass for Amy Smith's double when Amy was a teenager. Surely, the man who fathered Leslie Anne hadn't been a blood relative of Amy's!

"There's Daddy," Tessa said, then groaned. "Oh, God, she's with him."

"Why did he have to bring her?" Leslie Anne echoed her mother's sentiments.

Dante watched while G.W. approached, a strikingly attractive, petite redhead clinging to his arm. *The girlfriend?* When they drew closer, Dante noted that the woman was not as young as she appeared to be at a distance. No doubt Olivia Sizemore—Dante guessed her to be in her midfifties—had been a beauty in her youth and was still quite a lovely woman.

G.W. rushed forward and wrapped his arms around his granddaughter, encompassing her in a bear hug. "Don't you ever do anything like that again, honey pie. You had us scared half out of our minds."

"I'm sorry. I just didn't know what else to do." Leslie Anne began crying again.

G.W. petted her lovingly. "Enough of that. Whatever's wrong, we'll fix it."

"Some things can't be fixed." Leslie Anne glanced over G.W.'s shoulder and glared at Olivia.

"Mercy, G.W., don't keep the girls out here in this night air any longer." Olivia smiled and batted her eyelashes as she scolded G.W.

"She's right, Daddy," Tessa said somewhat reluctantly, apparently hating to agree with her father's girlfriend. "We need to get Leslie Anne home."

"Hal has the car waiting." G.W. inclined his head to where the Mercedes was parked on a paved area not far from the airstrip. He took his granddaughter's hand. "Let's go."

She wouldn't budge. "Wait!"

"What's wrong?" G.W. asked.

Leslie Anne pulled free and ran back toward Dante. "You're coming, too, aren't you?"

He hadn't intended to go to the Leslie Plantation with the family at this hour of the morning. He'd planned to get a good night's sleep at the local motel, where Dundee's had reserved rooms for their agents, and then finalize this assignment sometime tomorrow.

"Yes, please, Mr. Moran." Tessa placed her hand on her daughter's back in a supportive gesture. "I doubt any of us will get much sleep tonight. Leslie Anne deserves answers to the questions that drove her away from home. She seems to like you, to trust you. If she wants you to come home with us, then so do I."

"Is that what you want?" Dante asked Leslie

Anne. "Do you want a perfect stranger to be with you when your mother answers your questions?"

"You're not a perfect stranger," Leslie Anne said. "You're the man who saved me from— Please, Dante...Mr. Moran..."

"I'd appreciate it if you'd come home with us." Tessa looked at him pleadingly. Their gazes met and locked for a minute and during those sixty seconds, he studied her there in the shadows cast by the airstrip lighting.

"Sure thing. You two go on and I'll follow. I see the agency has a car waiting for me, too." He motioned to the driver.

"No, please, ride with us." Leslie Anne grabbed Dante's arm.

"There isn't room for all of us in the Mercedes," G.W. said. "Honey pie, let Mr. Moran—"

"Daddy, you and Olivia go on with Hal." Tessa clasped her daughter's hand. "We'll ride with Mr. Moran."

For a second there, it looked as if G.W. was going to protest, but as if realizing this wasn't a battle worth fighting, he acquiesced. "Very well."

Within minutes the Mercedes pulled out onto the road and Vic Noble followed. Settled into the front seat beside Vic, Dante turned halfway around and looked into the back seat.

Tessa had her arm around Leslie Anne, who cuddled against her mother, her head on her mother's shoulder. Leslie Anne's eyelids fluttered. Poor kid, Dante thought, she's been through hell.

"Are you two all right?" Dante asked.

"We will be," Tessa replied, and he understood her meaning.

He already felt awkward being this personally involved with his client's family. Technically, G. W. Westbrook was the client, since the old man was picking up the Dundee tab, but as far as Dante was concerned, he was working for Tessa. At least for the time being.

"Thank you for coming home with us, Dan—Mr. Moran." Leslie Anne yawned.

"Call me Dante," he replied.

A fragile smile lifted the corners of Leslie Anne's lips moments before she fell asleep. Tessa looked right at Dante and, by God, he felt as if he'd been hit by a bolt of lightning. The last time something like that had happened had been over seventeen years ago—when he realized he'd fallen hard and fast for Amy Smith.

SO THE LITTLE BRAT is coming home. Too bad. It would have made things so much easier for me if she'd disappeared completely. Or better yet, if someone else had gotten rid of her for me. But now she's my problem again. Not to worry. I'll figure out a way to remove all the obstacles standing between me and what I want, what I deserve. Besides, the world

will be better off without that demon seed. G.W.
should have insisted that Tessa have an abortion the
moment the doctors discovered she was pregnant. If
it hadn't been for that lily-livered Anne begging
Tessa not to abort her precious grandchild, everything would have been different. For Tessa, for me,
for everyone involved. If only I'd known then what
had really happened to Tessa, that the "accident" that
had supposedly killed her baby's father and left Tessa
near death had been nothing but a ruse to protect the
family from the hideous truth. Despite the fact that
Anne was dying slowly from cancer, I would have
told her the truth and spared all of us.

I've tried everything I know to avoid taking this
next step. As much as I dislike Leslie Anne, I rather
hate the idea of killing her. Of killing anyone. But it
must be done. There is no other way.

It galls me to think that Tessa gave her bastard
child not only Anne's given name, but the honorable
family name, too. The Leslie family goes back generations in southwest Mississippi and has been part
of a dynasty formed in the days preceding the War between the States. The offspring of a murderer doesn't
deserve to bear such a distinguished, revered name.

I must think of a way to get rid of Leslie Anne, a
way that will not implicate me. I could hire a hit
man. But what if he were caught and named me as
his employer? No, no, that would never do.

I could shoot her myself. Or stab her. Or poison her.

If only I were good at this sort of thing. But I'm not. I've never plotted someone's murder.

Think. Think about what can be done.

Revealing the truth about her father was an excellent first step in destroying the spoiled little princess's self-confidence. Her running away was an unexpected bonus.

But she's back now, in the bosom of her loving family.

Yes, she has returned to the Leslie Plantation, but not unscathed. She's been emotionally wounded and is now quite vulnerable. She knows me, trusts me. It should be quite simple to catch her unaware.

TESSA WATCHED while Dante lifted a sleeping Leslie Anne into his arms. For just a moment, the sweetest, strangest thought went through her mind. The gentle, caring way Dante handled Leslie Anne was the way a father would treat his daughter.

If only…

Tessa followed closely behind as Dante carried Leslie Anne onto the veranda. Hal held the front door open for them and G.W. waited quietly in the foyer. Much to Tessa's great relief, G.W. had deposited his current lady love at her house on their way home from the airstrip.

When he entered the foyer, Dante paused. Tessa walked to the staircase and motioned for him to follow, which he did. She led him up the stairs, down the hall and straight to Leslie Anne's suite. After hurrying inside, Tessa switched on a dim light in the bathroom to softly illuminate the suite. One step ahead of Dante, Tessa pulled down the covers so that he could deposit her child in her own bed. He slipped the black leather coat from beneath her and tossed it to the foot of the bed.

Tessa removed Leslie Anne's shoes, then lifted the sheet and blanket to cover her. She stood with Dante at the foot of the bed and looked at her daughter. When Dante eased his arm around her shoulders, Tessa almost cried out with gratitude. Despite having the loving support of her devoted father, she felt so alone. How many times had she dreamed of a man to stand by her, to love her, to be a father to her child? But there had been no one, even though she'd had numerous offers. In recent years, she had dated some, but had been unable to form a strong attachment to anyone, not even to Charlie Sentell. Dear, sweet, pompous Charlie. How many times had he professed his undying love? How many times had she broken his heart?

Her therapist had helped her understand that it was perfectly normal for her to fear committing herself to a sexual partnership. Not only had she endured a vicious rape, but she had survived a brutal beating that had left all of her assailant's other victims dead. After years of therapy, she had finally accepted a bitter truth—no matter how hard she tried to find love, to open herself up to the possibility of forming a lasting relationship with a man, she seemed doomed to failure.

So, why now, after all these years, did she find herself interested in a man she barely knew? What was it about Dante Moran that drew her to him, that made her instinctively trust him, that ignited a sexual longing inside her?

Dante led Tessa out of Leslie Anne's room, but left the door open. "Her falling asleep on the way here gave you a temporary reprieve from having to answer her questions," he said. "But come morning, she'll confront you. You know that, don't you?"

"Yes, I know."

"What do you intend to tell her?"

"The truth." She had hoped to never have to reveal the truth of Leslie Anne's true parentage. But she realized that lying to her daughter would hurt her far more, now that she suspected the truth.

"Is there anything I can do?" Dante looked at her with such intense concern that she longed to wrap her arms around him and beg him to stay with her.

Barely holding herself together, she shook her head sadly. "Not unless you think you can convince a sensitive, high-strung sixteen-year-old girl that it doesn't matter who her biological father was, that just because…" Tessa simply could not bring herself to say it again.

"Sorry. I'm not a miracle worker. I wish I were."

"Of course you're not. It's just I'd rather die than have to tell her what happened."

"I believe she already knows," Dante said. "All she wants is to hear you admit it."

"That's not what she wants. What she really wants is for me to tell her it's not true, that it's a terrible lie, that she really is the daughter of some man named John Allen."

"Telling her the truth won't be easy for you, either."

Dante reached out and caressed her cheek with the back of his hand. That soft, tender touch exploded inside her, as if she'd been struck by lightning.

When she stared at him, her mouth open, but silent, he continued. "It will be even more difficult for Leslie Anne to accept the truth. She's going to need all your love and support, as well as her grandfather's and her entire family's. And my guess is, it wouldn't hurt to take Dr. Ellison's suggestion and throw a really good therapist into the mix, too."

"She likes you, Mr. Moran…Dante. I believe after what happened at the hotel last night, she sees you as her knight in shining armor."

Dante harrumphed. "Believe me, that's not a role that suits me."

"I disagree," Tessa told him. "I'm in total agreement with my daughter. But if you prefer the title of guardian angel to white knight, then—"

"Hold on there." He held up his hand in a stop signal. "All I did last night was what I'd been hired to do—find your daughter and bring her home."

"Didn't anyone ever tell you that when you're given a compliment, you should simply say thank you?"

He smiled. "Thank you."

"I'll call Hal and he can show you to a room and if you need anything—"

"I think I'll just go downstairs," Dante said. "I should make a few phone calls and arrange to return to Atlanta tomorrow. So, don't bother Hal. I'll catch a quick nap in one of the chairs in the library."

"Are you sure?"

He nodded. "You'd better get some sleep."

"I'm going to stay in Leslie Anne's room with her. I doubt I'll get much sleep, but I will rest."

Dante turned and walked away. She watched him until he disappeared down the hall, then went back into her daughter's room. Leslie Anne slept peacefully, like the innocent child she'd been before last night. Tessa eased a cashmere knit throw from the back of the overstuffed floral lounge chair in the corner, sat down in the chair and covered up with the deliciously soft, warm afghan.

As she sat there in the semidarkness, she thought about the fact that for as long as Leslie Anne lived, she would remember the night she'd come very close to being raped. She might have nightmares for years, might see the man's face in her dreams, hear his voice, feel his foul touch. Tessa wished that she could erase her daughter's memories of what had happened.

But would that make it easier for her? Has being unable to remember what happened to you made it easier to accept that you were raped, brutalized and impregnated by a subhuman psychopath?

DANTE HAD CATNAPPED in the biggest, most plush chair in the library after he finished his phone calls and concluded his business. He'd awakened fifteen minutes ago, found the nearest bathroom and washed his face. He badly needed a shower and a shave. When he glanced in the mirror, the guy staring back at him looked like a seedy bum with scruffy stubble on his face wearing an expensive but wrinkled black suit. Since his usual morning routine of a shower, a shave and a cup of coffee was out of the question at the moment, because his suitcase was at the local motel, he would have to settle for just the cup of coffee.

When he finally found the kitchen, he was surprised to discover a plump, gray-haired woman buzzing about in the huge, state-of-the-art kitchen. After all, it was barely five-thirty. The moment he opened the door, he smelled the heavenly aroma of coffee brewing.

"Good morning," the woman said. "Come on in, Mr. Moran. Coffee's almost ready."

"Thank you. I'm afraid I don't know your—"

"Eustacia Bonner," she told him. "I'm the house-keeper and cook, although I mostly do the cooking. I oversee an outside staff who comes in daily to do the cleaning. I've been with the Westbrook family since I was a girl. My mama worked for old man Leslie, Miss Tessa's grandpa."

"Nice to meet you, Eustacia."

"You the only body up?" she asked.

"As far as I know."

She surveyed him from head to toe. "Looks like you slept in your clothes."

"I did. I caught a nap in the library."

"I want to thank you for finding our Leslie Anne and bringing her home to us." Eustacia lifted her large white apron and dotted the tears from her eyes. "She's a sweet thing, just like her mama. And spoiled just like Miss Tessa was when she was a girl, but it hasn't made her a little hellion the way it did her mama when she was that age."

Puzzled by her comment, Dante stared quizzically at the old woman. "Tessa Westbrook was a hellion as a teenager?"

Eustacia chuckled. "She sure was. You'd never believe it to see her now, would you? Ever since she recovered from that bad accident she had when she was eighteen, she's been the sweetest, kindest person I've ever known. And such a devoted daughter. You should have seen the way she was with her mama when Miss Anne was dying, one slow, difficult day after another. She would sit with her and read to her and hold her hand. And if it hadn't been for Miss Tessa and little Leslie Anne, I don't think Mr. G.W. would have survived after his wife's death. That man worshipped the ground Miss Anne walked on."

"Before the accident, Tessa…Miss Tessa wasn't kind and sweet?"

"Lordy no! That gal was wild as a buck and downright hateful sometimes. I swear she was the bane of her mama and daddy's existence."

"I suppose what happened to her—the accident and all—would have changed anybody."

"I suppose so. Terrible thing, the automobile accident that killed Leslie Anne's daddy. But it sure did perform a miracle on Miss Tessa." Eustacia reached up in the cupboard, got a mug and handed it to Dante. "Coffee's ready."

Just as he poured the cup full of steaming hot coffee, Hal Carpenter entered the kitchen. "Morning."

"Good morning," Eustacia replied.

"Mr. Moran, you've got a visitor," Hal said. "Ms. Evans is waiting in the library for you."

"Lucie's here?" What was she doing here this early? "Yes, sir."

After taking a sip of coffee and sighing quietly, Dante exited the kitchen and headed back to the library. He found Lucie, looking fresh as a daisy, standing in front of the fireplace, gazing up above the mantel at the oil painting of a young and lovely blond woman.

"You're out and about mighty early." Dante entered the room.

"Wonder if that's Anne Leslie Westbrook?" Lucie turned around and smiled at Dante.

"I don't know. I suppose it is. The dress is rather old-fashioned, so it could even be Mrs. Westbrook's mother, couldn't it?"

"Hmm." Lucie nodded to a small package on the massive mahogany desk. "I brought Leslie Anne's things from her friend Hannah's car."

"You've already exchanged the cars? I'll bet the servants at the Wright household appreciated being roused so early."

"The housekeeper was already up," Lucie said.

"Thanks for bringing the—"

"You'd better take a look inside that padded envelope," Lucie told him. "It'll explain why Leslie Anne Westbrook ran away."

"I already know why."

"You know that someone sent her a letter telling her that her biological father was a serial killer who raped and tortured his victims?"

"What?"

Lucie walked over, picked up the package and dumped the contents onto the desk. "Not just a letter, but dozens of newspaper clippings from when the man was finally arrested, put on trial and convicted. By that time he'd killed at least ten women whose bodies had been found and the police suspected him of murdering many more whose bodies were never found."

Listening to Lucie, thinking about the monsters out there who preyed on innocent people made Dante's blood run cold.

Following his graduation from college, he'd joined the FBI. One major reason he'd chosen the FBI as a career was because he'd thought he could use the bureau's vast resources to find out what had happened to Amy. After years of probing into various possibilities, he'd finally come to the conclusion that Amy might have been the victim of a serial killer. Amy had fit the description of all the other victims. All the women he had kidnapped and murdered were young, pretty blondes. Not one of his victims had been older than twenty. The madman had operated in several states—Louisiana, Texas, Arkansas, Oklahoma and Mississippi—over a period of nearly six years. Definitely at the time of Amy's disappearance.

Dante placed his coffee mug down on a heavyweight ceramic coaster on the desk, then picked up a couple of the newspaper clippings. The moment he read the name of the man who had brutalized Tessa Westbrook, his heart stopped beating for a split second.

Eddie Jay Nealy.

Dante closed his eyes in an effort to shut out the pain, but the rage and hatred burning inside him couldn't be contained. Eddie Jay Nealy was the man who had terrorized five states for half a dozen years, each of his victims a beautiful, blue-eyed, blond teen-age girl.

The man Dante believed could have murdered Amy—although her body was never found—was the same man who had raped and beaten Tessa. And that man was Leslie Anne Westbrook's biological father.

CHAPTER SEVEN

TESSA FOUND Dante in the kitchen eating breakfast with Hal. The two were drinking coffee and discussing football. She paused in the doorway and studied Dante, trying to discern what it was about the man that attracted her so. He was good-looking, but not drop-dead gorgeous. It was more an aura of raw masculinity, that dark brooding male of fiction women seemed to be drawn to even when they knew said male was dangerous. Not that Tessa believed for one minute that Dante Moran posed a physical threat to her or any woman. She'd seen the gentleness in him when he'd dealt with Leslie Anne. No, the threat was to a woman's emotions. This man could easily break her heart, and she simply couldn't take that kind of risk. In her thirty-five years, she'd experienced enough suffering. None of her making. But if she chose to pursue her interest in Dante and got hurt, then it would be her own fault.

When Eustacia said, "Good morning, Miss Tessa," Hal and Dante glanced up at her.

Squaring her shoulders, Tessa breezed into the kitchen, smiled at the three other occupants and headed straight for the coffee. "Good morning." She looked directly at Dante.

"How's Leslie Anne?" he asked.

"She's still asleep." Tessa lifted the coffeepot from the warmer and filled her cup.

"Do you have any idea why that child ran off the way she did?" Eustacia asked as she placed two slices of wheat bread into the toaster. "Anything could have happened to her out there all alone the way she was."

When Tessa didn't respond immediately—after all what could she say that wouldn't be a lie?—Eustacia shook her head. "It's just the age she is, I guess. Lord knows she came by it honestly. You were wild as a buck at sixteen. Yes, sirree, you sure kept your mama and daddy on their toes."

"So I've been told." Tessa placed her coffee cup on the table and sat down with Dante and Hal.

"You about got Mr. G.W.'s breakfast ready?" Hal asked. "It's almost seven-thirty."

"Just as soon as I get Miss Tessa's toast ready, I'll set things up on a tray for Mr. G.W."

As if on cue, the crisp browned bread popped up. Eustacia removed the two slices, buttered them lightly, put them on a plate and brought them over to Tessa. "You should eat more than toast and coffee for breakfast. No wonder you're so skinny."

Hal finished off his coffee and rose to his feet. "I

don't think you're skinny, Miss Tessa. I'd say you're just right. What do you think, Mr. Moran?"

Apparently taken off guard by Hal's direct question, Dante jerked around and stared at Tessa for several seconds before responding. "I imagine Ms. Westbrook knows she's a very attractive woman."

"Attractive, but skinny," the plump Eustacia said.

"Can't win with that woman." Hal removed a large breakfast tray from the bottom drawer in a massive oak cupboard.

Tessa ignored Hal and Eustacia's conversation as they prepared her father's breakfast tray. G. W Westbrook ate breakfast in his bedroom suite every morning promptly at seven-thirty. The menu seldom altered—bacon, eggs, grits and biscuits laden with butter, real butter, topped off with one of Eustacia's homemade jellies or jams. All the warnings from his doctor and the pleadings from Tessa hadn't changed G.W.'s eating habits.

"If I die," he'd said on numerous occasions, "I'll die happy with a full stomach."

Tessa sipped on her black coffee and waited for Dante to say something to her. He remained oddly quiet. She sensed something had changed between them since they'd put Leslie Anne to bed.

Don't be silly, she told herself. After all, there's really nothing between you two. Just a mutual attraction. How could that have changed in a matter of hours?

"Did you get any sleep?" she asked.

"I caught a catnap in the library."

"Hmm…"

"As soon as your father comes down, I'll finalize my business with him, then I'll meet up with the other Dundee agents at the motel and we'll head back to Atlanta."

No, please don't go, she wanted to say, but didn't. "I have a request. I'd like you to delay your departure."

Furrowing his brow and narrowing his gaze, he stared at her.

Tessa wasn't in the habit of asking favors. She'd spent the better part of the past seventeen years struggling to be strong and independent; her goal had been to become self-sufficient. After she'd been raped, beaten and left for dead, she had been at the mercy of doctors, nurses, therapists and psychiatrists. And she'd been totally dependent on her family. Only her father and her aunt Sharon had known the complete truth. Everyone else believed the lie her father had told—that she'd been in a horrible car wreck.

Whenever she brought up the past with her father, or asked him any questions about how he'd been able to keep the truth hidden, he always told her not to concern herself with those details. She suspected that G.W. had used his money and vast political connections to manipulate the law. It never ceased to amaze her how powerful her father was, not only in Mississippi, but in the entire South.

Whatever he'd done, he'd done it for her. And her

mother. And Leslie Anne. To protect them. He had rewritten history so that no one, especially her mother, would ever know the truth. In doing so, he'd given his wife one final gift in the last days of her life.

But now those once protective lies had become a threat to Leslie Anne. The safe, secure world she'd known had now become a dangerous, ugly place. A place where monsters preyed on teenage girls. Where innocent children were born as a result of rape. Where children couldn't trust their parents.

Dante cleared his throat. Tessa's mind jumped from introspection to the moment at hand. "Sorry," she said. "My mind wandered."

"What's the request?"

"Oh, yes, the request. I'd appreciate it if you'd stay until Leslie Anne wakes up and has a chance to say goodbye. She apparently formed some type of bond with you."

He hesitated, then spoke quickly, as if he really didn't want to see Leslie Anne again, but would do it anyway. "Sure, I'll stay long enough to say goodbye to her."

What was wrong with him? Tessa wondered. The change in him, in his attitude, was subtle, but it was quite apparent.

"Would you mind if we finish our coffee in the library?" she asked, wanting to get him alone before she asked him, point-blank, why he was acting so strangely.

"I've finished." He rose to his feet.

She nodded, then stood, left her cup on the table and walked to the door. Dante followed, leaving Hal and Eustacia bickering good-naturedly while preparing G.W.'s tray.

Once in the hallway, out of earshot of the others, Tessa paused and confronted Dante. "Want to tell me what's going on?"

He gave her an I-don't-know-what-you're-talking-about look.

"Something has changed with you," she said.

"The only change is that my job here is finished."

"No, it's something else. You're acting different—"

He grabbed her arm. Her mouth opened on a surprised gasp. "Let's discuss this in private." He glanced back at the closed kitchen door.

"All right."

She allowed him to lead her down the hall and into the library. Once he closed the sliding pocket doors, he turned to her. Her stomach fluttered with nervous trepidation. Instinct told her that she wasn't going to like whatever he told her.

"Lucie came by earlier." Dante pointed to the large mahogany desk that dominated the room. "She brought a package she'd gotten out of Hannah Wright's car. It's a package that was delivered to Leslie Anne via the U.S. mail before she ran away from home."

With her heartbeat thundering in her ears, Tessa glanced at the large padded envelope on the desk. "What's inside that envelope?"

"Take a look for yourself," he told her. "But be prepared to come face-to-face with your past." He watched her with a mixture of sympathy and sadness.

Fear clutched Tessa's chest, momentarily making it difficult for her to breathe. Garnering her courage, she walked across the library to the desk. For several moments, she simply stared at the padded paper bag. She could do this. She had to.

After lifting the envelope, she turned it upside down and dumped the contents onto the desk. Her hand trembled when she reached for the newspaper clippings scattered on the green felt blotter.

"Are these newspaper articles about *him?*" Tessa asked.

"Yes," Dante replied. "They're all about Eddie Jay Nealy."

Tessa clutched her throat. She couldn't— wouldn't—look at those newspaper clippings. Just the mention of the man's name shot a dose of instant fear through her mind and body. She laid the clippings on the desk hurriedly, as if by merely touching them she could somehow become contaminated. "This doesn't make sense. Are you telling me that someone sent these—" she eyed the clippings "—to Leslie Anne?"

Dante nodded. "Someone who wanted her to know the truth about her biological father."

He came over to where Tessa stood by the desk. She sensed that he wanted to touch her and she wished he would. Right now, she needed a strong shoulder to lean on.

"There's a note enclosed," Dante told her. "Typed. No signature."

"I don't understand how this is possible. No one, except Daddy, Aunt Sharon and I knew the truth—other than the authorities who were involved at the time. I seriously doubt any of them would dare risk Daddy's wrath."

"Obviously someone else knows. Or at the very least suspects. Someone who wants to hurt your daughter or you. Possibly both of you."

"Whoever sent Leslie Anne that package must hate her…or hate me."

"Do you know of anyone who—"

Tessa whirled around and glared at Dante. "You think it's someone I know?"

"Yeah." Dante looked at her as if she'd grown an extra head. His simple yeah response had sounded a great deal like duh.

"Stupid question. Of course it's someone I know. But I can't imagine who." *We will have to find out who. Once Daddy realizes…* "You can't leave Fairport. Not yet. We'll need the Dundee agency to investigate and find out who sent that package to my daughter."

"I agree you need to find out this person's identity

and there's no agency better than Dundee's to do the job, but I may be the wrong man for this assignment."

"What do you mean by that?"

"Don't get me wrong. I want to stay on this case. I want to help you. But I have my own agenda. A very personal reason for being interested."

"What do you mean?"

"There's something you have a right to know," Dante said. "You may not want me involved once I tell—"

"What is it?" Without even realizing she was leaning toward him, her body language told him she needed his touch.

He took both of her hands into his and held them, then looked into her eyes. "Years ago, the girl I loved—my fiancée—disappeared one night from Colby, Texas. She was waiting for me to pick her up after work, but when I got there, she was gone. She became a missing person who has never been found."

Tessa maneuvered her hands so that she could grasp one of his. "Oh, Dante, I'm so sorry. How terrible that must have been for you."

After taking a deep breath, he caressed her cheek. A shiver of pleasure rippled through her, a feeling like none she could ever remember.

"I don't know for sure what happened to her, but I've done some digging over the years and…" He gazed into Tessa's eyes.

"What are you trying to tell me?"

"Amy was a blue-eyed blonde. About your size.

There's even a slight resemblance between the two of you."

He's attracted to you because you remind him of her. Disappointment surged up from deep inside her. She wanted Dante to like her for herself, not because of some vague resemblance to his lost love.

"I remind you of her."

"Yes, you do. And so does Leslie Anne, who's closer to the age Amy was when she disappeared."

"How old was she when—?"

"Seventeen."

Tessa knew then what he was going to tell her. Oh, God, she knew. Don't cry, she told herself. Don't cry. She was strong enough to talk about what had happened to her all those years ago without falling apart.

"You think Eddie Jay Nealy killed your Amy, don't you?"

Dante swallowed. "Nealy kidnapped, raped, tortured and killed women in several connecting states, including Texas and Mississippi. When he was finally captured, stood trial and was convicted, he admitted that he'd killed dozens of pretty young blondes, but he would never tell the police where the missing bodies could be found."

Tears misted her eyes, drops gathering in the corners. "I vaguely remember being told how lucky I was to be alive. My memories of that time aren't clear, but I think it was a police officer or maybe a doctor who told me that my attacker's other victim hadn't survived. Or maybe he said other victims."

"You were the only one of Nealy's victims who survived until Helene Marshall," Dante said. "She's the young woman whose testimony, along with some overwhelming evidence, sent Nealy to death row."

"I didn't keep track of his trial," Tessa confessed. "Daddy told me when the man was captured, when he was convicted and when he was executed. Other than that, I didn't want to know any details. I couldn't bear to think about him. About what—" Her voice cracked.

Dante moved away, putting some distance between them. "Tell me something—why isn't your name listed as one of Nealy's victims? I've studied his records backward and forward. There's no mention of Tessa Westbrook."

"When your father is G. W. Westbrook, he can handle things so that you aren't involved, so that any mention of you or what happened to you can be erased from the records."

"Nothing like having local law enforcement in your daddy's hip pocket."

"That's true enough," she said. "But I wasn't attacked in Fairport. At least that's not where I was found."

"Where were you found?"

"I was lying in a ditch off Interstate 20, over in Louisiana somewhere."

Scowling, pain etched on every feature, Dante clenched his teeth and his eyes darkened to pitch-black. "Interstate 20 cuts straight across Louisiana and into Texas. Colby is about forty-five miles southwest of where that highway goes through Abilene. All the reports on Nealy stated that almost all of his victims were found near Interstate 20. I found out through my personal investigation after I joined the FBI that only a few days after Amy disappeared, a silver hair barrette with the initial A was found just off Interstate 20, along with a pair of white tennis shoes. The authorities figured they might have belonged to one of Nealy's victims, but they never found a body."

Tessa held her breath, knowing what he was going to say next.

"Amy was wearing white tennis shoes when she disappeared," Dante said. "And—" he took a deep breath "—and I'd given her a silver hair barrette with her initial on it for her seventeenth birthday." He glared at Tessa, as if wondering why she'd been the one girl who had survived. Why her and not his Amy? "Who did G.W. know in Louisiana powerful enough to bury any records of your being one of Nealy's victims?"

"Daddy and the then governor of the state were fraternity brothers."

Dante chuckled humorlessly. "Figures."

"What difference does it make to you that Daddy

protected me by using his influence?" That wasn't what was bothering Dante. It was something else. But what?

"You're right. It doesn't really matter to me."

"Then what is it? Suspecting your Amy was one of that monster's victims, just as I was, should make you the ideal candidate to investigate who sent Leslie Anne—" Oh, God, that was it. The truth hit her like a bolt from the blue. Dante's reluctance to be a part of the investigative team had nothing to do with her and everything to do with her daughter. "It's Leslie Anne, isn't it?"

Dante turned from her, that move and his silence speaking for him.

"Learning that *he* is Leslie Anne's biological father changed the way you feel about her, didn't it?"

Silence.

Tessa felt as if she'd been abandoned. Strange as it might seem, she had come to rely on Dante, as her daughter had. Men like Dante inspired confidence on short acquaintance.

What could she say to him now? What was there left to say? God only knew that if she could alter the circumstances of her little girl's conception, she would. And not for Dante Moran's sake!

"I'd like to hear the answer to that question," a small, quivering voice said.

Crying out faintly when she recognized that sweet voice, Tessa looked toward the partially open pocket doors. Leslie Anne stood there, a stricken expression on her face.

"I was hoping you'd sleep late," Tessa said, unable to think of something more profound to say. "I had planned to bring you breakfast in bed."

Ignoring her mother entirely, Leslie Anne entered the room and walked directly to Dante, who had turned to face her. Heaven help him, he looked like a condemned man on the verge of being hanged.

"You hate me now, don't you?" Leslie Anne looked Dante right in the eyes. "You can't even stand to look at me because I'm that awful man's child."

"No, honey, no," Tessa cried. "Mr. Moran doesn't—"

"I'm talking to him, Mama, not you."

Tessa said a silent prayer, pleading with God to bless Dante with wisdom and humanity so he could give Leslie Anne the answer she so desperately needed.

"I don't hate you," Dante said. "No one could hate such a sweet, lovely, young woman."

"You're lying. Someone hates me. Whoever sent me those newspaper clippings about my father—" She glared at Dante. "Eddie Jay Nealy was my biological father, wasn't he?"

"No one should be judged by who their biological parents are," Dante said. "My old man was no prize. He was a half-Italian, half-Irish hood from Chicago. He did a stint in the army, then came back

home to a life of crime. He got shot in the back of
the head when a drug deal went bad. But I had a great
mom who took me home to Texas when I was twelve
and surrounded me with her big, loving family. I've
spent my entire adult life on the right side of the law.
I'm not my father's son. And you—" he grasped
Leslie Anne's shoulders "—are not your father's
daughter."

Tears streamed down Leslie Anne's cheeks. "Oh,
God, it is true, isn't it? He is my father!"

Tessa rushed to her daughter, but before she
reached her, Dante opened his arms and pulled Leslie Anne into a comforting embrace. His big, dark
hand stroked Leslie Anne's back. The diamond cen-
tered in the onyx ring he wore caught the morning
sunlight coming through the windows.

While Dante held Leslie Anne and allowed her to
cry until she was spent, he glanced at Tessa and they
exchanged a knowing look. Tessa understood that despite the fact Dante had concerns about her daughter having been fathered by the man who had
probably murdered his fiancée, he was not the type
of person who would blame the innocent for another's crimes.

Dante was a good man. Of that, she had no doubts.
He wouldn't leave them, not now when they needed
him. She knew she could count on him to help them
find out who had sent those newspaper clippings.
Whoever he or she was, they had wanted Leslie Anne

to know the truth and they hadn't cared how deeply they would hurt her. But what reason would anyone have to want to hurt Leslie Anne? What did anyone have to gain by exposing a long-buried secret?

CHAPTER EIGHT

"WHAT DO YOU MEAN you've asked Moran to stay on?" G.W. bristled. His cheeks reddened and his brow wrinkled as he frowned.

"Don't get upset, Daddy. I thought you'd want him to stay on and help us find out who sent Leslie Anne those newspaper clippings about..." Pausing, she took a steadying breath. "Eddie Jay Nealy." There, she'd said the man's name. And it hadn't been as difficult as she'd thought it would be. Not once in all these years had she said his name aloud, even though it had echoed inside her mind way too many times. And today she'd said it twice!

"What difference does it make who sent them? The damage has been done." G.W. reached out and clasped Tessa's hands. "We can still lie to her, somehow convince her that John Allen—"

"No!" Tessa jerked her hands from his grasp. "It's too late for that. You're right—the damage has been done and my daughter has been emotionally shattered. All we can do now is try to pick up the pieces and put her back together."

"We don't need Moran for that."

"I think maybe we do. She's formed an attachment to him. She trusts him."

"And you? Have you formed an attachment to the man?" G.W. eyed her speculatively.

"Don't be silly. I hardly know him."

"Then send him on his way. We have Leslie Anne back safe and sound—"

"Safe, but hardly sound. She's not going to stop asking questions. She wants answers, and I'm going to give them to her." When her father didn't reply, simply looked at her with great sorrow in his eyes, Tessa put her arms around his waist and hugged him. "I don't want to argue with you about this. I want us to form a united front. For Leslie Anne's sake. Agreed?"

Huffing loudly and blinking the tears from his eyes, G.W. nodded. "If we're going to do it, then we should do it now. Get it over with and deal with the consequences."

"I've already telephoned Dr. Barrett. He'll be here at eleven."

"You called Arthur?"

"Yes. I thought the therapist who helped me come to terms with what had happened to me was the ideal person to help Leslie Anne now. After all, Dr. Barrett already knows the whole story."

"Yes, yes, he knows the whole story."

Tessa picked up on something odd in her father's voice.

"Daddy?"

"Yes?"

"What is it? What's wrong? What aren't you saying?"

He patted her on the arm affectionately. "I hate to dredge up the past. It was such a painful time for all of us. You, me…and your mother."

"I'd rather not dig up the past, either, but we must. For Leslie Anne's sake. And we have to find a way to convince her that just because *he* was her biological father doesn't mean she's his daughter in any sense of the word."

"If only you had married Charlie…."

"How could I have married Charlie? I didn't even know him. I didn't remember him at all. And I knew I was carrying another man's child."

"I wish we'd never told you the baby wasn't his. If I'd been thinking straight, I'd have lied to you, just as I lied to your mother. Charlie would have married you. He loved you. And he would have backed us up in whatever story we chose to tell the world. No one would have ever known he wasn't Leslie Anne's father."

"You would have known."

"It doesn't matter now anyway, does it?" G.W. lifted his hand to Tessa's face and caressed her cheek. "You gave Anne so much joy in those final years of her life. You and Leslie Anne. And no man could have asked for a better daughter. I'm so very lucky. I thank the good Lord every day for you. You know that, don't you?"

"Oh, Daddy, you old softie, you. I'm the lucky one. What would I have done without you? If it hadn't been for you, I'd have given up after…after the rape. Without being able to draw on your strength, I wouldn't have made it. You forced me to keep on living when I wanted to die."

"Don't sell yourself short, young lady. You're the strongest, bravest person I've ever known. I'm proud to be your father."

Tears clouded Tessa's vision. "We're both going to have to be strong and brave for Leslie Anne. She needs us now more than she ever has."

"We'll be there for her," G.W. said. "All of us. Her family. Sharon's on her way home, you know. Myrle says she should be here no later than this afternoon."

"Good. I've missed her since she started spending so much time in Key West. Aunt Sharon and Leslie Anne adore each other. I just know she'll be able to help Leslie Anne get through this nightmare."

G.W. put his arm around Tessa's shoulders. "We don't need outsiders involved in this, do we?"

Tessa stiffened. "Daddy, why are you so opposed to letting the Dundee agency find out who sent Leslie Anne those newspaper clippings?"

"That's not it, not at all. I—I'm being foolish, aren't I? Of course, we'll want to find out who sent those clippings. But why don't you let me handle it? You concentrate on Leslie Anne and I'll deal with Mr. Moran and the Dundee Agency myself."

"All right, if you'd prefer it that way." Her gut instincts warned her that her father was keeping something from her. But what? She'd thought they didn't keep secrets from each other.

G.W. DECIDED TO MEET with Dante Moran privately in the library. He'd made a couple of phone calls and had gotten the lowdown on this particular Dundee agent. Of course, the info he'd gotten just skimmed the surface, but it was enough for G.W. to form an opinion. Moran couldn't be bought off or scared off. He liked that about the man, and under different circumstances, he might have tried to steal him away from the Dundee agency. Westbrook, Inc. could always use a talented go-getter like Moran. But in this particular situation, G.W. would have preferred an agent who could be bribed.

When Leslie Anne had run away, all he'd thought about was hiring the best agency to search for her. And Dundee was the best. The agents were the cream of the crop, highly trained professionals. But the very thing that made them the best now proved a problem for G.W. If Moran—or any other Dundee agent— started digging around in the past and somehow dug a little too deep, G.W. wouldn't be able to keep him quiet with a hefty payoff. What would he do if anyone found out the complete truth?

That can't happen, G.W. assured himself. Only three other people knew all the facts—the former

Richland Parish sheriff, the coroner and one deputy. The coroner had died ten years ago at the age of seventy. Now suffering from Alzheimer's, Sheriff Wadkins was in a nursing home, his care paid for by G.W. And Deputy Summers was now the sheriff, his income supplemented by a monthly check from G.W. Summers wasn't about to open his mouth.

Let Moran dig as deep as he wants, G.W. thought. He won't find out anything except the basic facts. My daughter was kidnapped, raped and left for dead seventeen years ago. She was one of two girls who survived Eddie Jay Nealy's brutal attack. And my granddaughter is the result of that vicious rape.

G.W. shivered. He didn't usually allow himself to think about those heartbreaking days, about that black, evil deed that had almost destroyed his life. Without Tessa, his beloved Anne wouldn't have survived as long as she had. If they had lost their daughter…

As G.W. inspected his appearance in the floor-to-ceiling mirrors in his dressing room and made his way through the house and into the library, he dismissed his concerns about the secret buried deep in his heart. The present was what mattered—Leslie Anne—and finding out who had dared to send her those vile newspaper clippings about Eddie Jay Nealy.

Only he, Tessa and Sharon knew the truth about Leslie Anne's paternity. Even the doctors and nurses at all of the hospitals where Tessa had been treated hadn't known for sure. He had backed up one lie with another, and then another, until the day came when he halfway believed all the lies himself.

A knock sounded on the library door.

"Yes?"

"You asked to speak to me alone," Dante Moran said through the closed doors.

"Come in, please."

The pocket doors opened and Moran entered the library.

"Close the doors," G.W. said. "I don't want anyone overhearing our conversation."

After Dante did as G.W. had requested, he turned and faced his client.

"My daughter tells me that she wants to retain your agency to search for the person who sent Leslie Anne those newspaper clippings."

Moran nodded. "Yes, sir, she did mention it."

"If that's what Tessa wants, then it's what I want." G.W. understood that the best way to deal with Moran was to be straightforward. "It doesn't matter to me what agent handles the case, but Tessa seems to trust you and she expects you to head up the investigation. Will that be a problem?"

"No, sir."

"You're a man of few words, aren't you?"

Narrowing his gaze, Moran focused directly on G.W. "If you'd prefer another agent—"

"No, no." G.W. waved his hand. "It's just that I'd rather not dredge up the past. During your investigation, I'd appreciate it if you'd run everything you find out by me first. That way I can protect my daughter and granddaughter as much as possible. Do you have any objections to that?"

"No, sir. You hired the Dundee agency, so for all intents and purposes, you and you alone are our client."

"Good. Good. That's all I needed to hear."

"Then I take it that we're officially hired for the investigation."

"Definitely."

"I'll contact my superior, Sawyer McNamara, and make arrangements. In order to expedite the investigation, I plan to ask for Lucie Evans and Dom Shea to remain as part of the investigative team. You'll be paying for three agents instead of one."

"Money is no object. You should know that."

"Yes, sir, but I had to get your okay."

"You've got it. Use all the agents you need. Three or ten. Just do the job right."

"We always do."

"Yes, I'm sure you do."

"I need some information and I believe you'd rather I get it from you than from your daughter."

"Absolutely."

"All right then." Moran concentrated his gaze on G.W., a man-to-man exchange. "Tessa—Ms. West-brook told me that only you, your sister and she knew that Eddie Jay Nealy was Leslie Anne's biological father. Is that correct?"

"Yes."

"Your wife didn't know?"

"My wife had terminal cancer when our daughter was kidnapped," G.W. said. "I thought it best for her to never know the truth about what happened to Tessa. Until the day Anne died, she believed Tessa had been in a terrible car wreck and that the child she gave birth to was Charlie Sentell's daughter."

"Have you ever told anyone about—"

"No! Never."

"What about your sister? Do you think she would have—"

"Absolutely not. She would never do anything to harm Tessa or Leslie Anne."

"I didn't mean to imply that your sister might have sent those clippings. I only meant do you think it's possible she shared this secret with anyone? A close friend? A lover?"

"No." Could he be certain Sharon didn't tell someone? Yes, of course he could. His sister would never betray such an important confidence.

"Other people must have known at the time," Moran said. "The lawmen—police or sheriff's department—where Tessa was found. The doctors and nurses at the hospital—"

"They might have suspected, but they didn't know for sure. After all, Tessa was eighteen and as far as they knew she'd been sexually active before—" G.W. gulped. "The child could have been her boyfriend's."

"And that's what you chose to tell everyone?"

"She hadn't been dating anyone except Charlie, of course, for over six months. The baby could have been his." G.W. closed his eyes for a moment, gathering his thoughts and fortifying his courage. He'd told so many lies that sometimes it was difficult to keep them all straight.

"Could have been Charlie's, but wasn't? How could you be sure?"

G.W. took a deep breath. "When Charlie came to the hospital to see Tessa, I fed him the same story I'd told everyone else about Tessa being in a car wreck. I told him she was pregnant—only a few weeks along. Charlie had been away at college for over six weeks before…. He told me himself that he and Tessa hadn't…not in a couple of months. When I told him I had no idea who had fathered Tessa's baby, he offered to accept responsibility, to marry her and claim her child as his."

"If that's the case then why—"

"Tessa refused to marry him and wouldn't allow him to claim her baby, but she did agree that we'd tell her mother the child was Charlie's." To this day, G.W. couldn't think about Anne without hurting deep inside. She'd been the love of his life. He would have done anything—absolutely anything—for her. And that included protecting her from the truth.

"You and Tessa have told a great many lies over the years," Moran said. "It's possible that somewhere along the way, somebody put two and two together and came up with four. If we're going to unearth this person who sent Leslie Anne those newspaper clippings, I need for you to be honest with me. I need to know all the lies you've told and I need to know the truth. Start with Tessa being kidnapped."

You can do this, G.W. told himself. Tell him everything, except… "When Tessa first disappeared, we assumed she'd been kidnapped for ransom, considering our vast wealth. I made up a lie to protect my wife. I told her Tessa was off on a trip with Sharon. My sister was always jaunting all over the place."

"And that was the first lie?"

"Yes." The first of many. So many, G.W. wasn't sure if he could actually remember them all. Odd how, after all these years, the lies seemed more like the truth than the actual truth.

"How long was Tessa missing?" Moran asked.

"How long?"

"Yes, how long?"

"Uh, nearly two weeks."

"Tessa told me that she was found off Interstate 20 in Louisiana. Is that right?"

G.W. nodded.

"Who notified you?"

"The Richland Parish sheriff," G.W. said. No need to lie to Moran. It wouldn't be difficult for him to find out that bit of information since G.W. hadn't been able to arrange for all of the evidence to be destroyed. The hospital records, though confidential, still existed. "A motorist who'd stopped to take a leak just off the highway had found her body and thought she was dead. When the sheriff arrived, he discovered she was still alive. Just barely. They rushed her to the hospital. She'd been raped and brutally beaten, then left for dead."

"Eddie Jay Nealy's M.O."

"Yes." G.W. clenched his jaw. As long as he lived, he would never forget that day. His beautiful daughter had been battered unmercifully and the sight of her lying there motionless had devastated him.

"You went to Louisiana and found Tessa in the hospital, right?"

"Right. As soon as she was stable—ten days later—I had her transferred to Fairport. It was a couple of weeks after that when the doctors told me Tessa was pregnant. Simple calculations indicated that she'd been impregnated on or around the time she'd been raped."

"You told your wife and everyone in Fairport that Tessa had been in a terrible car wreck. But the doctors treating her would have known that wasn't true."

"Dr. Harlan was Tessa's doctor. He knew, of course, but he kept quiet. He never lied about Tessa's condition to anyone, but he didn't confirm any suspicions.

"You do realize that the doctors and nurses who

treated Tessa in Louisiana and here in Fairport knew she'd been raped and beaten. So when Nealy was captured and put on trial and that news hit the front pages of every newspaper in the South, someone could have remembered that Tessa fit the description of Nealy's victims. A young, pretty blonde who'd been raped, beaten and left for dead."

"If you suspect one of the doctors or nurses, can you explain why he or she would have waited all these years to contact Leslie Anne or what on earth they'd have to gain by telling her about Nealy?

"If someone wanted money, they would have sent the clippings to you or Tessa and blackmailed you," Moran said. "Whoever we're looking for has a different motive. He or she targeted Leslie Anne. If we knew why, we'd have a better idea of who."

"If I could get my hands on that person, I'd—"

"Let me handle this, Mr. Westbrook."

"Yes, of course."

"Let's start with a list of people closest to Leslie Anne. I'm not saying they're suspects, and I'm not ruling out someone from the past—a doctor or nurse or even a lawman. But my experience tells me that the man or woman we're looking for has a personal motive."

"I refuse to believe that anyone close to the family would have done such a thing, even if one of them might have figured out the truth."

"Your sister Sharon has always known the truth,

but you're certain of her loyalty. What about your sister-in-law and her daughter? What about your current girlfriend and her son? And what about Charlie Sentell?"

"My God, man, you can't think one of them would—"

"I'm not ruling out anyone. Not even the servants. There's Hal Carpenter and Eustacia Bonner. Servants have a way of knowing a lot more about their employers than they let on."

"Hal and Eustacia have been with the family for ages. I trust both of them implicitly. They're completely loyal."

"Someone is guilty," Moran told G.W. "And it's highly likely the guilty party is someone you know. It's just a matter of figuring out which of these trustworthy people sent Leslie Anne the newspaper clippings and told her that her father was a serial killer."

TESSA KEPT PACE with Leslie Anne's long-legged stride as they headed for the stables. She'd tried her best to dissuade her daughter from leaving the house, knowing that Dr. Barrett should be arriving shortly. But once Leslie Anne decided on something, it was practically impossible to talk her out of it.

"We can go riding this afternoon," Tessa said.

"You don't have to come with me, if you don't want to. I didn't invite you." Leslie Anne raced on ahead, waving at Luther Osborn, who cared for the small stable of four horses and oversaw the grounds of the five-hundred-acre estate. Luther had come to work for them three years ago, after old Toby Chapman had retired.

"Morning, Luther," Leslie Anne said. "How's Passion Flower this morning?"

"She's fine as a fiddle, missy. You come to ride her?" Pie-faced, bug-eyed, short and squat, the twentysomething young man had a troll-like appearance. But he was sweet and mannerly and did his job well.

"I most certainly did," Leslie Anne replied.

Catching up with her daughter, Tessa smiled at Luther.

"Morning, Miss Tessa. You riding, too?"

"Yes, Luther, I am. Would you please saddle our horses?"

"Yes, ma'am." Luther headed into the stables.

Leslie Anne whirled around, planted her hand on her hip and glared at Tessa. "What if I want to be alone to think?"

"You're in no state of mind to go off riding by yourself."

"I'm not going to do anything stupid, like kill myself or anything."

"I never thought you were." Oh, God, had the thought of suicide actually entered her child's head? Please, God, no!

"You know that riding helps me think. It's been

that way ever since I was a kid. But I'm not a kid any-more and I really don't need you to tag along."

"I can appreciate your wanting some time alone, but not today. Not until we've talked more and you understand why your grandfather and I have lied to you all these years."

"I understand. You didn't want me to know my father was a serial killer who raped you."

"Lower your voice. Do you want Luther to hear you?"

"What difference does it make who knows? I know. I know that I'm the devil's child, that I have bad blood running through my veins."

Tessa grabbed her daughter's shoulders and shook her. "Don't ever say such a thing. Not ever again. Do you hear me?"

Leslie Anne jerked away from her mother. The lost and confused look in her eyes frightened Tessa. She knew what it was like to feel helpless and hope-less, to wonder if it was worth the effort to keep on living. How could she protect her child from such damaging emotions?

"Here we are," Luther said as he led two beauti-ful Arabian horses from the stables.

Without glancing back at Tessa, Leslie Anne mounted Passion Flower and urged the mare into a gallop.

"Is she all right?" Luther asked, sincere concern in his voice. "I'm glad she's home now and safe."

Tessa smiled at Luther and nodded. "She'll be okay. She's sixteen going on thirty." The less anyone knew about the reason Leslie Anne had run away, the better.

Luther returned Tessa's smile. "Yes, ma'am, I know how that is. My mama's having a time with my two sisters. One's fifteen and the other's seventeen."

He led the horse to Tessa and dropped the reins. She mounted Mr. Wonderful, a now eight-year-old gelding that she'd chosen for herself several years ago, after the mare she'd ridden since childhood died at the ripe old age of twenty-five. Learning to ride again had been one of the many things she'd had to relearn following her recovery from the "accident." After using that term—the accident—for the past seventeen years, the word came to mind as easily as the lie rolled off her tongue. She had discovered that if you told a lie often enough, it soon began to seem like the truth.

But she had also discovered that the old adage was true—once you told a lie, you had to continue lying, backing up the initial lie with more and more lies. Sometimes it seemed as if she could no longer tell the truth from fiction.

But there was one fact she could never change— no matter how much she wanted to or how many stories she and her father fabricated—Leslie Anne's biological father was Eddie Jay Nealy. The man who had tried to kill her. The man who had probably murdered Dante Moran's fiancée.

THERE THEY GO, mother and daughter, riding off into the meadow like a couple of spoiled princesses, while I hide here in the bushes like some lowly serf. Seeing them together, so proud and regal, no one would ever guess the truth about either of the young Westbrook ladies. But I know the truth. And I intend to use that knowledge to gain everything that's due me. Everything that should be mine.

No one even suspects that I'm here watching and waiting for the right opportunity. I can't keep putting off the inevitable. I have to act soon, need to stir the pot while it's boiling. Once those Dundee agents clear out, I'll form a plan and put it into action. Perhaps I should have acted sooner, but I kept hoping there would be some other way. I realize now that there's only one way to get what I want.

Leslie Anne Westbrook must die.

CHAPTER NINE

DANTE STOOD in the corner of the room, feeling damned uncomfortable being present for this family meeting. Yet he wanted to be here, needed to be here. And not simply because Leslie Anne had asked him to stay close by or because he had any perverse need to hear the details of Tessa's personal tragedy directly from her. But if the same man who had kidnapped and tortured Tessa had done the same to Amy, he hoped that by learning everything about Tessa's experience, it might help him learn the truth about the fate of the only woman he had ever loved.

It seemed strange now that he'd once thought of Amy as a woman. Looking back, he realized she'd been a young girl, only a year older than Leslie Anne was now. Actually, he and Amy had both been a couple of kids. Young love. First love. Everybody had probably thought it wouldn't last. But they'd have been wrong. He and Amy would have proved them wrong. They'd been in love, deeply and completely. In love for a lifetime.

"You promise you'll stay." Leslie Anne walked over to Dante and stood in front of him, a pleading look in her dark brown eyes.

"I promise," he assured her.

Tessa came up beside Leslie Anne and looked directly at Dante. "Daddy isn't too happy about your being here, so if he says or does anything unfriendly, just ignore him. This is a very sensitive subject for him and he tends to be overly protective of me."

"As he should be," Dante said. "He's your father. Being overly protective is a father's job, isn't it? I know if I had a daughter, I'd be a damn grizzly bear to anyone I even suspected might hurt her."

"If you had a daughter, she'd be the luckiest girl in the world," Leslie Anne said.

The way she looked at Dante broke his heart. Poor kid. How would she ever come to terms with knowing that a man like Eddie Jay Nealy was her father?

If only he had picked up Amy on time all those years ago, how different Dante's life would be now. He would be married and probably be a father. He and Amy might even have had a daughter not much younger than Leslie Anne. Maybe they would even have a couple of kids. A boy and a girl.

Suddenly a viciously painful thought entered his mind. If Amy had been one of Nealy's rape victims and had gotten pregnant, how would Amy and Dante have handled the situation? Would Amy have gotten an abortion? Would he have asked her to get rid of her

rapist's baby? How would they have known for sure
that early on if the baby was Eddie Jay's or Dante's?

God help him, he didn't know what he would have
done under those circumstances. *What if you could
have had Amy back only if you accepted the child she
might have been carrying?* he asked himself. He
would have taken her back in a heartbeat. Amy *and*
the child. He would have done anything, accepted
anything, if Amy had come back to him.

He would still do anything—pay any price—if he
could find Amy alive somewhere.

*Shit! You're an idiot, Moran. Do you hear your-
self? You're talking nonsense.* Amy Smith died seventeen years ago and whether she might have been
impregnated by Nealy was a moot point. Hell, Dante
didn't even know for sure Nealy had raped and killed
Amy. He would prefer to believe she hadn't suffered
such a horrendous ordeal, but in all likelihood she had
experienced the same inhuman treatment that Tessa
Westbrook had somehow miraculously survived.

Tessa laced her arm through her daughter's and
led the girl across the room toward one of the two floral sofas that faced each other in front of the fireplace.
The main parlor of the old Leslie Plantation house
possessed an elegance that only money and good
taste could produce. And Dante had the oddest feeling that generations of Tessa's family wouldn't approve of some half-Italian, Yankee hoodlum's kid
even being here, let alone him having the hots for one

of their own. And he did have the hots for Tessa Westbrook.

The woman was way out of his league. Despite years of polishing his rough edges and achieving a degree of sophistication, he didn't come close to being the kind of man Tessa Westbrook deserved.

What difference does that make? He sure as hell hadn't deserved Amy Smith, but she'd been his— body and soul. Amy had been way too good for the wiseass, rowdy kid he'd been back then, but she'd loved him anyway. And he'd loved her. God, how he'd loved her.

Dante kept his place in the corner of the room, determined to be as inconspicuous as possible. He was here by invitation only. His job was to watch, listen and keep his mouth shut. To simply stand by in case he was needed. Any fantasies he had about Tessa would have to remain just that—fantasies. The woman's life was already complicated enough. The last thing she needed was an affair that would complicate things even further.

The moment he entered the parlor, G.W.'s huge presence filled the room, which was why it took Dante a good sixty seconds before he noticed the man who'd come in with the lord of the manor. Dr. Arthur Barrett, Dante assumed. A man of medium height and build, with thick gray hair and a neat mustache. He wore dress khakis and a blue button-down shirt. He didn't look like a psychiatrist paying a house call, he looked more like a friendly uncle who'd come to spend the day.

"Leslie Anne, this is Dr. Barrett," G.W. said. "He was your mother's therapist for many years."

Leslie glared at the doctor.

"Arthur is here to help us." G.W. glanced at Tessa.

"Years ago, Dr. Barrett helped me deal with what had happened to me." Tessa reached for Leslie Anne's hand, but her daughter scooted away from her, all the way to the other end of the sofa. "He can help you, too, if you'll let him."

"Can he change my DNA?" Leslie Anne asked. "Can he wave a magic wand and remove all of Eddie Jay Nealy's genes from my body?"

Tessa sighed.

"I'm afraid I don't have a magic wand," Arthur Barrett said, his voice gentle and kind. "I can't work miracles, but I am here to help you."

"Sure, doc. Help away." Leslie Anne turned to Tessa. "But first I want to hear the truth from you. And don't leave out anything. I think I have a right to know everything from the moment you were kidnapped—"

"I'm afraid I can't tell you everything," Tessa said. "I can only tell you what I remember."

"What do you mean by that?" Leslie Anne glowered at her mother.

"Your mother has no memory of her kidnapping or…the rape," G.W. said. "And thank God she doesn't."

"I don't understand." Leslie Anne looked toward Dante. "Do you believe she can't remember, or is she lying to me again?"

Dante hadn't wanted to be involved at all, certainly not this soon. He had planned on staying completely in the background, there only for moral support. "Yes, I believe her. Often a victim of a vicious attack has what's referred to as hysterical amnesia where his or her mind blocks out the horrible memory. It's a self-protective mechanism." He glanced at Arthur Barrett. "Am I right, Dr. Barrett?"

"Yes," the doctor replied. "Although technically Tessa's amnesia involved more than—"

"Anybody would have blocked out such a terrible thing," G.W. interrupted. "You should be glad your mother can't remember. And you shouldn't accuse her of lying to you. You've asked her for the truth and she'll tell you the truth."

Dante wondered why G.W. had stopped Dr. Barrett midsentence. Was the old man afraid the doctor might expose some information that G.W. wanted kept under wraps? If so, what was it? And why keep it a secret?

"All right. I'll buy that you don't remember being kidnapped and raped. So, just what do you remember?" Leslie Anne watched Tessa like a hawk, as if she thought she could determine whether her mother was telling her the truth simply by looking at her face, by gazing into her eyes.

"I remember waking up in the hospital, in Louisiana." Tessa sucked in a deep breath. "At least the nurses told me I was in Louisiana. I didn't have any idea where I was or what had happened to me. And even now, my memories of those first few days after I was found are rather blurry. I think a policeman or maybe one of the doctors told me what had happened to me. And they told me that my father was waiting to see me."

"The sheriff told you," G.W. said. "Sheriff Wadkins."

"I remember your grandfather coming in to see me and I didn't recognize him. He told me who he was and that he was going to take care of me and that everything would be all right."

Dante not only heard and saw the pain Tessa was experiencing, but he felt her agony at having to relive the trauma she had no doubt worked so hard to put in the past. How was it that he sensed Tessa's emotions, that he hurt for her, that he cared so deeply?

Because you can't separate Tessa and what happened to her from Amy, that's why, he told himself. *You've gotten the two women all mixed up in your mind.*

"Granddaddy didn't know you were pregnant, did he?" Leslie Anne asked.

Tessa shook her head. "No one knew. Not then. Not until several weeks later, after Daddy brought me back to Mississippi."

"Did you hate me when you found out? Did you want to get rid of me?" Leslie Anne's eyes widened into big circles of despair.

God in heaven, lie to her if you have to, Dante thought. *Whatever you do, don't tell this child that you ever hated her or wanted her dead.*

"I—I didn't hate you," Tessa said, her voice very quite, little more than a whisper. "I considered an abortion, but I didn't have one. I couldn't. I—I wanted you."

Dante knew Tessa was lying. If Anne Leslie Westbrook hadn't begged her daughter not to abort the child she carried, Tessa would have gotten rid of her rapist's baby. But that was one truth Leslie Anne didn't need to know.

"You're lying!" Leslie Anne jumped up and stood over Tessa, tears streaming down her cheeks. "You couldn't have possibly wanted me."

"Don't do this to your mother!" G.W. shouted, his voice quivering. Not with rage, but with fear and pain.

"No, Daddy, leave her alone," Tessa said. "She's right." Tessa rose to her feet and faced her daughter. "I did not want to be pregnant by the man who had raped me. Your grandfather and I decided I'd have an abortion, but your grandmother accidentally found out I was pregnant and because she didn't know about the rape, she begged me not to abort my baby."

Leslie Anne wrapped her arms around herself in an apparent effort to steady her trembling body. "So you did hate me, didn't you? You hated me and didn't want me."

When Tessa tried to touch Leslie Anne, she drew back and glared at her mother.

Tessa's hands remained in front of her, reaching out in a pleading gesture. "After you were born, the minute the nurse placed you in my arms, I felt this overwhelming maternal love. And I realized that I did love you. I always loved you—the whole nine months I carried you. Because you were *my* baby. Mine. And no one else's."

Leslie Anne gulped down sobs, then wiped her face with her fingertips. "Did you still love me later on, after you brought me home from the hospital?" She glared at G.W. "What about you, Granddaddy— did you love me right from the beginning, too, or did you still hate me after I was born?"

"God, what a question!" G.W. looked everywhere but at his granddaughter.

Dante watched Tessa and wondered how much more of this she could take without breaking. She looked as if she might shatter into a million pieces at any moment. Everything within him wanted to go to her, wrap his arms around her and promise her that he would take care of her, that somehow, someway, he would make everything right. It had been seventeen years since he'd cared this much about another human being. There had been a time when he'd desperately wanted to lay the world at Amy Smith's feet, to love her, take care of her and give her anything her heart desired.

"I cannot change the past," Tessa said calmly. "If I could, I would. I had no control over what happened to me. But you are not that vile man's daughter. Do you hear me? You're *my* daughter. You're Leslie Anne Westbrook. You're beautiful and smart and good and kind. I love you. Your grandfather loves you." With her hands outstretched, Tessa took a tentative step toward her daughter. "Everyone who knows you, loves you, sweetheart."

Leslie Anne backed farther and farther away from Tessa until she stood halfway across the room, close to the French doors leading to the side porch. "Did you take care of me when I was a little baby? Did you bathe me and feed me and rock me to sleep? I'd think you couldn't bear to look at me without thinking of him."

"When I look at you, I see you, my daughter. My precious Leslie Anne."

"You didn't answer my question."

"You had a nanny when you were an infant," Tessa admitted. "Don't you remember Leda? She was with us until you were six years old."

"Yes, I remember her," Leslie Anne said. "But I remember you taking care of me when I was a little girl. You gave me baths and read me bedtime stories and we made cookies with Eustacia and…"

"We had a nanny for Tessa," G.W. said. "For generations, all the Leslie children have had nannies."

"When you were an infant, I didn't take care of you," Tessa said. "I—I couldn't. I wasn't physically or mentally capable of caring for a baby."

"What are you talking about?" Leslie Anne stared at Tessa, her face contorted in a fierce scowl.

"Haven't you heard enough!" G.W. stormed toward his granddaughter, stopping a few feet away and facing her with a stern look. "Can't you see that you're tormenting your mother with these endless questions?"

"Leave her alone, Daddy, please," Tessa said. "She has a right to know." Tessa went to her father's side, took his hand in hers and looked right at Leslie Anne. "I was beaten so severely that I had to spend a long time in the hospital and then in rehabilitation centers during most of my pregnancy. And for almost a year after you were born, I needed daily therapy."

"Physical therapy?" Leslie Anne asked.

"Yes."

"What did he do to you?"

"He cracked her ribs, broke both of her arms and one of her legs," G.W. said. "He battered her unmercifully…" G.W. clenched his teeth. "Her skull was cracked, too, quite possibly from having been thrown from a moving vehicle."

Leslie Anne's eyes widened in horror.

"The broken bones healed within a few months, but my injured brain didn't heal so quickly." Tessa spoke with little emotion, as if she were discussing someone other than herself. "I had to relearn how to do almost everything. I could talk, but I often got my words all mixed up. It was almost like being a toddler who had to learn to walk and talk and think. I was practically helpless for a long time."

"It's a miracle that your mother recovered," Dr. Barrett said. "It took over a year of intense physical therapy and several years of psychiatric therapy for her to become a fully functioning person again. She worked long and hard and whenever she even thought of giving up, two things kept her going." The doctor looked at G.W. "Your grandfather wouldn't let her give up. Whenever Tessa became frustrated or felt she'd never get better, G.W. would remind her that she had a daughter to raise. And that's all it took. She'd tell me she had to get well for Leslie Anne."

Dante turned away, unable to bear watching both Tessa and her daughter in such emotional agony. And to make matters worse, he couldn't stop thinking about what he feared his sweet Amy had gone through at the hands of a deranged killer. Images of Amy flashed through his mind. Her beautiful face, her glorious smile. And then blood. Blood everywhere. All over Amy's face. All over Amy's body…

Tormented by those thoughts, Dante screamed silently, demanding those images to vanish from his mind. But they lingered.

"Leslie Anne, please come back!"

Tessa's pitiful cry snapped Dante from his anguished thoughts. He turned around just in time to see Leslie Anne fling open the French doors and run out onto the side porch.

"I'll go after her," Dr. Barrett said. "I believe she needs to talk to someone who can be objective."

G.W. slumped down into the nearest chair, bent his head over and hung his hands between his spread knees. Gasping for air, Tessa tossed back her head and balled her hands into tight fists. Acting purely on instinct, Dante rushed across the room, came up behind Tessa and wrapped his arms around her. She tensed, then when he jerked her backward, pressing her against him, her shoulder blades to his chest, she relaxed into him and sighed.

"Don't hold it all inside," he whispered in her ear. "Let it go. Let it all go. I'm right here to catch you when you fall."

As if all she'd been waiting for was his vow to take care of her, Tessa let out a high, shrill keen. The dam burst and tears flooded her eyes, poured down her cheeks and dampened her chin and neck. Dante turned her into his embrace and held her as she wept. The last time a woman had felt so right in his arms, he'd been nineteen and crazy in love with Amy.

Amy was gone and there was nothing he could do for her.

But Tessa was a different matter. She was alive.

She was suffering. And if there was anything he could do for her, he would.

G.W. cleared his throat. "Everything's going to be all right. Leslie Anne will calm down and see reason. She's a smart girl. She won't let this business about Nealy change her. Dr. Barrett will see to it. He helped you and he'll help her."

Tessa lifted her head from Dante's shoulder and looked at her father. "I hope you're right. I know she's a smart girl, but she's also a very sensitive six-teen-year-old. Dr. Barrett can help her only if she'll let him."

G.W. grunted. "I think I'll take a walk. Would you like to come with me, Tessa?" He glared at Dante, who understood the old man was issuing him a warning.

Tessa shook her head. "No, I…I want to talk to Dante. Alone."

G.W. eyed Dante curiously, as if wanted to ask him something but thought better of it. "Just remember that he's not a doctor or a lawyer, so whatever you say to him is not privileged information."

"We'll be fine, Daddy. Go take your walk," Tessa said.

G.W. stood up straight and tall, then with one final intimidating glare in Dante's direction, he left them alone in the parlor.

"He doesn't like the idea of your being in my arms," Dante said. "Even if my only motive is to comfort you."

"I appreciate the comfort, but…" Tessa eased out of Dante's arms. "Perhaps it would be best if another Dundee agent heads up the investigation."

Puzzled by her request, Dante stared at her inquisitively. "Why?"

"I'd think that's obvious."

"Spell it out for me, will you?"

"All right. My life is a mess. I've never fully recovered emotionally from what happened to me seventeen years ago. And now I have to deal with my daughter's emotional problems. I don't have anything to give you. The last thing you or any man would want is to become personally involved with me and my crazy, mixed-up life."

"Should I pretend I don't know what you're talking about?"

Shaking her head, she offered him a fragile smile. "It won't work, you know. The two of us. I'm terribly needy. It would be so easy for me to turn to you, to lean on those big, broad shoulders. But I don't want to use you that way because I know it isn't me you want to help and take care of and protect. It's Amy. Your Amy. You've gotten us all confused, all jumbled up together, in your mind. Maybe in your heart, too."

"Tessa…"

"I think you should go now, while you still can. Before—" she swallowed a sigh "—before you become too involved."

"I'm already involved," he told her. "And yeah, maybe I have gotten you and Amy all jumbled up together up here—" he tapped the side of his head "—and possibly even in here—" he pointed to his heart "—but, lady, you've got to know that I can't walk away from you."

With tears in her eyes, she laughed softly. "Then heaven help you, Dante Moran, because I don't want you to go. I want you to stay."

CHAPTER TEN

SHARON REMOVED her sunglasses and slipped them into her coat pocket as Tad escorted her to his car, a sleek little silver Chrysler Crossfire. It wasn't that she knew much about automobiles as a general rule, but since she'd purchased this vehicle as a gift for Tad on his twenty-ninth birthday last year, she was well aware of how much it had cost her—thirty-five thousand dollars. No one except the two of them knew about this special gift or the fact that it was only one of many expensive items she'd given her young lover. If G.W. had any idea that she had been having an on-again-off-again fling with his lady friend's son, he would blow a gasket. But then G.W. tended to be old-fashioned about such things as women dating younger men. Her brother was such a hypocrite sometimes. It was perfectly all right for him to fool around with Olivia, who was at least a dozen years his junior. And it was totally acceptable for him to supplement Olivia's income by paying her rent on a lovely waterfront home and giving her a monthly allowance. But God forbid his little sister pay for services rendered by Olivia's son or any other man.

The moment they settled into the sports car, Tad leaned over and kissed Sharon's cheek. "I've missed you something awful, sugar. I wish you'd taken me with you to Key West. I've been bored to tears around here without you."

"I wasn't gone that long. Only a few weeks." She reached over and patted Tad's smoothly shaven cheek. He was such a pretty thing with his curly auburn hair and dark eyelashes that any woman would envy. "Besides, you know I have friends in Key West who keep me busy and amused."

"Another man, you mean." Tad mimicked a sulky pout.

Sharon laughed. "You are adorable when you play-act that way, but I'd prefer you save all your talent for the bedroom. That's where I most appreciate you."

"You're cruel, Sharon. Why do you treat me this way when you know I'm mad about you?"

"Pooh. You've probably been out with a different young thing every night while I've been gone."

Obviously peeved at her comment, Tad revved the engine, screeched out of the parking area at the airstrip and zoomed up the road. Sharon struggled to put on her safety belt, but finally gave up and just sat back to enjoy the wild ride.

"Who flew you into Fairport?" Tad asked. "One of your millionaire boyfriends?"

Sharon laughed again, but didn't bother telling Tad that her old friend, Stuart Markham, with whom she'd been staying in Key West, had flown her straight from Florida to Mississippi. The last thing she wanted was to argue with Tad. What she did want was to savor every moment of freedom she had before they reached the Leslie Plantation. It wasn't that she didn't love her brother and his family. She did. But she and her brother didn't get along. Mostly because G.W. had never approved of the way she lived her life. He was eleven years her senior and after their father died, he'd taken it upon himself to act as her domineering parent.

G.W. had married well. You didn't do better in Fairport, Mississippi, than to marry a Leslie. Of course, giving the devil his due, her brother had loved Anne Leslie almost beyond reason. Sharon had been twenty when G.W. and Anne married, twenty-two when Tessa was born. And from the very second he'd gotten himself engaged to the older Leslie daughter, G.W. had judged his little sister by an impossible standard. He had wanted her to be a lady. God, she would have suffocated in such rarified air, if she'd tried to please him. Which she hadn't. Of course, the more he tried to rein her in, the more she'd rebelled.

Marriage and babies weren't for her. Not when she'd been twenty or thirty or even forty. The thought of belonging to a garden club and the Junior League had bored her, as had most of the suitable young men G.W. paraded through the Leslie Plantation in the hopes she would marry one of them. She had wanted to live life to the fullest, to travel the world, to meet and bed exciting men. And that's exactly what she'd done. But her big brother hadn't understood her hunger for an exciting life; and he couldn't forgive her for being a constant embarrassment to him. She supposed the thing he would really never forgive her for was encouraging a teenage Tessa to spread her wings and fly into the wild, glorious blue yonder. She and the teenage Tessa had been two peas in a pod, more like sisters than aunt and niece. Sharon had introduced Tessa to beer, marijuana and men, not necessarily in that order.

But after Tessa's so-called accident, the fun-loving girl Sharon had so enjoyed tutoring became a different person. The rebellious hellion that had been the bane of her parents' existence, matured by a trial of fire, had become the ideal daughter. Dutiful, respectful, dependable. And dull. Poor Tessa. The trauma to her brain had erased more than her memories. It had altered her personality.

To this day, Sharon felt partly responsible for what had happened to her niece. If she hadn't led Tessa off the straight and narrow, it was possible she wouldn't have been in the wrong place at the wrong time. And she wouldn't have encountered that monstrous man, Eddie Jay Nealy. Although her sister-in-law, Anne, who'd been a kind and loving lady, had forgiven her, she had never quite forgiven herself. And God knew G.W. hadn't forgiven her.

While Tad chatted nonstop, about this, that and nothing, Sharon started thinking about Leslie Anne. When Sharon had left Fairport less than a month ago, her great-niece had been little more than a carbon copy of her saintly mother, so it had come as a complete shock when Myrle had phoned her in Key West to say that the little princess had run away from home.

"Have you seen Leslie Anne since they brought her home?" Sharon asked, interrupting Tad midsentence.

"No, but Mother went with G.W. early this morning to meet them when they flew home in a helicopter from somewhere over in Alabama. From what little G.W. told Mother, it seems the girl ran into a bit of trouble and some man tried to rape her in a motel."

"What?" Had she heard Tad correctly? "Did you say somebody tried to rape Leslie Anne?"

"Those things happen to little girls who run away. You hear about it happening all the time. It's on the news and in the papers nearly every day. She's just lucky that one of the agents G.W. hired found her and rescued her before—"

"Agent? What agent?"

"Haven't you talked to G.W. or Tessa?"

"No, only to Myrle, and she didn't seem to know much of anything. First she called to tell me to rush home immediately because Leslie Anne had run off.

Then she called to say that the child had been found and brought home."

"G.W. hired this high-priced private security and investigation agency to locate Leslie Anne," Tad explained. "According to Mother, your brother paid a small fortune to bring in four agents to do the job."

"Does anyone know why Leslie Anne ran away in the first place?"

"I don't have a clue. G.W. hasn't told Mother anything. The reason seems to be some major secret. I thought surely you'd know."

A shudder of uneasiness wound its way up Sharon's spine. Totally crazy, wildly ridiculous thoughts went through her mind. What would possess a happy, well-adjusted sixteen-year-old to suddenly run away from home?

"I don't have the slightest idea why she ran away," Sharon said. "Teenagers do crazy things."

"Not Leslie Anne."

No, not Leslie Anne. And that's what worried Sharon. "Maybe she got sick and tired of being little Miss Goody Two-Shoes."

Liar. You know there could be another reason. A more compelling reason. No, it can't be. It just can't be.

There's no way that sweet kid could have found out the truth about her father, was there? Neither G.W. nor Tessa would have told her. And Sharon knew that she sure as hell hadn't. And no one else knows, do they? She'd never told a living soul about

Tessa being raped. At least as far as she knew she hadn't. Even when she was zoned out on liquor or occasionally on pills, she wouldn't have revealed such a heartbreakingly tragic family secret.

When the iron gates guarding the Leslie Plantation came into view, Sharon tensed. Something instinctive within her balked at coming home. And despite the fact that she loathed this pretentious old house and all it stood for, it was still home because her family—G.W., Tessa and Leslie Anne—was here. As much as she loved traveling and having fun with friends, she had found that as she grew older, family had come to mean a great deal more to her than it had in the past.

If Leslie Anne was in trouble, she would need her aunt Sharon. After all, she wasn't likely to get any sympathy from G.W. He thought the girl was perfect or at least should be. Maybe her niece had a secret boyfriend and had gotten herself pregnant. If that was the case, Auntie Sharon would find a way to help her. Or maybe the problem was something a lot less serious. Something as silly as she'd failed geometry. First and foremost, G.W. and Tessa expected Leslie Anne to maintain her straight-A average.

Whatever the reason Leslie Anne had run away, it wasn't because she'd found out the truth about her mother being raped by a maniac. No, no, that wasn't the reason. It just couldn't be. There was no way G.W. or Tessa could deal with having to face the past. And there was no way anyone could have found out about Tessa's horrible ordeal, not after G.W. had done everything in his power to bury all evidence of what had happened.

TESSA KNEW that with just the least bit of encouragement, Dante would kiss her. And even though she longed for that intimacy, she feared losing control. It seemed unreal to her that she could want a man—any man—but that she would yearn to be with a man she barely knew astounded her.

"Don't shut me out, Tessa," he said.

"I'm not—"

He gently placed his index finger over her parted lips. "Yes, you are."

"Not intentionally."

His finger traced the outline of her lips, then moved across her chin and down her neck. Momentarily lost in the sensual pleasure of his touch, Tessa closed her eyes, then drew in a deep breath and held it until Dante spread his hand out over her throat and cupped her chin.

Her eyelids flew open. Their gazes connected and melded, neither able to look away. "I don't really understand what's happening to me," she admitted, wanting to be completely honest with this man.

"It's called sexual attraction." The corners of his mouth lifted ever so slightly in a hesitant smile. "You know, it's that feeling that makes a man and woman want to rip off each other's clothes and go at each other like a couple of wild animals."

"I know what it is." She made an effort to return his smile. "But I've never experienced it. Maybe before the…the rape, but not since then."

"You aren't saying you haven't been with a man since—"

"No, that's not what I'm saying. As part of my healing process, I had sex, but… Let's just say I couldn't work up very much enthusiasm. I haven't really wanted someone. Not until now. And it shouldn't be you."

"Why shouldn't it be me?"

He reached for her; she sidestepped him.

"You don't want me to touch you?" he asked.

She shook her head. "That's not it. The problem is that I want it too much. And my life is far too complicated right now for me to deal with a love affair. The first real love affair I've ever wanted."

"Ever? What about before you were raped? You said maybe before then. Why maybe? Either you did or didn't. It's my understanding that most women never forget their first lover."

"I've been told that Charlie Sentell was my first lover. At least that's what he told me," Tessa said. "But Aunt Sharon swears I was sexually active long before Charlie. She said her guess is that my first time was when I was fifteen and—"

"You're confusing me with all this Charlie told me

and Aunt Sharon says. You talk as if you—" His eyes widened in realization. "My God, you don't remember, do you? When you woke up in that hospital in Louisiana and didn't know your own father or remember what had happened to you, it wasn't just hysterical amnesia, not some temporary loss of memory. You can't remember anything before that time, can you?"

Tessa clenched her teeth, trying to control her emotions. She didn't want to think about how she'd felt all those years ago when she had awakened in that hospital ICU and had no memory of who she was or what had happened to her. Terrified didn't begin to describe how she'd felt.

"I suffered minor brain damage," Tessa said. "It took endless months for me to relearn how to do almost everything. How to put sentences together so they made sense. How to dress myself and feed myself and even to read and write. Actually, it took me several years to become somewhat normal again."

"Oh, Tessa, honey…" He socked his right fist into the open palm of his left hand. "Damn, I wish I could have gotten hold of Eddie Jay Nealy. I'd have—"

"You're thinking about her, aren't you? About Amy and what he probably did to her."

"There's no telling how many young women he raped and tortured and killed. But you somehow survived. Not only survived, but recovered. God, Tessa, you're living proof that a person can endure anything."

"Maybe your Amy survived, too. Maybe she's out there somewhere and has no memory of her past." Unable to resist the urge to comfort Dante, she ran her hand up and down his arm.

He grabbed her hand and held it over his biceps, then squeezed. "If only that were possible."

"Why isn't it possible? I survived. And if my father hadn't been notified that there was a woman fitting my description in that Louisiana hospital, I might never have discovered my identity. I could be out there somewhere alone, with no memory whatsoever of my past. If it nearly happened to me, it could have happened to Amy."

Dante slipped his arm around her waist and pulled her to him, his dark eyes boring into her as if he were searching beyond the exterior, seeking something inside her. In her soul.

"Until Helene Marshall survived, you were the only one of Nealy's victims who was found alive. But I didn't know anything about you. I didn't know you even existed because there is no record of your being raped and beaten. Believe me, I've done my research over the years, and I've done some more since meeting you. There was no other young, blond woman reported raped and beaten around the time of Amy's disappearance, not anywhere in the South or Southwest. If I hadn't come to Fairport on this assignment, I'd have never known about you. Your father did a great job of covering up what happened to you."

"Oh, Dante, I'm so sorry. I wish, for your sake that—"

He kissed her. It happened so quickly, so unexpectedly that she had no time to prepare herself. His wide mouth was soft and moist, but the kiss was hard and demanding. As a trickle of fear crept up her spine, she stiffened in his arms. Then suddenly the kiss changed from aggressive to tender, as if he instinctively understood her reaction and tempered his passion with gentleness. Giving herself over to the delicious sensations bombarding her body, Tessa returned his kiss, opening her mouth, inviting him in. His tongue licked a quick path over her lips, then delved between her teeth and raked over the roof of her mouth. Tessa sighed. Her tongue darted out shyly, wanting to participate, but not sure exactly how. As Dante deepened the kiss, took it to another level of intimacy, primeval feminine instinct took over and Tessa's inhibitions dissolved in the heat of her passion.

The kiss exploded into raging hunger that Tessa could not control. She grasped Dante's shoulders, her nails biting into the fabric of his jacket. Throbbing, moistening in preparation, her femininity clenched and unclenched. All rational thought ceased.

And then without warning, Dante ended the kiss, grabbed her by the shoulders and held her away from him. His breathing was harsh and labored; hers was the same. They stood there staring at each other, the chemistry between them electrified.

"Dante?"

"It's all right, honey. We just got a little carried away. It was all my fault. I shouldn't have let things get so out of hand."

She shook her head. "I wanted it…needed it."

"Ah, babe…"

He stared at her with such longing, the hunger in his eyes so raw, that it hurt her to look at him. "Were you kissing me or were you kissing Amy?"

He released her abruptly. "You want the truth?"

"Yes."

"I don't know. I honest to God don't know who I was kissing."

Tessa told herself that she would not react in any way to his admission. After all, she'd already known what he would say, hadn't she?

"Maybe you're right. Maybe another Dundee agent should take over the investigation. I can't seem to handle things in an objective manner."

He gave her one last look, his gaze saying how sorry he was, before he walked away. Out of the parlor. Leaving her alone.

His name echoed inside her head. *Dante. Dante.* She wanted to cry out, to call him back, to beg him not to leave her. Did it really matter that he was still in love with his teenage sweetheart? Amy Smith was dead, wasn't she? How could Tessa possibly be jealous of a dead woman?

But she was jealous of Amy. And it did matter that

Dante still loved her, or at least the memory of her. *Let him go,* Tessa told herself. *Let him go before he breaks your heart.*

CHAPTER ELEVEN

"WHAT'S THE MATTER, Dr. Barrett?" Leslie Anne glared at the therapist. "I thought you were the wise one, the great psychiatrist who helped my mother recover from being raped and savagely beaten by my father, and yet you don't seem to have any words of wisdom for me."

She hated the way the doctor looked at her, with such pity in his eyes. What was he thinking—that Leslie Anne Westbrook would make a fine case study, perhaps be the ideal subject for a book on inherited deviant behavior?

"Do you really think of Eddie Jay Nealy as your father?" Dr. Barrett asked.

Leslie Anne shrugged.

The truth of the matter was that she didn't think of her mother's rapist as her father. But she also didn't think of some fictitious guy named John Allen as her father, either. Even though she'd been curious about her paternity for years and had suspected her mother and grandfather were lying to her about John

Allen, she had clung to the childish hope that who-ever her father was, he and her mother had loved each other. Boy, what a dummy she'd been. Nothing could be further from the truth.

"You can't expect to digest all the information you received today in a matter of hours or even weeks," the doctor told her. "It took your mother years to work through her fears and doubts, to be able to move forward and live a normal life."

"Is that what she has—a normal life? She isn't married. She doesn't date. Her whole life revolves around three things—her job with Westbrook, Inc., Granddaddy and me. If you'd actually cured her, don't you think she'd at least have a boyfriend?"

"Is that what you want, Leslie Anne? Would you like to see your mother married?"

"I didn't say that. I just said I don't think you fixed her a hundred percent and you're not going to be able to fix me, either. I'm like Humpty Dumpty, all broken into a bunch of pieces and not you or any-body else can put me back together."

Dr. Barrett paused in their stroll along the path that led through the well-maintained gardens on the es-tate. He crossed his arms over his chest and looked into her eyes. "If your mother got married, you'd have a stepfather, someone you might be able to think of as a father. Is that the reason you'd—"

"Ha!" Leslie Anne smiled, spreading her arms wide in a phony pose. "Of course, that's it." She snapped her fingers. "Instant cure. Find me a step-daddy with whom I can bond. That's all I'll need to forget the fact that some psychopath's blood flows through my veins, that I could possibly have inherited his demonic need to kill." She walked up to the doctor, stood on tiptoe and got right in his face. "Maybe I'll start by killing you. Doesn't that worry you?"

His ruddy face paled. Despite the fact that she was crying inside, screaming with pain and humiliation, she laughed. Dr. Barrett wasn't as unaffected by her threat as he tried to pretend, even though he managed to maintain his composure.

"I can't help you if you don't want to be helped," he told her in a calm voice. "Your mother desperately wanted help. Apparently you're not ready. Not yet."

"I'm ready for you to leave me the hell alone." With her chin tilted, her gaze defiant, she stood her ground.

"If that's what you want."

"It's what I want."

"Very well. Why don't I walk you back to the house and we can tell your mother how you feel about therapy? That you're not ready to begin sessions with me. Not yet."

"Why don't you tell her yourself? And while you're at it—tell her I want everybody to leave me alone. And I mean everybody!" Feeling an overwhelming need to escape, Leslie Anne turned and fled.

"Leslie Anne!"

Dr. Barrett kept calling her name, but she didn't pause in her flight, didn't look back. She kept running down the path, hurrying away from the doctor and from her home and family, running from a truth too horrible to bear. But where was she going? What was her destination? She didn't know, didn't care.

By the time she realized which pathway she'd taken, she had reached the river. Winded and perspiring, she skidded to a halt near the edge of the embankment that overlooked the dark, lazily flowing waters of the mighty Mississippi. Gazing down, over the tops of the brush that clung tenaciously to the jagged, sloping earth, she suddenly wondered why she shouldn't jump. If she threw herself over the edge, into the river, all her problems would be solved. She wouldn't have to deal with the knowledge that Eddie Jay Nealy was her father. Not now. Not ever.

"Are you thinking about jumping?" a familiar male voice asked.

Leslie Anne gasped, then whirled around to face Tad Sizemore. "What's it to you?"

"Nothing really," he replied, a silly grin on his much-too-pretty face. "Jump if you'd like. But you should know that if you do jump, there's a very good chance you'll break your fool neck."

"Is that so? Well, maybe I want to break my fool neck. Did you ever think of that?"

"Now, tell me, princess-of-all-she-surveys, why would you want to kill yourself?"

"I didn't say I wanted to kill myself."

"Sugar, if you break your neck, it'll more than likely kill you."

She crossed her arms over her chest and glared at him. "Why don't you go away and leave me alone? What are you doing out here anyway?"

"Mother and I are having lunch with G.W. today," Tad said. "I'm early because I stopped by the airstrip to pick up your aunt Sharon and give her a ride home. Mother will arrive shortly, so there's no point in my leaving and returning later. But I did feel that I might be in the way up at the house, so I decided to take a leisurely walk and not butt in while your aunt informs the family she's returned."

"How considerate of you."

"Hmm. They're probably talking about you, you know. You certainly upset the household when you ran off the way you did. I'm curious. Whatever possessed you to run away? You've got the world by the tail, little girl. Old G.W. dotes on you. He'd cut off his right arm for you. And you seem to be the beginning and end of your mommy dearest's whole world."

"You don't like me very much, do you, Tad?" Well, she didn't care if he hated her. She certainly despised him and his butter-wouldn't-melt-in-her-mouth mother.

"Other than the fact that you're G.W.'s heir, you really aren't even a blip on my radar screen. But you and your mother are definitely thorns in Mother's side. She's bent over backward to make you two like her and yet—"

"Your mother doesn't care anything about Granddaddy. All she's interested in is his money."

"Words straight out of Tessa Westbrook's mouth. But then you are your mother's daughter, aren't you? A spoiled little rich girl who snaps her fingers and gets whatever she wants."

"And you're your mother's son," Leslie Anne retaliated. "Blood-sucking leeches, the both of you."

Tad's face reddened and for just a moment, Leslie Anne thought he might hit her. Instead, he laughed.

"Heredity is a bitch, isn't it, kid? We don't get to choose our mommies and daddies, but we have to spend our entire lives trying to overcome their influence."

What did he mean by that? Did he know about Eddie Jay Nealy? Had Tad learned about who her biological father was from somebody in the family? Had Granddaddy told Olivia?

"Who told you?" she demanded.

"Who told me what?"

"Don't play dumb with me. You know about my father, don't you? Did Granddaddy tell Olivia and then she told you? Did you two get a big laugh at my expense? G.W.'s precious little princess is the devil's daughter. Bet you found that funny."

She hated Tad. She hated Olivia. And she hated Granddaddy, too!

"The devil's daughter?" Tad laughed.

Leslie Anne reached out and slapped him, then gasped and jerked her hand away. What had she done? Rage boiled inside her. Murderous rage?

"Why you little minx." Tad rubbed his cheek. "You've got quite a temper, don't you? I'd say you need the same thing I needed growing up—a father who'd put you over his knee and give you a good walloping."

Horrified as much by the fact that she'd hit him, that she had reacted violently, as by his comment about her needing a father to beat her, Leslie Anne ran past Tad, back up the path toward the garden area. With tears blinding her, she couldn't see where she was going. But she didn't care. God, she wished the ground would open up and swallow her.

TESSA STOOD in the shadows of the arbor and watched her father and Olivia in the gazebo. That woman had no shame. She'd chased G.W. unmercifully, calling him five times a day, dropping by the house unexpectedly several times a week, arranging to be invited to every social occasion where she knew he would be. She'd worn him down, little by little, and all with Aunt Myrle's help. Didn't her mother's sister see Olivia Sizemore for the gold digger she was? The woman had been married four times. She'd buried two husbands and divorced two. And she seemed damned and determined to make G.W. number five.

Over my dead body, Tessa thought.

It wasn't that she objected to her father dating. He'd kept company with several very suitable ladies since her mother had died over thirteen years ago. If he wanted to remarry, why hadn't he chosen someone halfway worthy of him? Olivia might have been Aunt Myrle's sorority sister, but she certainly wasn't the same type of woman. She wore too much makeup, dyed her hair that hideous red to cover the gray, laughed too loud and talked like a magpie.

Tessa crept closer, wanting to hear what Olivia was saying to her father. She didn't trust that money-hungry floozy any further than she could throw her. If she didn't protect her father from the woman, then who would?

"Oh, G.W., I do wish you wouldn't fret so about that child." Olivia forked her fingers up the back of G.W.'s neck in a playful, petting gesture. "Children will act up from time to time. They all do. Even my darling Tad sowed a few wild oats."

"You don't understand," G.W. said.

"Then tell me, sugar. Explain what's going on. Maybe I can help." She nuzzled his neck as she laced her arm through his and cuddled against him. "You know little old me would do just about anything for you."

Oh, God, Daddy, don't tell her! Tessa said silently, praying her father had better sense than to divulge a family secret to Olivia.

G.W. wrapped his arm around Olivia's tiny waist. "I appreciate your concern, but it's a family matter."

"I'm practically family, aren't I?" The woman cooed the words.

Tessa thought she might throw up.

"Now, Olivia, honey, we've discussed this before and—"

"I don't know why Tessa and Leslie Anne don't like me," Olivia whined. "I just adore both of them and I've done everything I know to do to make them like me. Thank goodness my Tad thinks the world of you. Why he said to me only this morning how he surely did wish G. W. Westbrook was his daddy."

G.W. chuckled. "Did he now?"

Oh, get real. Daddy, you've got to know what a lie that is. Tessa inched closer and closer to the gazebo, hiding behind a massive live oak tree and staying just out of sight from the gazebo's two occupants.

"A man like you should have had a son," Olivia said. "Someone to carry on the Westbrook name and take over the reins of Westbrook, Inc." Using the tip of her finger, she caressed G.W.'s lips, then pulled his bottom lip down and stuck her finger in his mouth. "If we got married, I know Tad would gladly let you adopt him and legally change his name to Westbrook."

"I'm sure he would," G.W. said, then bit down on Olivia's finger.

She yelped and jerked her finger away. "You naughty boy you."

He grasped her shoulders and gave her a gentle shake. "I'm not ready for marriage. Not to you or anyone else. And although I appreciate the fact that Tad would very much like to be my son, he's not. As for carrying on the Westbrook name—I have a daughter and a granddaughter who carry that name. And as for Westbrook, Inc., Tessa has already proven she's more than capable of taking over when I'm gone."

Good for you, Daddy. That's telling her! Tessa felt like jumping for joy.

"Eavesdropping?" Sharon Westbrook whispered as she sneaked up behind Tessa.

Tessa gasped. "My God, Aunt Sharon, you scared me half to death." Tessa turned around, grabbed her aunt and hugged her. "When did you get home?"

"Just a little while ago. Olivia's darling boy, Tad, picked me up at the airstrip and brought me home. When did she arrive?"

"About five minutes ago. She's a couple of hours early for lunch." Tessa gave her aunt a condemning look. "Tad's bad news. He's just like his mother, out for whatever he can get."

"Give me some credit, Tessa. I know what that beautiful boy is all about." She nodded toward the gazebo. "And G.W.'s got Olivia's number. He just enjoys screwing her. He's not going to marry her."

"Aunt Sharon, you're outrageous."

G.W. cocked his head to one side and looked out toward the big live oak. "Is somebody out there?"

"We've been caught," Sharon said.

"It's just us, Daddy," Tessa called to him. "Aunt Sharon's home."

"Well, come on up and say hello to Olivia."

Sharon laced her arm through Tessa's. "Come on, kiddo, let's go face the enemy."

Tessa laughed.

When they entered the gazebo, Olivia reached out and hugged Sharon first and then Tessa, before Tessa could sidestep her grasp.

"How's our little Leslie Anne?" Olivia asked. "She will be joining us for lunch, won't she?

"Leslie Anne's fine," G.W. replied.

"I'm not sure she'll be joining us," Tessa said. "She's rather tired after her...er, her adventure."

Lowering her voice and putting a concerned look on her face, Olivia asked, "Did she ever tell y'all why she ran away?"

Silence. Loud, profound silence.

How could they answer such a direct question? Tessa wondered. Why Leslie Anne ran away was none of this nosy woman's business.

"She did it on a dare," Sharon said, in a matter-of-fact way that brooked no doubt.

"On a dare?" Olivia's hazel eyes widened quizzically.

"You know how teenagers are." Sharon offered the

woman her most sincere smile. "One of her friends dared her to run away from home and our bold Leslie Anne accepted the challenge."

"Is that right?" Olivia forced a smile, obviously uncertain whether Sharon was lying or telling the truth. "It's unfortunate that her adventure almost ended in tragedy. G.W. told me that the poor child was almost raped."

"Daddy!"

"Oh, Tessa, don't scold him," Olivia said. "Your father was overwrought early this morning when y'all brought Leslie Anne home. He needed someone to talk to, didn't he? And after all, I am practically family."

"Where is my favorite great-niece?" Sharon asked, apparently hoping to prevent a scene between Tessa and Olivia.

"She's taking a walk," Tessa replied, then looked directly at her father. "She was walking with a friend who came for a visit earlier. He stopped by and spoke to me before leaving. It seems he and Leslie Anne had a little misunderstanding, but he said he'd be back to see her another day."

"Oh, how sweet. A lover's quarrel." Olivia stayed cuddled against G.W.

The woman's an idiot, Tessa thought.

G.W. huffed loudly. "Sharon, why don't you and Olivia go to the house and check on lunch. Tell Eustacia to set another place for you."

"I believe we've been dismissed," Sharon said. "Come on, Olivia, let's leave father and daughter alone to talk about us."

Flustered by Sharon's comment, Olivia nevertheless did as she'd been told. She kissed G.W. on the cheek and then went with Sharon toward the house. As soon as they were out of earshot, G.W. turned to Tessa.

"Did Leslie Anne refuse to cooperate with Arthur?" he asked.

"Oh, yes, she most certainly did. Not only did she tell him to leave her alone, she even made some silly comment about killing him."

"What?"

"He didn't take her seriously. He's quite certain she said it to shock him."

"She's got it in her head that she has some sort of evil inside her," G.W. said. "We've got to get that ridiculous notion out of her head, prove to her that she's still the same wonderful girl she's always been, that—"

"If I could get my hands on the person who sent her that letter and those newspaper clippings, I just might be capable of murder myself," Tessa told her father. "Whoever did it has done irrevocable harm to my child. She'll never think of herself the same way she once did, not ever again."

"Mr. Moran and the Dundee agency will find this person and when they do, I'll make certain they regret hurting my family. Nobody crosses G. W. Westbrook without paying a stiff penalty. Dante Moran is the type who understands a man doing what must be done."

"I should tell you now that Mr. Moran is going to send another agent out here to the house. He plans to take charge of the actual investigation and work in the field."

"What happened?" G.W. grabbed Tessa's arm. "Why is he sending someone else to work directly with us? Leslie Anne likes Dante. She trusts him."

"I'm sure Mr. Moran has his reasons. After all, he is the professional, isn't he? He knows best."

G.W. nodded. "I suppose you're right. But still…"

Tessa could hardly tell her father the real reason Dante wouldn't be coming back to the Leslie Plantation. G.W. might like Dante, but she wasn't sure he'd approve of him as his daughter's lover.

DANTE CAUGHT a glimpse of Leslie Anne as he headed toward the rental car Lucie and Dom had left for him. She was halfway up the long, winding driveway. Where was she going? he wondered. Maybe he should say goodbye to her before he left. After all, it wasn't likely that he would see her again anytime soon. Probably not until they'd discovered the identity of the person who'd made sure she knew the truth about her paternity.

"Hey there," he called to her as he waved. "Leslie Anne!"

She stopped suddenly and turned around. When she saw him, she threw up her hand and waved back at him. "You headed somewhere?" she asked.

Increasing his pace to a fast walk, he caught up with her in a couple of minutes. As he looked at her, he was once again reminded of her uncanny resemblance to Amy. "I'm going into town for a meeting with the other Dundee agents," he told her. "We have to plot a strategy for finding the person who sent you those newspaper clippings."

"What difference does it make?" She shrugged. "Whoever it is, he—or she—did me a favor. They told me the truth when my own mother and grandfather wouldn't."

"Don't be so hard on Tessa and G.W. You know they lied to you to protect you."

"You wouldn't lie to your kid, if you had one," she told him with great certainty.

"I'm not so sure about that. If I had a kid, I don't know what I'd do, what lengths I'd go to or what lies I'd tell, if I believed it would protect her from something that could cause her great harm."

"Yeah, I guess finding out your father raped, tortured and killed dozens of women could cause a girl a lot of harm, couldn't it?"

When he looked at Leslie Anne, he saw Amy. Amy, young and beautiful and alive. As hard as he tried to shake the notion that there was some connection between Leslie Anne and Amy, he couldn't.

Logic dictated that there had to be a reason, other than coincidence. If Amy died seventeen years ago, she couldn't have given birth to a child sixteen years ago. And if by some miracle Amy was still alive somewhere and she'd had a baby, it wasn't possible that Leslie Anne was that baby. Not unless Tessa was lying about being Leslie Anne's mother.

Maybe Tessa doesn't know the truth. Maybe Tessa's baby died at birth and G.W. arranged to swap babies. Or maybe the hospital switched babies.

You're doing it again, Dante told himself. *You're creating impossible scenarios. Ridiculous scenarios. None of it makes sense.*

"Why are you staring at me like that?" Leslie Anne asked.

Dante cleared his throat. "Sorry. It's just that you remind me of someone I knew a long time ago."

"Really? Who?"

"A girl named Amy."

"Was she your girlfriend?"

"Yeah."

"Do you have a girlfriend now?"

"No, not right now."

"My mother doesn't have a boyfriend."

"Is that right?" Dante knew where this conversation was going, but he didn't know how to end it without hurting Leslie Anne's feelings.

"I think she likes you."

"I like her, too, but—"

"But you wouldn't want to date a woman whose daughter was fathered by Eddie Jay Nealy. Is that it?"

"No, that's not it. You put words in my mouth."

"Then why wouldn't you be interested in my mother? She's smart and beautiful. And she really is a good mother. And a good daughter to Granddaddy."

How could this sweet girl be Eddie Jay's daughter? It didn't seem possible. He had studied the photographs of the man, searching for any resemblance. And found none. Leslie didn't look like Eddie Jay. But other than her being blond and a few other vague similarities, she really didn't look like Tessa, either.

Leslie Anne Westbrook looked like only one person—Amy Smith.

CHAPTER TWELVE

AS HE SETTLED into the booth in a quiet corner of the restaurant where he was meeting with fellow Dundee agents, Dante couldn't get Leslie Anne off his mind. He had intended to tell her that another agent would take his place as the liaison between her family and the agency, that he'd be working in the field for the rest of this assignment. But he'd changed his mind at the last minute, deciding it was best to leave that unpleasant job up to Tessa. She was the child's mother, wasn't she? She was better equipped to deal with her daughter than he was. Besides, the less Dante was around Leslie Anne Westbrook, the better.

But what if Leslie Anne isn't Tessa's daughter?

That one thought tormented him in a way nothing had since he'd had to face the fact that Amy was dead, that she'd never come back to him. Now here was this teenage girl who looked so much like Amy. Could it be nothing more than a strange coincidence? Or was he blowing the resemblance between the two totally out of proportion? Maybe the teenager didn't look as much like Amy as he thought she did.

He needed an unbiased opinion. That's why he'd asked Lucie to meet him a little earlier than the other agents. She was that rare breed of woman who could, despite being an emotional creature, act and react in a rational manner when the occasion called for logic.

Dante watched Lucie as the hostess pointed her in the right direction. He waved at her, then eased out of the booth and stood while she walked toward him.

"Thanks for meeting me," he said.

"Sure thing. What's up? You sounded sort of odd when you called and asked if I could get here a little earlier than we'd planned."

After Lucie slid into the booth, Dante slipped in on the opposite side and faced her. "I need to ask you to do something for me and I need you to keep it strictly between the two of us."

"All right." Apparently curious, she studied him for a moment. "I take it this is something personal and has nothing to do with the Westbrook case."

"Right and wrong."

She stared at him questioningly. "Right that it's personal?"

"Yes."

"And wrong about—"

"In a roundabout way, it does have something to do with the Westbrooks. With Leslie Anne in particular."

"Hmm. You've got me dying of curiosity."

Dante removed his wallet from the inside pocket of his jacket, flipped it open and stuck his finger into a slot beneath his driver's license. "I want you take a look at this picture and tell me if she resembles anyone you know."

Carefully, Dante eased the senior high photograph of Amy from his wallet. He'd been carrying this picture around for seventeen years. He tried not to glance at it as he slid it across the table to Lucie, but he couldn't stop himself. God, how it still hurt. Sometimes the pain was as fresh and raw as it had been in those first few weeks and months after Amy had disappeared. Her beautiful blue eyes stared up at him from the faded picture. But it was her smile that still captured his heart, as it had all those years ago. Removing his finger from the edge of the picture, he lifted his hand and curled his fingers into a loose fist.

Lucie turned the photograph around, picked it up and looked at it. Her mouth opened on a silent gasp, then she shook her head. "Who is this?"

"Who does she look like?"

"I'm confused. Where did you get this old picture? Who's the girl?"

Dante breathed in deeply and out slowly. "Damn it, Lucie, just tell me if you think she looks like anybody you know."

"Well, if her eyes were brown instead of blue, if the hairstyle was updated and if it wasn't obvious that this photograph wasn't taken recently, I'd say this is Leslie Anne Westbrook."

Dante swallowed hard, inwardly reeling from the strength of his emotions. Joy and total despair fought within him for dominance. If Lucie saw the resemblance, then it hadn't been his imagination playing a cruel trick on him. Leslie Anne did look enough like Amy to be her—? Her what? Sister? Daughter? Niece?

"Obviously this isn't Leslie Anne." Lucie laid the photo on the table and scooted it back toward Dante. "Is it a photo of a relative? Leslie Anne's aunt or grandmother or—"

"That picture is of a woman named Amy Smith. She was seventeen when this senior picture was taken." Dante lifted the photo, gave it one quick glance, then stuck it back in his wallet. "She disappeared seventeen years ago and has been presumed dead all this time. She fit the description of all of Eddie Jay Nealy's victims— young, pretty, blond. And she lived in Texas, one of the states where quite a few of Nealy's victims lived."

As if puzzled, Lucie shook her head. "Whoa. Wait a minute, will you? I'm really confused here. How do you know about this girl—Amy Smith? And where did you get her picture? And how is she connected to Leslie Anne Westbrook?"

"Amy gave me this picture," Dante said, taking a leap of faith by trusting Lucie in a way he trusted very few people. "When I was nineteen, I was engaged to Amy."

"My God!" Lucie's big brown eyes flew open wide. Narrowing her gaze, she stared hard at Dante. "When Sawyer called us all in for a briefing on the Westbrook case and he handed out the files containing a picture of Leslie Anne, you saw the resemblance right away. That's why you volunteered for the job."

"Yeah. I jumped at the chance to take this assignment because I wanted to know how it was possible that a sixteen-year-old girl could look enough like a woman who supposedly died seventeen years ago to be her daughter."

"Have you asked Tessa Westbrook if—?"

"She swears she gave birth to Leslie Anne. But she also admitted that she has no memory whatsoever of her life before she woke up in the hospital in Louisiana."

"What's one got to do with the other? Leslie Anne was born nine months later, after the attack. Tessa would know whether or not she gave birth to Leslie Anne."

"Tessa would know that she gave birth to a child, but what if—" Dante let out a harsh, exasperated breath. "Damn it, I know I'm grasping at straws here…."

"You think there was a baby switch? Dante, that doesn't make any sense. That would mean Amy Smith had to be alive and that she gave birth at the same time Tessa did and in the same hospital."

"I realize what a ludicrous scenario I've drawn up

in my head, but I keep thinking about the possibility that Tessa's baby might have been born dead or died shortly after birth."

"It still doesn't add up," Lucie told him. "Neither Tessa nor G.W. really wanted the baby in the first place. The only reason Tessa went through with the pregnancy was for her mother's sake. So if the child had died, I doubt G.W. would have tried to replace it, especially not with another child belonging to one of Nealy's victims."

"I know. But the only other possibility I can think of is impossible."

As Lucie continued looking at Dante, she suddenly seemed to realize what he was thinking. She grunted. "Huh-uh, don't go there, my friend. There's no way in hell that Tessa could be—"

"Yeah, I know. I know. Other than being the same height and general physical description, Tessa bears only the most superficial resemblance to Amy. Add to that the fact G.W. and Anne Westbrook would have known their own daughter even if she didn't know herself, as would all of Tessa's friends and relatives. But you tell me how it's possible that Leslie Anne—"

Lucie grabbed Dante's hand and held it tightly. "I don't know, but my gut instincts tell me that there's definitely something rotten in the state of Mississippi."

"Then you don't think I'm crazy?"

Lucie grinned. "I'm not sure about that. But you

have every reason to suspect something's definitely screwy about who Leslie Anne Westbrook really is."

"What would you do if you were me? How would you handle things?"

"You need to put some distance between yourself and the Westbrooks, especially Tessa. You already know that I picked up on some chemistry between you two, so don't deny it." Lucie pointed her index finger in his face. "After what you just told me, you can't let yourself become involved with Tessa Westbrook."

"I plan to send someone else to work personally with the Westbrooks," he said. "I'd thought maybe Dom, but—"

"Send me. I can work both sides of this. I doubt Tessa knows anything that can help you, but it's possible I'll hear something, pick up on something or just figure something out simply by staying at the Leslie Plantation. I'll consider this a twofold assignment. One is to find out who sent Leslie Anne the clippings about Nealy and number two will be to learn anything I can about why Leslie Anne looks like Amy Smith. It could be that there's a family tie we don't know about. Could Amy have been a distant relative of Tessa's? Does Amy have family still in Texas that you could—"

"Amy was an orphan. Her parents were killed in a car wreck when she was six. If either had any family to speak of, Amy didn't know them. She couldn't remember any grandparents or aunts and uncles. And social services never located any relatives."

"Look, there are several different scenarios that would explain why Leslie Anne resembles Amy Smith so much, but to be honest with you, all of them seem implausible."

Hearing familiar voices on the other side of the restaurant, Dante glanced up and saw Dom Shea and Vic Noble talking with the hostess. She looked his way, then pointed the Dundee agents in the right direction.

"Here come Dom and Vic," Dante told Lucie. "Let's shelve this for now."

Before Lucie could respond, the other two agents joined them. Dom sat by Lucie, while Vic slipped into the booth by Dante. Lucie gave Dante a mum's-the-word look.

"Nothing I like better than a dinner meeting," Dom said jokingly. "Makes it easier to digest your food when you're talking business."

"I'm flying to Rayville, Louisiana, tonight and picking up a rental car," Dante said. "While Lucie takes over with the Westbrooks, I want you, Dom, to start digging around Fairport. Find out everything you can on the people closest to G.W., Tessa and Leslie Anne. And find out who would have anything to gain by harming Leslie Anne." He glanced at Vic. "I had intended to send you back to Atlanta because I figured Sawyer might need you on another case, but

I checked with him about an hour ago and he said he can spare you for a few more days."

"Fine by me," Vic said.

"Why are you going to Louisiana?" Dom asked.

"I want to talk to Sheriff Summers," Dante explained. He'd tell Dom and Vic only what they needed to know. "Summers was a deputy in Richland Parish seventeen years ago when Tessa Westbrook was found half-dead just off Interstate 20. It's possible he'll remember something that might affect our case."

"Don't you think it's odd that G. W. Westbrook thought it necessary to cover up what had happened to his daughter?" Dom said. "And believe you me, he covered things up pretty good. There is no record on file in Richland Parish on Tessa Westbrook—not a report from either the police in Rayville or any surrounding towns or the parish sheriff's department. But there is a record of her having been a patient at the medical center in Rayville for ten days."

"Do you have any idea what's in those records?" Lucie asked.

Dom shook his head. "Nope. But we've got somebody working on the inside to find out. It's costing us—" he rubbed his thumb against his index and middle fingers "—*mucho dinero*. Spies and informants don't come cheap."

"What do you want to bet the hospital records either vanish from thin air or they've been doctored so they read as if Tessa Westbrook was in a terrible car wreck?" Vic Noble glanced around the table. "Daddy Warbucks was damned and determined to keep the truth about what happened to his daughter under wraps. The old man called in a lot of favors and doled out a heap of money."

"He wanted to protect his daughter," Lucie said. "He didn't want the scandal of her being raped and impregnated by her rapist to become public knowledge. I can understand, can't y'all?"

"He had to have put the cover-up in action almost immediately after he was notified about Tessa being found," Dom said. "That means he formulated a complicated lie about what had happened before he knew his daughter was pregnant."

"One thing's for sure—we have a lot of questions and very few answers," Dante told them. "Lucie will handle the family exclusively from now on. Dom, you and Vic will investigate locally. And I'll start at the beginning, with where Tessa was found seventeen years ago."

THE LAST THING Tessa felt like doing was entertaining, even if their guests were only family and friends. And she couldn't fault her father for thinking it would be helpful to surround themselves with people he believed truly cared about them. It was almost as if he had called in reinforcements after the battle had been lost. But the war wasn't over, Tessa reminded herself as she sipped on her wine—a vintage she would have, under normal circumstances, appreciated. But not tonight. Not when her mind was so preoccupied with one thought. Only when the beast who'd sent Leslie Anne those newspaper clippings had been unearthed and punished would the next battle be won. As for the war itself—it might not ever end. Not unless her daughter could come to terms with the truth.

"I do wish our darling Leslie Anne could have joined us this evening," Myrle Poole said. "But I suppose the dear girl is embarrassed by that silly stunt she pulled. Can you imagine her running away from home because some other teenager dared her to do it?"

"Did y'all find out who dared her to run away?" Celia asked. " I think his or her parents should be notified and the proper punishment doled out." She turned to Charlie, smiling like a besotted fool. "Don't you think so, sweetheart?"

"Most certainly." He looked straight at G.W. "And if I were you, I'd make sure Leslie Anne wasn't allowed to see this person ever again."

"Quite right." G.W.'s cheeks flushed. "But I doubt we'll be able to pry the person's name out of her. Leslie Anne can be quite stubborn."

Listening to the conversation, Tessa marveled at how easily her father lied. At least he had the decency to seem slightly embarrassed by his bold-faced lie. But what else could they have done except fabricate a believable story about why Leslie Anne ran away from home? It wasn't as if they could announce to one and all that the Westbrook clan—G.W., Sharon and Tessa—had been harboring a dark, ugly secret all these years.

Olivia laughed, the sound shrill to Tessa's ears, but then everything about the woman rubbed Tessa the wrong way.

"G.W., from whomever do you suppose the child inherited her stubborn streak?" Olivia cooed the question.

Tessa didn't know who was worse—Olivia or her cousin Celia? Both women were making spectacles of themselves by the way they were fawning over their men. But she supposed desperate women acted that way. A woman who was unsure of how a man felt about her often pushed too hard for assurance.

G.W. chuckled, the sound only slightly wooden, and Tessa doubted anyone other than she and Aunt Sharon knew how phony that laugh was. "I'll take full blame for any of Leslie Anne's bad traits, including her stubbornness. And I'm damned proud to be her granddaddy."

Sharon and Tessa exchanged a look that said only they knew what G.W. really meant. He was proclaiming to one and all that his granddaughter was a Westbrook. And be damned with who her biological father was. Of course, his declaration was lost on the rest of his audience.

Suddenly Tessa wondered if they all really believed the car wreck story? Dear God, what was she thinking? Of course they believed it. Surely no one here in her home, sharing dinner with her, might actually have been the person who'd sent Leslie Anne those clippings. No, no, that wasn't possible. None of the others knew. And even if they did, who would have—?

Olivia! That damn woman was capable of anything. But why? What motive did she have to want to hurt Leslie Anne?

Tessa could understand if Olivia or Tad had tried to blackmail her for money to keep the secret from being revealed, but what did either of them have to gain by exposing Leslie Anne to the story of Eddie Jay Nealy's murdering spree?

Think about it, she told herself. A person doesn't do something so sadistically cruel without a motive. And no one here had a motive.

Olivia and Tad might be money-grubbing sycophants, but what would they have gained by hurting Leslie Anne? And the others here this evening were all family. Aunt Sharon had always known the truth and could have revealed it at any time. But she adored Leslie Anne and would never harm her. Aunt Myrle could be annoying and often silly, but she had a heart of gold. How often did she refer to Leslie Anne as "my sister's precious little namesake?" Tessa wasn't overly fond of Celia, mainly because Celia hadn't kept her jealousy of Tessa a secret. Celia had been panting after Charlie for ages now and up until recently, he'd been panting just as hard after Tessa. But was Celia capable of deliberately hurting Leslie Anne simply because she hated Tessa?

Yes, I believe she is.

But how would she have learned the truth?

Last but not least was Charles Sentell. She couldn't imagine him doing anything so unkind, not when he'd begged Tessa to marry him and allow him to adopt Leslie Anne. He'd always had a soft spot in his heart for Tessa's little girl, a child he'd said, more than once, might have been his had circumstances been different.

But as with the others, even if Charlie was capable of doing such a thing, how could he have found out about Eddie Jay Nealy?

"You're awfully quiet this evening." Celia zeroed in on Tessa. "But finding out that you aren't the perfect mother must be worrying you terribly."

"Why, Celia, what an unpleasant thing to say." Myrle frowned at her daughter.

"Was it, Mommie?" Celia feigned ignorance. "I do apologize if my innocent little comment seemed unkind. I certainly didn't mean it that way." Celia offered Tessa a wide, toothy smile, one that was as fake as a three-dollar bill.

"I think you'd better get that kid some help." Tad injected his opinion into the conversation, startling everyone into complete silence. "I talked to her earlier today and she was acting weird, like she might do something to herself."

"What!" Sharon's voice joined Tessa's and G.W.'s simultaneously.

"Tad, whatever are you talking about?" Olivia asked.

Tad shrugged. "Maybe I shouldn't have said anything, but I think y'all shouldn't buy her story of running away because somebody dared her to. There's something else going on with her."

"Are you implying that Leslie Anne might actually harm herself?" Charlie narrowed his gaze and glared pensively at Tad.

"I'm not implying anything," Tad said. "I'm just saying something's up with the kid."

Fear cut straight through Tessa, hitting first her heart and then her gut, the pain physical as well as emotional. Surely to goodness, Leslie Anne wasn't suicidal. Not her beautiful, smart, levelheaded child.

Yes, Leslie Anne was all those things, but she was also a young girl who had learned her mother and grandfather had been lying to her all her life. She had been forced to accept the fact that her mother had been raped and she was the result of that heinous act. Who knew how such knowledge would affect even the most stable person.

Don't ever forget that there was a time when you thought about suicide, when you longed to die, Tessa reminded herself.

But she hadn't picked up on anything from Leslie Anne that indicated the thought of killing herself had even crossed her mind. Didn't she know her child better than anyone? If her daughter's mental state was that fragile...

Hal Carpenter appeared in the doorway of the dining room, cleared his throat and said, "I'm sorry to bother you, Miss Tessa, but there's a Dundee agent here to see you. She says it's rather important."

"She?" Sharon asked.

"Yes, ma'am. A Ms. Lucie Evans." He paused, then said, "And Eustacia asked if she should take Miss Leslie Anne's dinner up to her on a tray?"

"You go speak to Ms. Evans," Sharon told Tessa, then looked across the room to Hal. "Tell Eustacia that I'll take a tray up to Leslie Anne."

Tessa and Sharon rose from the table in practically synchronized movements. Sharon didn't bother to excuse herself, but followed Hal out of the dining room.

"If y'all will pardon me," Tessa said. "Ms. Evans is probably here to tie up some loose ends."

"Do you need me to go with you?" G.W. asked.

"No, Daddy, please stay here and enjoy dinner with our friends and family. I'll try not to be long."

Tessa found Lucie waiting in the foyer, a small floral suitcase resting on the marble floor only a few inches from her feet.

The minute she saw Tessa, she said, "Dante sent me."

"He told you everything?"

A strange expression crossed Lucie's face. "Yes. Everything."

Tessa eyed the suitcase. "I assume you'll be staying here."

Lucie nodded.

"We'll have to think of a reason for your remaining here in Fairport and why, since Leslie Anne is home safe and sound, we need a Dundee agent on the payroll."

"Perhaps the best excuse is to say that until you're sure Leslie Anne won't pull another childish stunt, you and her grandfather thought she needed a bodyguard. Of course, you'll need to run that excuse by your daughter before we start using it."

Tessa sighed. "I suppose it's as good an excuse as we'll come up with, so we might as well tell Leslie Anne now and hope she'll cooperate."

"It could wait until after y'all have finished dinner."

"Leslie Anne didn't come down to dinner tonight. She's in her room, so why don't we go on up and talk to her?" Tessa eyed Lucie's suitcase. "Bring your bag and after we talk to Leslie Anne, I'll show you to your room."

Lucie followed her upstairs, straight to Leslie Anne's suite. The blare of loud rock music drifted down the hall, the sound bouncing off the walls and ceiling, all but shaking the old mansion to the ground. Tessa knocked on the closed door. No response. She knocked again. Louder. Harder. Still no response. She tried the door. Locked.

Leslie Anne never locked her door.

Lucie set her suitcase on the floor, pulled her bag from her shoulder and unzipped a front pouch. After removing a small leather case, she pulled a shiny tool from the case and inserted it in the door lock. After replacing the tool and returning the case to her bag, Lucie turned the doorknob and, voilà, the door opened.

Tessa lifted her eyebrows in a well-done comment, then walked into her daughter's room, preparing herself for a possible confrontation. Lucie came in behind her, but waited just over the threshold. Tessa found Leslie Anne sprawled out across her rumpled bed. She wore a pair of hot pink cotton knit sweats and her eyes were puffy and red from crying.

My poor baby. Tessa longed to pull her child into her arms.

Apparently sensing she was no longer alone, Leslie Anne looked up and gasped. "How'd you get in here?"

Lucie walked over to the entertainment center and turned off the deafening rumble of the hard rock CD. "I picked the lock."

Leslie Anne jerked around and glared at Lucie. "What are you doing here? Where's Dante?"

"Don't be rude," Tessa said. "Lucie is here to—"

Leslie Anne jumped off the bed and stood to face her mother. "Where is Dante?"

"Mr. Moran is going to head up the investigation." Tessa sensed her daughter's agitation and prayed she could soothe her and make her see reason. "Lucie is here to work with us—"

"I want Dante." Leslie Anne slammed her hands on her hips in a defiant stance.

"Mr. Moran felt he should take over in the field," Tessa tried again to explain.

"Does that mean he won't be back?"

"It means we won't see him for a while."

"What did you do?" Leslie Anne cried. "Or was it Granddaddy? Who made Dante go away? I thought you liked him. I thought you understood how much I need him."

"Leslie Anne, sweetheart, please—"

"Leave me alone." Leslie Anne stormed out of the bedroom, into the bathroom and locked the door behind her.

Tessa looked at Lucie, who said, "I can pick that lock, too, but what's the point? She's in no mood to listen to anything either of us has to say right now."

"What's happened?" Sharon called from where she stood in the open doorway, Leslie Anne's supper tray in her hands.

"Bring the tray on in and put it down," Tessa said. "Aunt Sharon, I'd like for you to stay here while Lucie picks the lock on the bathroom door, which she'll do in a little while. Once Leslie Anne comes out, tell her that I've gone to talk to Dante Moran."

"Are you sure you should cave in to her demands that way?" Lucie asked.

"What demands?" Sharon glanced from Lucie to Tessa.

"My daughter could well be on the verge of a nervous breakdown," Tessa looked from Lucie to Sharon and back to Lucie. "Tad Sizemore said that Leslie Anne gave him the impression she was suicidal earlier today. I believe he's wrong about that, but if bringing Dante back here to talk to her soothes her in any way, then that's what I'm going to do—bring him back."

"You shouldn't listen to Tad. He tends to be overly dramatic, even melodramatic sometimes," Sharon said.

"I realize that, but…" Tessa heaved a deep sigh. "I think Leslie Anne has built up some sort of fantasy about Mr. Moran. She sees him as her protector, as a father figure of a sort. If receiving some kind of reassurance from him can help her, then by God, that's what she'll get. I'll make Dante understand that he's needed here."

"We'll take care of Leslie Anne. If you'd like, part of my job here can be to act as your daughter's bodyguard, so you can rest easy about her. You go on and talk to Dante," Lucie told her. "He's at the Fairport Inn, Room Seven."

CHAPTER THIRTEEN

THE HELICOPTER would pick Dante up at nine-thirty tonight and transport him directly to the John H. Hooks Jr. airport in Rayville, Richland Parish's county seat, where a rental car would be waiting for him. He'd already booked a room at the Ramada Inn and first thing in the morning he would begin his investigation. His first stop would be the sheriff's department. Sheriff Earl Summers had been a deputy seventeen years ago, so Dante assumed he would remember any rumors within the department back then about a pretty blond girl being found out near the Interstate. Unless Summers had been in on the cover-up.

Don't go jumping to conclusions.

Hopefully the person Dundee's had working inside the medical center, where Tessa had been a patient, would be able to find and photocopy Tessa's medical records.

And what if those records tell you nothing you don't already know?

There had to be somebody in Richland Parish who knew something about Tessa. If not the guy who was now the sheriff, then perhaps another former deputy. Or maybe someone who'd been a hospital employee at the time. A naked girl—raped, brutalized and left for dead—found just off the side of the highway would had to have made the news, even if her name and details of her condition hadn't been released to the press. Maybe before he saw the sheriff or checked with their hospital spy, he should go by the local library and search through the old newspapers, which were probably on microfilm.

Rubbing his hand over his face, Dante grunted. He needed a shave. His heavy black beard grew like weeds, creating a permanent five o'clock shadow. If he wanted a smooth face in the evenings, he had to shave a second time. After lifting his vinyl bag onto the foot of the bed, he undid it, then removed his shaving kit and carried it into the bathroom. He took off his tie and button-down, draped them over the hook on the back of the bathroom door, and then yanked his T-shirt over his head.

Just as he turned on the hot water to fill the sink, he heard a loud knock at his motel room door. Who the hell? Probably Dom or Vic. But what would either of them want? They'd gone over the game plan at dinner. What else was there to say? It wasn't as if he was buddy-buddy with either guy, even though he figured that on longer acquaintance he'd probably become friends with both.

The knocking grew louder and more intense.

"Hold your horses, will you? I'm coming," Dante called as he hurried to the door, not bothering to put his shirt back on.

Always a cautious man, he peered through the peephole. Holy hell, it was Tessa! What was she doing here? He yanked open the door.

"I took a chance that you would still be here. I have to talk to you." Her gaze moved from his face to his naked chest.

"Sure, come on in." He stepped back to allow her entrance.

She hesitated for a couple of seconds, then walked into his room. He closed the door; she turned to face him.

"What's wrong?" he asked.

"It's Leslie Anne."

He gave her an inquisitive look.

"When Lucie showed up at the house a while ago, Leslie Anne threw a fit. A regular temper tantrum. And believe me, Leslie Anne hasn't acted like that since she was three."

"Why did she throw a fit? I thought she liked Lucie."

"She does, but she got upset because she thought Daddy or I had done something to run you off." Obviously exasperated, Tessa huffed softly. "She told me that she thought I understood how much she needs you. Then she locked herself in the bathroom. When I left, Lucie was planning to pick the lock and she and Aunt Sharon were going to try to reason with Leslie Anne."

"Damn!" Dante grunted. "Under normal circumstances, I'd say Leslie Anne needs discipline, not catering to by anyone. But considering what she's been through these past few days—"

"Tad Sizemore told us at dinner tonight that Leslie Anne implied to him earlier today that she was thinking about...about harming herself."

"What?"

"Tad Sizemore, Olivia's son, said he thinks Leslie Anne is suicidal."

"I didn't see any evidence of it, did you? Did Dr. Barrett say anything about—"

"No, no, he didn't say a word about it, and I don't get a sense that Leslie Anne wants to harm herself. She's angry and confused, but I think she'd rather stomp all over everyone around her rather than hurt herself."

"That's the impression I got, too," Dante assured Tessa.

"But I can't take any chances. Surely you understand. So Lucie has agreed to keep close tabs on Leslie Anne."

"Lucie's a top-notch bodyguard. You don't have to worry about Leslie Anne with Lucie on duty."

"I'm her mother. I'll worry regardless. It comes with the territory."

He nodded.

"I need to ask you for a favor," Tessa said. "For Leslie Anne."

"Whatever you want, if I can do it, I will."

"Come back to the house with me. Talk to her. Promise her that if she needs you, you'll be there for her. I think she believes you're the only person she can trust."

Tessa looked at him pleadingly and it was all he could do not to pull her close and kiss the breath out of her. If it were up to him alone, he would steer clear of Tessa Westbrook for as long as possible, but what he knew was good for him and what he wanted were two different things. Even if he wasn't obligated to help her because of his position as a Dundee agent, there was no way he would desert Tessa or permanently walk away from Leslie Anne. It was past time he admitted to himself that his fate was linked to this woman and her daughter because somehow, someway, they were connected to Amy Smith.

Ironic that the first woman since Amy who had brought to life more than just his lust was a woman whose daughter was Amy's spitting image, a woman who had been brutalized by the same animal who had probably killed Amy. Were the omnipotent powers-that-be playing some cruel cosmic joke on him?

"I'm taking a helicopter to Rayville, Louisiana, tonight," he told her. "I leave at nine-thirty."

"You're going to Richland Parish?"

He nodded.

"I wish you didn't feel it necessary to go there, but…you're the investigator. You know what's best." She held out her hand to him, then realized what she was doing and let her hand drop to her side. "Please, come by the house now and talk to Leslie Anne before you leave town."

She kept staring at his naked chest, her eyes filled with what he recognized as desire. He'd known enough women to be well acquainted with the signs. But the crazy thing was, he didn't think Tessa was aware of it herself.

He reached for her, all the while telling himself not to do it. Logic warned him that he was complicating an already ridiculously complicated situation. But when she came to him willingly, placed her trembling hand on his chest and looked up at him with those incredible blue eyes—eyes as blue as Amy's—he knew he was fighting a losing battle. He wanted Tessa. But it wasn't that plain and simple. He would want her regardless, but he realized that because his heart had her all mixed up with Amy, he couldn't be a hundred percent sure that when he made love to her, he wouldn't halfway be making love to Amy. Even though he knew she wasn't Amy, he kept reacting to her as if she were.

He tensed, then released her. He couldn't do this.

Not to himself. Not to her. Since the day he'd lost Amy, he hadn't had anything to give a woman other than his body. Tessa deserved better. She deserved more.

"I want…" She slid her hand up his chest and over his shoulder, grasping him, clinging fiercely. "I want to go with you…to Richland Parish."

"What?" He moved away from her, raked his fingers through his hair and grimaced. "Why do you want to go with me? You don't even know why I'm going to Rayville."

"You're going to find out what you can about what happened to me. And if there's anyone in that parish who might know the whole truth about me, you want to learn whether or not they could have had a reason to send Leslie Anne those newspaper clippings."

She had it partly right, but she knew only half of it. And he couldn't tell her all the reasons he was going to pilfer through her past, searching for any tidbit of information that might explain a mystery that had him totally stumped. He could hardly say to her, "Your daughter looks enough like Amy Smith to be her, and I've got to find out why."

"There's no reason for you to go with me. You're better off staying here," he told her. "Leslie Anne needs you."

"She needs both of us. You know that, don't you?"

"Tessa, honey—" God, he wished she'd stop looking at him that way, as if he were the answer to her prayers. "I'll do what I can to help you, to help your daughter, but you have to see how impossible it would be for anything—permanent—to happen between us."

"Because you're not a permanent type of man? Because you don't want me? Or because Eddie Jay Nealy is my child's father?"

Damn! No beating around the bush. She'd laid it all out there for him. The three most obvious excuses. And there was only one he could deny.

"I want you, honey. God, how I want you."

The corners of her full, pink mouth lifted in a hint of a smile.

"But I'm not a guy who forms permanent attachments. Not since Amy."

"You're still in love with her, aren't you?"

"Part of me probably always will be." No need to lie to Tessa. She had a way of seeing right through him.

"And no matter how much you like Leslie Anne, no matter what you're willing to do to help her, you can't look at her without remembering—"

He grabbed Tessa and covered her mouth with his to silence her. Surprised by his actions, she tensed at first, but within seconds her body melted against his and she returned the kiss with equal passion. She tasted like peppermint, zesty and sweet. So sweet. Had she used a breath mint right before she'd knocked on his door? She lifted her arms and draped them around his neck while he deepened the kiss, taking them one step further, arousing himself unbearably.

Clinging to him, hungry for all he could give her, Tessa whimpered with need. He eased his hands down her spine and cupped her buttocks, lifting her up and against his sex. He was hard and hurting. She was willing.

He skimmed his lips across her cheek, down her jawline and to her throat, then whispered in her ear. "If I make love to you, it doesn't come with any promises. No commitment. No forever after. Do you understand?"

Tilting her head back, she gazed up at him. "I understand."

He grabbed her by the shoulders. "Look at me, Tessa, really look at me." *And you look at her,* he told himself. *She's not Amy. She's Tessa. Amy's dead.* "Your daughter has put me up on a pedestal and I don't belong there. I don't want either of you making me out to be some glorified white knight. All I am right now is a guy who wants to fuck you real bad."

She stared at him, searching for the truth. Had he blown it by being too honest with her? Who was he kidding? He hadn't been totally honest with her. Yeah, he wanted to fuck her, but there was more to the way he felt about her. And it was that something more that scared the hell out of him.

"You're trying to run me off, aren't you? And by doing that, you just contradicted your own declaration that you're no white knight." She eased out of his loose grasp. "Maybe we *should* wait—" the words "until you want more" sizzled between them "—until we have more time. It's already nearly nine and if we're catching a helicopter ride to—"

"What do you mean *we?*"

"I'm going with you, Dante. It's *my* past you're going to be digging around in and it's *my daughter* whose sanity is possibly at stake." She focused on him, a determined look in her eyes. When he didn't respond immediately, she said, "We'll call Leslie Anne to tell her we're going out of town together and that when we return, you will come out to the house with me to see her. I want you tell her that she can count on you, that she and I can both count on you."

"Tessa, honey—"

"You don't have to mean it," she told him. "Just tell her what she needs to hear. I'll deal with any fall-out later on. Right now, you seem to be her lifeline, and I'm sorry if that's difficult for you, but I know you're the kind of man who can put his personal feelings aside long enough to help a girl in desperate need of your kindness."

"Lady, you give me more credit than I deserve."

Tessa reached in her coat pocket and pulled out her cell phone, flipped it open and dialed. Dante stood by and waited.

"Aunt Sharon, is that you?" Tessa asked. "I assume you're answering Leslie Anne's phone because she wouldn't."

Dante listened to Tessa's end of the conversation

and drew the conclusion that neither Sharon Westbrook nor Lucie had been able to talk sense to Leslie Anne.

"Tell her that I'm here with Dante and he wants to talk to her." Tessa held out her cell phone to him.

He took it. Reluctantly.

"Dante, is that you?" Leslie Anne asked, her voice suspicious, yet edged with hope.

"Yeah, kid, it's me."

"Please, come back," Leslie Anne said. "I need you. You're the only person I can trust."

You can't trust me and neither can your mama. I haven't been completely honest with either of you.

"I want to make a deal with you," Dante said. "How about it?"

"What sort of deal?"

"Your mother and I need to go out of town to track down some leads on who sent you those newspaper clippings, so while we're gone, I want you to let your aunt Sharon and Lucie Evans do what they can for you. Don't fight them about everything. And I want you to think seriously about starting therapy sessions with Dr. Barrett."

"And if I do all that, what do I get in return?"

"When your mother and I return from our trip, I'll come out to your house and stick around here in Fairport for a while."

"For as long as I need you?"

Dante chuckled. "You drive a hard bargain."

"I learned from Granddaddy and Mother. They're both tough negotiators."

"Okay, I'll stay as long as I think you need me."

"You changed the wording of our deal just a little."

"Just a little. So what do you say?" Dante asked.

"Okay. We've got a deal."

"Now, talk to your mother," Dante told Leslie Anne. "And be nice to her. She loves you a lot, you know."

"Yeah, I know."

He handed Tessa the phone.

"Dante and I won't be gone too long and I'll be only a phone call away," Tessa said. "Are you sure you're all right with my going away?" When Leslie Anne said something to her, Tessa laughed. "Okay. I'll keep that in mind. I love you, sweetheart."

Tessa closed her phone and dropped it into her coat pocket.

"What did she say?" he asked.

"She told me that if I was half as smart as she thought I was, I'd seduce you."

"Are you sure she's only sixteen?"

"Sixteen going on thirty. She's become a little too worldly-wise to suit me."

"It's not your fault," Dante told her.

"No, not entirely. But I should have done a better job of protecting her."

"What more could you have done?"

"I could have told her the truth sooner," Tessa said.

CHAPTER FOURTEEN

How obliging of Tessa to leave town. But how inconsiderate of her to instate that redheaded Amazon to protect Leslie Anne. Then again, Lucie Evans being assigned to guard duty won't make much difference in the grand scheme of things, not now that I've revised my plans somewhat. I'll simply work around the Dundee agent, as I will any obstacles thrown in my path. I still have to get rid of Leslie Anne, but I'm more convinced than ever that the best way to do that is to persuade everyone that the girl is suicidal. It shouldn't be too difficult to push the little brat over the edge. A nudge here and there. Subtle but deadly. If I can make her believe that there is no hope for her, that she will never be able to overcome her heritage, then perhaps she'll come to realize that she should end it all—before it's too late and she exhibits some type of deviant behavior. Or at least before everyone finds out the truth and they believe it's only a matter of time before she zones out and commits some terrible crime.

Naturally, the death of her only child will devastate Tessa. She'll never be able to recover from such a loss.

Oh, yes, that would be the ideal outcome, wouldn't it? Poor little Leslie Anne Westbrook, so overwrought finding out her biological father was a serial rapist/killer that she takes her own life. And then her mother has a complete nervous breakdown. Two birds with one stone. Eliminate the daughter and the mother self-destructs.

Brilliant. Absolutely brilliant.

And if Leslie Anne doesn't do the job herself? Considering that stubborn streak she inherited from G.W., as well as the grit, determination and strength that G.W., Anne and Tessa passed on to her, it's possible she'll resist the idea of doing away with herself. In that case, she'll leave me no other choice than to arrange for her suicide. After all, how difficult could it be? A goodbye-cruel-world note left on her computer, after days of erratic behavior, should cinch the deal.

I must put my plan into action immediately. If I work things just right, those closest to Leslie Anne will see just how disturbed the child really is.

LESLIE ANNE woke with a start. She thought she heard someone calling her name. A strange voice. Neither male nor female. Just eerily jarring.

She sat up on the side of the bed and listened. She heard only the rapid beating of her heart, the rhythm strumming in her ears. Not fully awake and halfway convinced the voice hadn't been part of a nightmare, she scanned her bedroom.

Get real. There's no way anybody could have gotten into the house and be hiding in the closet or under the bed.

She'd imagined the voice. Either that or dreamed it. She should forget all about it.

But instead of putting the voice out of her mind, she suddenly remembered that the voice had spoken more than her name. *Think, Leslie Anne, think. What did it say?*

Leslie Anne. Leslie Anne. Who's your daddy, little girl?

Oh, God, that's what the voice had said. Not just her name. And it hadn't been a dream. It couldn't have been, not when it had been the sound of that voice that had awakened her. Someone inside the house had come into her room and—

Leslie Anne jumped out of bed and searched high and low. Under the bed. Behind the drapes. In her huge, twelve-foot-square closet. Inside the shower enclosure. When she dropped to her knees and peered into and up inside the fireplace, she fell back onto the floor and laughed. What an idiot she was, searching for an intruder up the chimney. Who did she think the weird voice belonged to—Santa Claus?

"What's so funny?" Eustacia asked as she walked into the suite carrying Leslie Anne's breakfast tray.

"Nothing you'd understand." Leslie Anne scooted around on her bottom and staying put on the floor, looked up at the cook. "What time is it? I suppose everyone else has had breakfast already."

"It's ten 'til eleven, young lady," Eustacia said crossly. "Mr. G.W. insisted I bring your breakfast to you by eleven o'clock, but I'm telling you right now—" she placed the tray on the round table flanked by two striped silk chairs "—this had better not become a habit. I'm too old to be toting your meals up here to you when you're perfectly capable of coming downstairs to eat."

"I'm sorry you had to bother with this." Leslie Anne bounced to her feet, then went over and gave Eustacia a hug. "Am I forgiven?"

"Of course you're forgiven." Eustacia swatted Leslie Anne's backside. "I don't know why, and I don't want to know what possessed you to run away. All I know is that you're worrying your granddaddy to death. You ought to make a point of calling him at the office right now or maybe even—"

"He went into work today?"

"Sure did. Some reason he shouldn't have?"

Leslie Anne shook her head. "No, of course not. I guess the house seems pretty empty with Grand-daddy and Mama both gone."

"It would, even with Miss Sharon home, but we've got a houseful today, not counting that Lucie Evans person."

"Who else is here?" If they had visitors, wasn't it possible that the strange voice that had awakened her with such a hateful taunt belonged to one of them?

"Your great-aunt Myrle and Miss Celia came to visit Miss Sharon and naturally Mr. Charlie came along. I swear that man is here more than he's at work. It's a wonder Mr. G.W. doesn't get on to him about that."

"Charlie's just Charlie," Leslie Anne said. "And nobody, not even Granddaddy, would change him, even if they could. Besides, when he and Celia get married, he'll be one of the family for sure and you know how Granddaddy is about family."

"Family means everything to Mr. G.W. and if that Miss Olivia has her way, your family will be expanding even more. That woman has set her sights on your granddaddy and I wouldn't be the least bit surprised if she doesn't finagle a marriage proposal out of him before Christmas."

"Hush your mouth." Leslie Anne frowned. "Granddaddy isn't going to marry that awful woman."

"Well, if he doesn't, it won't be for her lack of trying. Her and that worthless pup of hers is downstairs, too. Just showed up about twenty minutes ago. Unannounced and uninvited. But you know Miss Sharon, she made them welcome."

"If Mama had been home—"

"Where's your mama gone off to anyway?" Eustacia asked. "And what would she think about your missing school again today?"

"Mama's off on business over in Louisiana. I expect she'll be gone several days. And as for school— I don't care what anybody thinks. But fall break starts next week, so I just got a head start on it. Believe me, my missing a few days of school is the least of Mama's worries."

"Just what do you mean by that?"

Leslie Anne groaned, shook her head and clicked her tongue. "I didn't mean anything, just that she's busy. That's all."

Eustacia gave Leslie Anne a skeptical look, then said, "That Evans woman wanted me to let her know when you woke up. She came down around seven for breakfast and since then she's checked on you I don't know how many times. Just what's she doing here anyway? I couldn't get a straight answer out of your granddaddy or your aunt when I asked them."

"She's my guard dog." Leslie Anne offered the cook a genuine smile. She loved old Eustacia, who was for all intents and purposes a member of the Westbrook family, just as Hal was. "Lucie's here to make sure I don't run off again while Mama's gone."

"If that's the case, I'll be especially nice to her." With that said, Eustacia left, waddling out of the room as quickly as her short, fat legs would carry her.

Leslie Anne walked over to the table, lifted the white linen cloth that covered the tray and studied the neatly arranged items. A bowl of her favorite cereal, Sugar Pops. A cup of two-percent milk. A glass of freshly squeezed orange juice. Two slices of cinnamon toast. Silverware, a linen napkin and— *What's that?*

Leslie Anne dropped the white linen cloth to the floor, then reached out and touched the piece of folded paper stuck inside her napkin. Her heartbeat accelerated. She shouldn't be so afraid. After all, it was only a piece of paper. Before she had a chance to think about it and chicken out, she grabbed the sheet of paper and yanked it away from the napkin. She held it in her hand for a couple of minutes before she managed to gather up enough courage to open it and take a look.

What she saw turned her stomach. Her hand trembled, but she held the paper tightly and continued staring at a computerized splicing of two pictures so that it looked as if both had been only one newspaper photograph. This photo of her had been snipped out of the *Fairport Journal*, the town's weekly newspaper. When she'd been elected sophomore class president at the beginning of school, her photo, and those of the other class presidents had appeared in the *Journal*, along with a brief article on each of them. The other photo in this spliced picture was one that had run in a Texas newspaper and showed Eddie Jay Nealy the day he'd been arrested on murder charges.

Above the spliced photo was a typed caption. *Who's Your Daddy, Little Girl?*

Oh, God, she hadn't imagined the voice. It had been real. Someone had actually been in her room, whispering to her. And that same someone had managed to put this damn little message on her breakfast tray. Without thinking what she was doing, Leslie Anne ripped the photo into pieces and threw the fragments down on the floor.

A loud knock sounded at her door. She jumped.

"May I come in?" Lucie Evans asked.

"Yeah, just a second, okay?"

Should she or shouldn't she tell Lucie about the voice that woke her and about the photo? Leslie Anne glanced down at her handiwork lying on the floor. Damn, she'd destroyed the evidence. But what difference did it make? She didn't need to show Lucie the photo or ask her help in figuring out what it meant. It hardly took a genius to figure out that whoever had awakened her with cruel taunts and had managed to sneak the photo onto her breakfast tray had to be someone inside her house right now. Someone who was visiting. Someone her family trusted.

Oh, God, what if it was a member of her family?

If only Dante was here, she would tell him what had happened. He would know exactly what to do. But she didn't trust anyone else, not even Lucie. She would do a little investigating on her own and maybe by the time Dante and her mother got back into town, she would have some real evidence to give them. But maybe she should call them to let them know there was no point in searching in Louisiana for the person who'd sent her the newspaper clippings because he or she was here at the Leslie Plantation right now.

No, I can't do that. Not yet. Mama needs time alone with Dante so they'll both realize how perfect they are for each other.

Okay, so maybe snagging Dante for a stepfather was an impossible dream, but didn't she and her mother deserve someone great like Dante Moran? If she were his kid, he would never let anything bad happen to her ever again.

"WELL, THAT DIDN'T amount to anything," Tessa said as she and Dante left the Rhymes Memorial Library on Louisa Street. "After searching through months of seventeen-year-old newspapers, we found only two small articles that might or might not have been about me."

Dante opened the door of the rental car for Tessa. Then after she was safely inside, he rounded the hood, opened the driver's side door and slid behind the wheel.

"We knew it was a long shot." Dante tapped his fingers on the steering wheel. "But I'm puzzled by those two articles. They appeared nearly a week apart. The one about an unidentified woman's body being found was dated six days before you were admitted to the hospital. And the other one, about a car wreck that left a young woman critically injured, came out four days after your hospital admission."

"Okay, so neither article was about me," Tessa said. "Puzzle solved."

"Or what if both articles were about you."

"How's that possible?"

"Maybe you were found a week before the date on your hospital admission," Dante said. "Maybe for some reason, G.W. told you the wrong date. I assume you don't remember the exact date yourself."

She shook her head. "No, I don't remember very much about those days I spent at the medical center before Daddy had me transferred back home."

"G.W. could have had the second article put in the paper when he decided on the cover-up story about your being in a car wreck."

"Possibly. But what difference does it make? The bottom line is that we didn't find any new information. So where to next?"

"The sheriff's office is next," Dante said. "Then from there to the City Café. I spoke to our spy at the medical center while you were still in your room this morning and he told me to meet him at the City Café at one this afternoon."

"Did he say whether or not he'd seen my medical records?"

"All he said was that he'd have some info for me by then."

LESLIE ANNE joined the others for lunch. She had taken extra pains to look nice, to show them all that she wasn't some crazed teenager who might follow in her father's footsteps. Among these genteel members of her family and family friends was someone who hated her, someone who had deliberately destroyed her safe and happy world. And she intended to find out just who that person was.

When Lucie had told her that her grandfather had called to check on her and would be coming home for lunch at twelve-thirty to see about her himself, she'd decided to make an extra effort to be nice to him. After all, she was well aware of the fact that her grandfather had a heart condition. The last thing she wanted was for her actions to cause him any health problems. If she'd been thinking straight several days ago, she would have realized how her running away might affect him. Even if he and her mother had lied to her all her life, she knew, deep down in her heart, that they'd fabricated a fictitious story about her father in order to protect her.

She might not fully trust her mother or her grandfather, but she did love them. And they loved her. If she didn't believe anything else, she believed that.

When she entered the parlor where everyone had congregated, her grandfather paused in his conversation with Charlie and surveyed her from head to toe.

"Well, look at you," G.W. said. "Don't you look pretty."

"Thank you, Granddaddy." Smiling sweetly, she breezed across the room and planted a kiss on his cheek.

"You seem to be bright and chipper today," Olivia said.

"Why thank you, Olivia." Leslie Anne blasted the hateful floozy with one of her thousand-watt smiles. "I am bright and chipper. As a matter of fact, I'm downright fine."

Her aunt Sharon eyed her skeptically. "And just what brought about this miraculous transformation?"

Leslie Anne danced her shoulders up and down as she smiled coquettishly, her gaze traveling over the room and settling on Tad Sizemore. Tad was suspect number one. And his mother was suspect number two. Wouldn't they just love to get rid of her and her mother, then move in to grab the entire Westbrook fortune?

"I decided that life is too short to stay in my room and pout." She laced her arm through G.W.'s. "Besides, I wanted to have lunch with Granddaddy."

"Well, I'm certainly glad you're feeling better." G.W. gazed at her tenderly and she sensed the same unconditional love he'd always given her. "My precious girl." He uttered the last three words so quietly that only Leslie Anne heard them.

She gave his arm a squeeze, then eased away and scanned the parlor. As she meandered around the room, she kept sensing that someone was watching her and soon realized that Lucie Evans was keeping a close eye on her. That was okay. After all, that was Lucie's job, wasn't it?

Charlie came up to her and put his arm around her shoulders. "It's good to see you acting more like yourself. You had us all terribly worried you know. Tad all but convinced us that you were on the verge of doing something…" He cleared his throat. "Well, I should have known better, shouldn't I?"

"Yes, you should have, considering the source."

Charlie chuckled in his usual good-natured manner. Always pleasant and mannerly. A gentleman to the core. There had been a time when she'd wanted her mother to marry Charlie. God knew he'd asked her a zillion times. But now that she was more mature, she understood that there just wasn't any sparks between Charlie and her mother.

But between Dante and her mother—well, a girl could hope, couldn't she?

Within minutes, her great-aunt Myrle cornered her and starting talking some sort of nonsense about boys and girls and being young and foolish.

"I imagine it was some young cretin that dared you to run away from home," Myrle said. "My dear, you simply mustn't associate with these uncouth teenagers."

She never thought she would welcome Celia's presence, since her cousin was far from her favorite person, but she was actually glad when Celia interrupted Aunt Myrle's spiel.

"You've certainly been a worrisome brat, haven't you?" Celia told her. "You should be ashamed of yourself for worrying Uncle G.W. half to death. Whatever were you thinking? You know the poor dear has a bad heart."

"You're so right, Celia," Leslie Anne said and relished the look on her cousin's face when she agreed with her. "Now, if you'll excuse me, I feel I should help Aunt Sharon play hostess."

Taking this one chance to escape Aunt Myrle and Celia, Leslie Anne started across the room to corner Lucie and ask if she'd heard from Dante today. But before she made it to her destination, Tad waylaid her.

"You're putting on a good act. This bunch has no idea what a good little actress you are, but I do."

"Takes one to know one, huh, Tad?"

"Touché."

"I can't have everyone thinking I'm suicidal, can I? They'd never leave me alone or let me have any peace."

"So this little act is to convince G.W. you don't need a bodyguard?" He glanced at Lucie. "Now, that's some woman."

"Let's just say that I have my reasons for wanting everyone to think I'm doing just fine." *There, Tad,* Leslie Anne thought, *I've given you a little rope. Not nearly enough to hang yourself, but just enough to draw you in.* In case he was the guilty party—and she'd lay odds he was—she didn't want him catching on to what she was up to. Not until it was too late and she'd trapped him.

Tad put his hand on her shoulder. "Look, kid, if you ever want to shake your shadow—" he glanced at Lucie "—let me know and I'll help you slip off from her."

"Would you really do that for me?" Leslie Anne acted innocent and grateful.

"Absolutely. After all, I'm practically family. At least I will be when Mother marries G.W."

"That's right, isn't it? Once Olivia and Granddaddy are husband and wife, you'll be G. W. Westbrook's stepson."

"And your uncle." He tapped her playfully on the nose.

She managed to laugh and smile, all the while wondering exactly what Tad Sizemore was up to.

SHERIFF EARL SUMMERS was a friendly guy in his early forties, with a potbelly that hung over his belt and a slightly receding hairline. He had the words "good old boy" written all over him. He'd welcomed Dante and Tessa into his office, ordered coffee for them and agreed to answer any questions they had. But when Dante asked him if he remembered when a young blond woman had been found naked and nearly dead off Interstate 20 seventeen years ago, his face went ashen and he got a severe case of amnesia.

"Are you sure that happened in Richland Parish?" Summers asked.

"Yes, we're positive," Tessa said. "You see, I'm that woman. I spent ten days in the hospital here."

Summers shook his head. "I was a deputy back then, just a green rookie, and I'm telling you that I don't remember nothing about a case like that, but I seem to recall a young blond gal being in a bad car wreck back a good fifteen or twenty years ago. I'm sure that, if he could, Sheriff Wadkins would tell you the same thing. Unfortunately, he can't. The poor old fellow's got Alzheimer's and doesn't know what day of the week it is."

Dante looked pointedly at Summers. "You're sure you don't remember anything about a young girl being found—"

"Sure don't!"

"You'd think that as unusual as the case was, everyone working in the sheriff's department when it happened would remember something about it," Tessa said. "Maybe if we could talk to everyone who was working here at the time."

"Wouldn't make any difference," Summers said. "Won't nobody remember any more than I did."

"Why do you say that?" Dante asked.

"Because like I told you, we never had a case like that. If we did, there would be a record of it and I can assure you there is no record of any blond woman being found off Interstate 20 and being brought to the hospital. No records here at the sheriff's department. No records at the hospital or the coroner's office. Because it never happened. Ma'am you must have our parish and our town mixed up with another one here in Louisiana somewhere. Have you checked with the sheriffs over in Madison or East Carrol or even West Carrol Parish? You know that highway cuts clean across the state."

"No, Sheriff Summers, we haven't checked other counties because I know for certain that—" Tessa gasped when Dante abruptly grabbed her arm and jerked her to her feet.

"Since the sheriff here is certain we've got the wrong town and even the wrong parish, I don't think we should take up any more of his valuable time."

"What?" Tessa glared at Dante, her look questioning his sanity.

"Honey, let's go. We can make a few phone calls and check out a couple of other parishes before suppertime, if we hurry."

Dante shook hands with Sheriff Summers while he held on to a fuming Tessa with his other hand; then he practically dragged her from the sheriff's department and outside onto Julia Street. When they got to their rental car, she stopped dead still and glared at him.

"Want to tell me what the hell is going on?"

"Sorry about the caveman act, but it was obvious Summers is hiding something and he had no intention of sharing it with us. The harder we'd have pushed, the more he would have balked. Besides, he told us something interesting without even realizing he'd let something slip."

"What did he let slip?"

"He adamantly vowed that there were no records of the case we described to him at the sheriff's department or at the hospital or at the—"

Tessa gasped. "Or at the coroner's!"

"Bingo."

"Why would the coroner have any records about a victim who survived?"

"Yeah, why would he?"

"How do we find out?"

"We wait to hear whatever our hospital spy has to say, then we'll see if we can make any connection between what the sheriff didn't tell us—" Dante grinned at Tessa "—and what our informant has found out."

CHAPTER FIFTEEN

THE CITY CAFÉ was a small, neat restaurant nestled between a shoe shop on one side and an empty two-story brick building on the other. A dark-haired guy in a quilted navy blue parka and a red hat hovered near the front door, his gaze downcast. The minute Dante and Tessa approached, the man glanced up and a pair of pale gray eyes studied them.

"You Moran?"

"Yeah. And you're—?"

"Somebody Dundee's hired to do a little dirty work for them." The man looked up and down the sidewalk, then grinned. "I live in this town, so if anybody asks, I'll tell them you're friends of my aunt Sadie, who lives out in Texas. You understand how it is. Okay?"

"Whatever you want," Dante said.

"Just call me Tug." He looked at Tessa and grinned. Deep dimples appeared in his cheeks and softened his rode-hard-and-put-away-wet appearance. "And you're…?"

"She's with me." Dante slipped his arm around Tessa's waist. Protectively. And possessively? Hell, he didn't want to feel possessive about her, but he did.

Tug waved his hand in an expression of unconcern. "Hey, man, I wasn't hitting on the lady, just asking her name."

"I'm Tessa." She held out her hand. "Hi, Tug. Nice to meet you."

Tug shook Tessa's hand quickly and let go, but he didn't make direct eye contact with her. Dante figured Tug wisely chose to not risk irritating him again. It wasn't that he tried to be intimidating, he just was. He'd been told once by a fellow FBI agent that he sent out some powerfully dangerous vibes.

"How about we talk while we eat lunch?" Dante suggested. "No point in wasting time."

"You in a hurry or something?"

"Or something."

"Sure thing," Tug said. "City Café's got the best down-home cooking you'll ever eat. They run a lunch special five days a week. Today's fried chicken."

Dante chose a back table, off by itself, in the crowded restaurant. He felt uneasy discussing business with so many strangers surrounding him. But when you dealt with informants, you usually had to let them choose the rendezvous point in which he or she felt the most comfortable.

After they removed their coats and settled in, the waitress brought three glasses of water, and put one down at each place setting. "Today's special is fried chicken, mashed potatoes, green beans and corn bread. If you want something else, the menu's on the wall over there." The middle-aged brunette, whose plastic name tag read Gert, nodded to the large white metal sign with red lettering that listed such things as hamburgers, hot dogs and chicken stew. "Our desserts are banana pudding and chocolate cake."

"Three lunch specials." Dante looked at Tessa. "Want dessert?"

"No, thanks."

"I'll have the banana pudding," Tug said.

"What do y'all want to drink?" Gert asked, glancing disapprovingly at Tug's hat.

"Sweet tea, please," Tessa said.

Tug jerked off his hat, folded it in half and laid it on the table. "Sweet tea for me, too."

"Make that three," Dante said.

As soon as the waitress headed off to put in their order, Dante leaned forward across the table and skewered Tug with a let's-get-down-to-business glare.

"What do you have for us?"

Tug reached around to where he'd hung his coat on the back of his chair, pulled a folded manilla envelope from the inside pocket and handed it to Dante. "That's the girl's medical records." Tug glanced at Tessa. "You're her, aren't you? You're Tessa Westbrook."

"Yes, I am." Tessa removed the paper ring from her paper napkin which was wrapped around her silverware. After nervously opening the napkin and placing it in her lap, she set her fork to her left and arranged her knife and spoon side by side on the right.

Tug watched her closely. "Ma'am, I'd like to say I think you're a mighty tough lady to have survived what you went through."

Tessa swallowed, then offered Tug a fragile smile.

Dante tapped the envelope against his open palm. "You read through these medical records?"

"I skimmed 'em," Tug admitted. "After I photocopied them. I had to do a rush job before somebody caught me."

Tessa eyed Tug curiously. "How were you able to—"

"How I get a job done is classified info, ma'am." Tessa nodded.

"Look, Moran, when Dundee hired me to get my hands on those confidential files, I was given the background information on Ms. Westbrook and told to compare what I found in the files with the info I'd been given. This is far from the first time I've done something like this, you know. If I wasn't trustworthy, people would stop coming to old Tug—" he patted himself on the chest "—to help them out when they needed to sidestep the law in order to get things done."

"Did my medical records confirm what you'd been told?" Tessa asked.

The waitress returned with three iced teas, which she set around the table. "Food will be out in a minute."

"Thanks," all three said in unison.

Tug looked right at Tessa. "Yes, ma'am, those records—" he eyed the manilla envelope Dante held "—paint a sad picture. Yes, they do. White female, age eighteen, raped, brutalized… It's a wonder you lived."

Not wanting to hear more details and concerned for Tessa, Dante asked hurriedly, "You didn't find any inconsistencies? Nothing that sent up a red flag and made you question the information?"

"Nope, nothing in the medical records. You can see for yourself when you read over them."

Dante heard an unspoken "but" in Tug's voice. "Just lay it on the line for me, will you? What else is there?"

Tug grinned. "When I'm hired to do a job, I tend to get creative, if I think it might mean a bonus."

"You want extra pay for extra information, is that it?"

"You give me your word that my check from Dundee will be, say a grand more than agreed on and—"

"If what you have to tell us is worth a thousand, you'll get it," Dante told him.

The waitress returned with a large, food-laden tray. "Three specials."

After she set the plates on the table, she laid the bill, facedown, beside Dante. "Anybody want refills on that tea—" she eyed the untouched, full glasses "—just holler."

Tug lifted his glass and took a hefty swig of tea, then wiped his mouth with the back of his hand. "Best iced tea in Rayville."

Neither Dante nor Tessa said a word, but both glared at Tug.

Tug set his glass down, picked up his fork and speared the green beans on his plate. "There's a woman—a close personal friend of mine, if you know what I mean—" Tug winked at Dante "—who works in medical records at the hospital and she's got an aunt who used to work over at Maitland's Funeral Home. The aunt's name is Deanetta Knight. That old gal's got a memory like an elephant. She don't forget nothing." Tug stuck the green beans in his mouth, then added a scoop of mashed potatoes. As he chewed, he eyed Dante, then swallowed. "Deanetta's willing to talk to y'all, if you promise not to never tell nobody that you got the information from her."

"What does she have to tell us that's worth your getting an extra thousand dollars?" Dante was fast losing patience with this good old boy.

"That's for her to say." Tug put his fork aside and picked up the chicken leg. "But I'll tell you this—she recalls when there was a gal found out on Interstate 20, about seventeen years ago. That's when Deanetta was working for the funeral home."

"What does one thing have to do with the other?" Tessa asked.

"Well, you see, Aaron Maitland, who owned the

funeral home, was the county coroner back then," Tug explained.

A knot formed in the pit of Dante's belly. "And?"

"And Deanetta remembers that Sheriff Wadkins called in Aaron Maitland when a body was found on the side of the road."

"What's strange about that?" Tessa glanced from Tug to Dante. "Isn't it usual procedure for the coroner to be called—?"

"Ma'am, the body Aaron did an autopsy on was a young, blond girl who'd been raped, beaten and dumped off the interstate."

Turning white as a sheet, Tessa gasped. Damn! She looked like she might faint.

THE LITTLE BITCH! She'd done a complete about-face, transforming herself from a hysterical, out-of-control child into an astonishingly calm young lady. The way she'd acted at lunch today, no one would believe she was suicidal.

I've never seen a better job of acting. Or was she acting? She had to be. She couldn't have recovered from such shocking news so quickly. She was putting on a show. But for whom? For G.W., no doubt. She knew the old man had a bad heart. Everybody was aware of the fact that G.W.'s doctor had warned him to change the bad habits of a lifetime before he had a severe heart attack. I suppose it's possible, even probable, that she loves her grandfather enough to do whatever is necessary to make him believe she isn't completely falling apart. I suppose that's well and good. After all, I can't have G.W. dying on me. Not yet anyway.

My plan for Leslie Anne's death to look like a suicide is a good one. Too good to abandon just because she decided she can bluff her way through this traumatic experience. I need to remind her of who she is, of the evil flowing through her veins. And I should make her realize that it's only a matter of time before her ugly little secret is out and everyone will know she's Eddie Jay Nealy's daughter.

As a matter of fact, perhaps I need to figure out a way to let those nearest and dearest to the family learn about Tessa's pitifully sordid past. And I need to do this while Tessa is out of town.

Hmm. What's the best way to go about this? A phone call, using the same device to disguise my voice that I used this morning when I taunted a sleeping Leslie Anne? Oh, it had been so easy to enter and exit her suite through the sitting room without anyone noticing. And if anyone had seen me, so what? Who wouldn't have believed me if I'd told them I was concerned about Leslie Anne and wanted to check on her?

DEANETTA KNIGHT lived a few miles outside of town in an old turn-of-the-century house that had been renovated, added on to and bricked sometime in the recent past. She met them on the porch, asked to see some identification, then invited them into her living room. The old woman walked with the aid of a cane, making her movements slow and slightly unsteady. Tessa guessed her age to be at least seventy, maybe seventy-five.

Deanetta looked back and forth from Dante to Tessa, her milky brown eyes studying them, obviously trying to discern their honesty. "Tug said I could trust y'all not to involve me if anything gets stirred up because of what I'm gonna tell y'all."

"That's right," Dante said.

"Swear it to me." Deanetta focused on Tessa.

"We swear, don't we, Dante?" Tessa said.

Dante nodded.

"You're that Westbrook gal, ain't you?" Deanetta looked Tessa over, from head to toe. "I never seen you up close back then. Once your daddy showed up at the hospital, they posted a private duty nurse in your ICU room. Never heard of such a thing. That's how everybody knew your daddy was somebody important."

"Mrs. Knight, I thought you worked at the Maitland Funeral Home at the time," Dante said. "How do you know what went on at the hospital?"

"My sister Flossie was an LPN who worked the night shift at the hospital back then. She's dead and gone these past five years." Deanetta sighed heavily. "Me and Flossie talked about it, you know, but when there was never no mention of it in the papers or nothing, and Mr. Maitland warned everybody who worked at the funeral home to never say a word about it, we figured it was best to keep our mouths shut. We didn't want no trouble."

"Tug said Aaron Maitland performed an autopsy on a young woman whose body was found out on Interstate 20 and he implied there was a connection between this woman and Tessa Westbrook. Is that what you're talking about? Is that what Mr. Maitland warned his employees to never talk about?" Dante asked.

"There was a connection." Deanetta studied Tessa again. "Two young gals, both blond, both raped and beaten and dumped out on the side of the road. The same thing was done to both of them gals. Awful things. Just awful."

Tessa's heart stopped for a split second. Snapping her head around, she looked at Dante. He'd gone still as a statue, his face without expression. But she knew what he was thinking—the same thing she was. That second girl, the other blonde who hadn't survived, had been Amy Smith. But why the cover-up? Had her father made certain that what had happened to the other girl was kept secret, too? But why?

Deanetta stared sympathetically at Tessa. "You poor little thing you. How you lived through that is beyond me. Flossie told me that the folks working in the emergency room when you was brought in said you was nothing but a broken, bloody mess."

"I really don't remember." Tessa tried her level

best not to picture herself as she must have looked when she'd been brought to the E.R. She barely remembered those days, when she'd been unable to think straight and had been totally helpless. Thank God her daddy had shown up so quickly and had made sure she received the best care money could buy.

"Yeah, Flossie heard you had amnesia and we agreed it was a blessing you couldn't remember nothing about what happened to you."

Dante's gaze met Tessa's. She wanted to reach out, grab him and hold him close. He had to be dying inside, halfway hoping he could lay Amy Smith to rest once and for all and yet maybe praying that the other blond girl Deanetta had told them about hadn't been his Amy.

"What happened to the other girl?" Dante asked. "What did the funeral home do with her body? Was it sent to the state—"

Deanetta lowered her voice as if she thought the walls had ears. "After the autopsy, her body was held for identification. You see, her body was found first, that is her body was found before they found you, Ms. Westbrook. And your daddy came to Rayville to take a look at the other girl because she fit your description. That was about five or six days after her body was found, best I can recall."

"Oh, poor Daddy. He must have been so relieved that it wasn't me." Tessa reached over and grasped Dante's hand, wanting to comfort him. God, how she wished that Dante's Amy had survived, too. "When Daddy told the sheriff that the girl wasn't me, what happened then?"

"To the girl's body?"

"Yes," Tessa replied.

"Well, strange thing was, the very next day you was found and brought to the hospital in the same shape that other poor gal had been in, except you was alive. Just barely. And the sheriff got hold of your daddy before he left town and he rushed right over to the hospital and saw that you was his little girl. Flossie said she saw him that day and he was a crying something awful. Right after that, Mr. Maitland sent the other girl's body off to be cremated."

Dante tensed. "Who ordered her cremation?"

"I ain't got no idea. But afterward was when Mr. Maitland told me and the others who knew about the girl to never tell a soul, that there was some sort of criminal investigation going on that would trap the man who'd killed her and nearly killed the Westbrook girl."

"What sort of criminal investigation?" Tessa asked.

"Don't know. That's all we was ever told."

Dante jerked his hand out of Tessa's grasp as he faced Deanetta. "What happened to the other girl's ashes?"

"That was something plum peculiar, you know. Don't reckon she had no kin folks. Nobody ever claimed her ashes, but somebody paid for a plot over in the cemetery and I went with Mr. Maitland the day they buried the urn with that poor little gal's ashes in it. Weren't nobody there except Mr. Maitland, me and Reverend Allsboro. And the grave digger, of course."

"Where's the cemetery?" Tessa asked.

"You want to go by and pay your respects?" Deanetta asked. "I guess it's only fitting, 'cause except by the grace of God, it could have been you who died and not her."

DANTE HADN'T said a word. Except for the fact she could see his chest rising and falling, Tessa wouldn't have been sure he was even breathing. Once Deanetta gave them directions to the cemetery, they'd left her house hurriedly. After he'd thanked the old woman for the information, Dante had all but run outside and straight to the car. Tessa had lingered only long enough to hug Deanetta.

"The other girl, the one who died…" Tessa had said. "We—we think she might have been Dante's fiancée. They were engaged when they were teenagers."

"Mercy to goodness!" Deanetta had held Tessa's hands tightly and looked deeply into her eyes. "You go help him say goodbye to her. And then you show him he's still alive."

The old woman's words repeated themselves over and over in Tessa's mind. She might be able to help Dante say goodbye to Amy Smith, if that was his intention. But she suspected it might be impossible to convince him to let Amy go.

Dante parked the rental car alongside the road, then got out and headed toward the cemetery. Tessa opened the door and stood by the car for several minutes, watching Dante as he walked among the headstones. He was so obsessed with finding Amy's grave that he'd all but forgotten Tessa.

"Look for the pink marble monument," Deanetta had said. "Only one like it in the whole cemetery."

She shouldn't let him do this alone. But did she have the courage to stand at his side and give him whatever support and comfort she could while he mourned for another woman? How could she be so jealous of Amy Smith when the poor girl wasn't even alive? Because Dante had loved Amy. Because he still loved her.

As her gaze kept pace with Dante's every move, she cried out quietly when he stopped and stared down at a small, pink marble monument. The afternoon sun hung midhorizon, its light hitting the row of pine trees lining the far side of the graveyard. Shadows cast by the tall, skinny pines flickered about on the ground, across the pink marble and over Dante's stoic face.

All thought for herself evaporated as loving concern for Dante filled her heart, and Tessa rushed across the cemetery. He needed her. Even if he didn't know he did. He was all alone, facing his worst fears, forced to accept the bitter truth. Although they had no proof that the other young, blond woman who'd been dumped out on the highway a week before Tessa was found had actually been Amy Smith, the odds were that she had been Dante's missing fiancée. Tessa only suspected that the date the girl had been found was close to the same time Amy had disappeared. If her suspicions were right, then Dante would have no choice but to accept the facts. Undoubtedly Nealy had dumped Amy's body, then kidnapped Tessa almost immediately afterward.

When Tessa came up behind Dante, he didn't even hear her. And when she placed her hand on his shoulder, he didn't flinch, although she felt his muscles tense.

"There's no name on the monument and the only date is the year," Dante said, his voice amazingly calm. Too calm.

Tessa took a good look at the monument. Pink marble, exquisitely carved, with the verse of a poem about the deceased living on in the gentle breeze, the morning sun, the soft rain, spanned the distance between two marble roses that graced either side of the headstone. No name. The only date, the year. Seventeen years ago.

There was no doubt in Tessa's mind who had paid for this young woman's cremation and her expensive monument. But why? Had her father been overcome with pity for the girl who had no family to claim her body and gratitude that it had been she and not his own daughter who had died? What other explanation could there be?

"It might not be Amy," Dante said.

Tessa squeezed his shoulder. "It might not be."

"You think it is, don't you?"

"I think it's highly probable. And so do you."

Tessa felt a slight tremor rippling through Dante. *Oh, God, help him. And help me to say and do all the right things, to give him whatever he needs to get through this ordeal.*

"It's my fault she's dead," Dante said.

Moving closer to his side, Tessa slipped her arm around his waist. "You're talking nonsense. It's not your fault. Eddie Jay Nealy preyed on young women. He's the one responsible for Amy's death, not you."

Dante trembled again. "She was waiting for me and I was late that night. I always picked her up after work so we could have a little time together. But I had a flat tire that night and when I got to the Dairy Dip, she wasn't there. I—I found the engagement ring I'd given her on the sidewalk, along with the chain she kept it on around her neck."

Tessa hugged up closer and closer to Dante, wishing she had the ability to absorb some of his pain. He was reliving the night he'd lost Amy, the night his world had come crashing down around him. In his own way, Dante had suffered unbearably, just as she had. Dante and she and Amy were all Eddie Jay Nealy's victims.

I refuse to allow that evil man to win. I rebuilt my life from the ashes of a broken body, a mind void of memories and a crushed spirit. If I did that, why can't Dante find the strength to accept what he cannot change, then move on and find love again?

Selfishly, Tessa wished that Dante could love her. Not as he'd loved Amy. Young love, first love could never be equaled, never be repeated. But if he could open his heart to the possibility of loving someone else, maybe she could be that someone.

But what about Leslie Anne?

Dante accepting Amy's death was only one of many hurdles they would have to overcome if there was any hope of them having a future together. Would Dante ever be able to forget that Tessa's daughter had been fathered by the monster who had killed Amy?

Tessa sighed softly as her dream of loving and being loved by Dante vanished like the phantom wish it had been. She and Dante had no future together, nothing beyond a fleeting moment in time. But surely fate had brought them together for a purpose.

Yes, of course, Tessa thought. *Dante and I are destined to help each other. He has come to me not only for Leslie Anne's sake, but to show me that I can feel passion. And I'm with him, here and now, because he needs me.*

"Have you blamed yourself all these years?" Tessa asked, knowing full well that he had.

"Oh, yeah," Dante said. "I know it's not logical. Fate conspired against Amy and me from the very beginning. I was a real bad boy and she was such a good girl. People warned her to steer clear of me and they were right to warn her. I went after her because I wanted to prove I could have her, but boy did I get the shock of my life. I fell for her like a ton of bricks. I was so crazy in love with her I couldn't see straight. And the funny thing is, she felt the same way about me."

Dante stared directly at Tessa, but she realized he was looking straight through and seeing a ghost from his past. How would it feel, she wondered, to love and be loved that way?

"Any other night, I'd have gotten to the Dairy Dip on time," Dante said, "and Eddie Jay Nealy would never have gotten his hands on her."

Dante clenched his teeth, balled his hands into fists and groaned. Tessa held on to him as he quivered from head to toe, shaking with the force of his barely suppressed emotions.

"Oh, God, Dante, don't," she pleaded. "Stop thinking about what he did to her. It all happened so long ago. Please, darling, please, don't think about it. I can't bear to see you in so much pain."

Jerking with emotion, agony ripping through him so fiercely that Tessa could practically see the slash marks on his body, Dante dropped to his knees before the pink marble headstone. He dragged Tessa down with him because she refused to release her tenacious hold on him. Together, both on their knees, they faced Amy Smith's monument.

"Deep down I've known for years what happened to her, but I held on to the hope that I was wrong, that somehow, someway—" He leaned over and beat the ground, his fists pounding repeatedly. "God damn son of a bitch!" He kept repeating those words over and over again as he continued clubbing his fists against the hard ground. Finally he crumpled over, holding his bloody hands between his knees.

Tessa wrapped her arms around him and held him. For what seemed like an eternity, she didn't say anything, didn't move, barely breathed. Dante's body shook uncontrollably. But he didn't cry.

"Don't hold it in any longer," Tessa said. "Let it go. Release it."

"I can't," he told her, his words spoken through tightly clenched teeth. "I don't dare."

"Yes, you can. I'm right here with you. I'm your lifeline. I won't let you drown."

CHAPTER SIXTEEN

G.W.'s AFTERNOON ROUTINE had been interrupted by three consecutive phone calls, giving him little time to regroup and think between the conversations. First, he had reluctantly accepted a phone call from Olivia, wondering at the time what was so urgent. After all, it had been only a little over two hours since he'd had lunch with her.

"I received the most dreadful phone call," Olivia had said and quickly went into this lengthy tirade about a mysterious voice telling her an ugly, vicious lie about dear little Leslie Anne.

G.W.'s blood had run cold when Olivia mentioned the name Eddie Jay Nealy.

While he was still on the phone with Olivia, G.W.'s personal assistant, Fay Harris, had interrupted, telling him that his sister-in-law needed to speak to him immediately, that she claimed it was a family emergency. He assured Olivia that what she'd been told was a pack of lies, then got off the phone with her as quickly as possible. He'd gone through a similar scenario with Myrle, who had been practically hysterical. By the time he'd persuaded her that someone was spreading vicious lies and he would deal with them harshly, G.W. realized that whoever had sent Leslie Anne those newspaper clippings was damned and determined for the whole world to learn the truth about his granddaughter's paternity.

As he'd prepared to leave the office and go home, Sharon had called. Before she'd said a word, he knew why she'd called him.

"I'm heading out the door," G.W. had told his sister. "Whatever you do, don't let Leslie Anne speak to anyone. And tell that Dundee agent, Lucie what's-her-name, about what's happened. I don't want Leslie Anne to hear about this before I get a chance to tell her myself."

When he pulled his Mercedes to a stop in front of the house, not bothering to park in the garage, G.W. had already planned and discarded several different solutions to the problem at hand. More than anything, he wanted to protect Tessa and Leslie Anne. But it would take a miracle to prevent the looming disaster. Out there somewhere was a person armed with the truth about Tessa's rape and Leslie Anne's conception. And apparently he or she was on a mission to see that the whole world knew the Westbrook family had been living a lie for the past seventeen years.

Before he even got out of the car, Sharon opened the front door and came rushing off the veranda, a look of panic on her face. His sister was rather dramatic and often overreacted to things, but in this case, he shared her sense of doom.

"God, G.W., what are we going to do?"

Leaving his briefcase lying on the front seat, he emerged from the Mercedes and faced his sister. "Did you recognize the voice of the person who called you? Was it a man or a woman?"

"Didn't I tell you that the voice was disguised?" Sharon reached out and put her arm through G.W.'s as they rounded the car's hood and headed toward the front veranda. "I probably didn't. I've been so upset that I'm not thinking straight."

He felt the slight tremor in her body and wondered if the shakiness inside him was apparent to her.

"Where's Leslie Anne?" he asked. "Does she know—"

"No, she has no idea that someone's calling everyone we know to tell them about Eddie Jay Nealy being her biological father. I explained what's been happening to Ms. Evans and she got Leslie Anne out of the house by suggesting they go horseback riding."

"Is that where they are now?"

"Yes, yes." Sharon paused, threw her arms around G.W. and hugged him. "I've been worried sick about you. This stress can't be good for your heart. Maybe we should call Dr. Lester."

"I don't need a damn doctor. What I need is the Dundee Agency to find out who's trying to destroy my family. What did Ms. Evans have to say about all this? Has she heard anything from Dante and Tessa?" He'd been damn upset to learn that Tessa had run off with Moran, that they were in Rayville, searching for ghosts. But what could they find out? Hadn't he spent a fortune to keep all their secrets buried? Nobody would dare admit to anything, not when anyone who knew anything had been involved in the cover-up themselves or were bound by ethics not to reveal confidential matters.

"Ms. Evans put in a call to the other two agents to alert them and they'll contact Mr. Moran," Sharon said, easing her tenacious hold on G.W. "I tried to call Tessa, but I got her voice mail. She's either out of range or she's turned off her cell phone."

"Damn time for her to be away." G.W. put his arm around Sharon and led her up the steps and onto the veranda. "She had no business going off with Moran. I don't understand her reasoning."

"Her whole life is falling apart, G.W. Don't you think she has a right to—"

"I gave her this life, and by God I won't let it fall apart. She should know that." G.W. opened the front door and held it for Sharon to enter. "I'll protect Tessa and Leslie Anne, no matter what the cost."

Sharon walked into the foyer, G.W. directly behind her. "I don't think all the money in the world can keep the truth from coming out and spreading like wildfire. Whoever this person is who made the phone calls, he—or she—isn't going to stop. This has become a damn avalanche that keeps growing bigger and bigger and picking up speed. This family is in the line of fire and we're not going to come out of it without taking a direct hit. We're going to be buried alive by seventeen years of lies."

G.W. slammed the door. "We have to come up with some type of damage control. You get on the phone and find out what you can from Olivia and Myrle and tell them to keep their damn mouths shut. I'm contacting Sawyer McNamara at Dundee headquarters and explaining the situation. I'll hire however many agents we need to get to the bottom of this mystery. I want to know who's doing this to us and why!"

"Myrle and Celia are already on their way over here," Sharon said. "I told them not to come, but you know Myrle."

"Then you'll have to handle them because I cannot deal with Anne's sister. Not until I decide the best way to handle this mess."

"What about Charlie?"

"What about him?"

"He's already here."

"What?"

"Myrle called him and told him about the phone call she received and he came right on over. He's worried about Leslie Anne and Tessa. And about you, G.W. You know how Charlie worships you."

G.W. glanced across the foyer at the parlor. "Where is he?"

Charlie had been like a son to G.W., and despite his deficiencies as a businessman, he was a charming, likable young man who reminded G.W. of Charlie's dad, who'd been G.W.'s best friend and his fraternity brother. Lieutenant James Sentell had died a hero's death in the last days of the Vietnam War, when Charlie had been little more than a baby. It was at that time G.W. had stepped in to help James's widow, Brenda, who was G.W.'s first cousin, once removed. And even after Brenda remarried, G.W. had remained a father figure to Charlie.

"I left him in the library," Sharon said. "The poor boy is terribly upset, just as we all are."

"What did you tell him?"

"Nothing, but…I put him off, then finally I lied to him and said I couldn't image how such a vile rumor got started. But, G.W., I know he didn't believe me."

G.W. patted her on the shoulder. "It's all right. I suppose I should have told Charlie the truth years ago, but I kept hoping he and Tessa would get married and he'd adopt Leslie Anne. I wasn't sure how he'd feel about Leslie Anne, if he knew Eddie Jay Nealy had fathered her. Brenda raised him to look down on anyone he perceives as beneath him. It's her fault he's such a damn snob."

"Go talk to him before you call Sawyer McNamara," Sharon said. "I'll phone Olivia to try to put her off and then I'll deal with Myrle and Celia when they arrive."

"Lock the damn door and refuse to let them in."

"I can't do that and you know it. It's no use trying to postpone the inevitable."

"When I find out who's responsible for this disaster, I'm going to make him wish he'd never been born."

G.W. stomped off toward the library, leaving his sister to handle things the best way she could. He'd spent a fortune, even broken the law, to keep his family's ugly secret. And he had no regrets about what he'd done. He'd do the same things all over again. Everything he'd done—every lie he'd told—he'd done for only one reason. To protect the people he loved. And he *had* protected the person he'd loved most in this world. Anne. Even now, after so many years, he missed her unbearably. But he was thankful she had not lived to see this day. The truth would have broken her heart.

The library doors stood partially open, allowing G.W. to see inside before entering. The room was empty. Where the hell was Charlie?

"Charlie?" G.W. called.

No answer.

He couldn't worry himself with his godson's whereabouts. Charlie had always had the run of the house. He'd probably gone to find Hal and ask for a drink. It was getting close to that time of day.

G.W. sat down behind the massive mahogany

desk, leaned his head back and closed his eyes. Was there any possible way to stem the tide before the dam broke? Or had the dam already broken? Were Olivia and Myrle the only people who'd received a call from the mysterious voice? Or had this person telephoned half the citizens of Fairport?

Trying to think rationally about a subject that was entirely emotional and extremely personal, G.W. reminded himself that even if the entire world learned the truth, he and his family would find a way to deal with it. So what if the worst happened and everyone knew that Tessa had been one of Nealy's victims and Leslie Anne was a result of Tessa having been raped? Most people would be understanding and sympathetic and to hell with those who weren't. Leslie Anne would have to undergo therapy whether the secret stayed within the family or spread through the whole county. And Tessa had already proved she was made of tough stuff. She had survived Eddie Jay Nealy; she could survive this, too.

So what do I do now? Should I admit to Olivia and Myrle that I covered up the truth about what happened to Tessa all those years ago? Do I confess to having committed a crime in order to save Anne a heartache I felt she couldn't endure?

He might not have any other choice. It seemed someone was intent on revealing the truth about the past. But who? And why? And just how much did this person really know?

TESSA HELD Dante as he knelt at Amy Smith's grave, time standing still for both of them. The crisp October wind picked up, whirling around them. Dead autumn leaves danced haphazardly over the graves and came to rest against the headstones. Tessa shivered. Dante glanced at her, his features tight, his eyes glazed by grief.

"You're cold," he said, his voice lifeless. "We should go."

She hugged him, his back to her chest, then laid her chin on his shoulder as she pressed her cheek against his and whispered, "We'll stay here as long as you need to."

"I don't want…to leave…her." His voice cracked with emotion.

"Oh, Dante."

He reached out and caressed the cold pink marble, his fingertips tracing the words of the heartbreakingly sweet poem etched into the stone. A low, guttural wail emerged from deep within him as he clutched the top of the monument and doubled over in pain, his forehead grazing the edge of the sculpted rose on the left. Tessa released him and came to her feet, then stood over him, allowing him this moment alone with Amy.

She longed to hold him. Comfort him. Ease his suffering.

When her father had stood by and watched her endure sheer hell as she'd slowly recovered from Eddie

Jay Nealy's handiwork, had he felt as helpless as she felt now? Had his heart broken in two seeing her suffer and knowing he could do so very little to help her?

Oh, Dante. She didn't understand why she cared so deeply, why he'd touched her heart in a way no other man ever had. He was little more than a stranger to her and yet she felt as if she'd always known him, as if they were soul mates. If she believed in reincarnation, she'd swear they'd been lovers in another life.

Was this connection she felt to him nothing more than a strong sexual attraction? Or was it because she shared a tragic history with Amy Smith? Dante's teenage sweetheart and Tessa hadn't known each other and yet fate had forever linked them by the vicious acts of a madman.

Tessa wasn't sure how long they stayed at the cemetery, how long Dante was trapped in the throes of inconsolable grief, but when he rose to his feet, the sun lay low in the western sky. Approaching twilight painted the horizon with glorious color.

After Dante turned around, he didn't look at Tessa; he simply walked away. She caught up with him and fell into step at his side. When they reached the rental car, he yanked the keys from his pants pocket and tossed them to her.

"Can you drive?" he asked.

"All right."

As soon as they were buckled into their safety

belts, Tessa started the car, then glanced at Dante. "Is there anywhere you want to go before—"

"Let's just go back to the motel for now."

"Sure."

They rode in silence for quite a while, although Tessa kept thinking of ways to approach Dante without mentioning what had happened at the cemetery. He'd fallen to pieces and yet hadn't shed one tear. Tessa knew from personal experience that he couldn't hold back the tears much longer without exploding. That's when he would need her. And she intended to be there for him when it happened.

LESLIE ANNE found herself laughing when she and Lucie returned to the stables and worked together to rub down the horses. They'd talked girl-talk for the past couple of hours, nothing serious, nothing to remind Leslie Anne of recent events. She'd given Lucie a tour of the Leslie Plantation and had been surprised that the Dundee agent rode like a pro.

"I grew up on a farm," Lucie had told her. "I was riding not long after I learned how to walk."

They'd stopped twice during the afternoon, once down by the river to let the horses drink and then again underneath the tree house her granddaddy had had constructed as a sixth birthday present for her.

"I don't know who loved that tree house more, me or Granddaddy," Leslie Anne had told Lucie. "Eustacia used to pack us picnic lunches and we'd climb the ladder and sit up there eating peanut butter and jelly sandwiches and drinking chocolate milk out of Thermoses."

"Sounds like you had a wonderful childhood."

"Yes, I did. Thanks to Mother and Granddaddy."

"Do you ever use the tree house now that you're older?"

"How'd you guess?" Leslie Anne giggled. "Every once in a while I climb up there and stay for hours whenever I want to be by myself."

After they finished cooling down Passion Flower and Mr. Wonderful, Luther led one horse and then the other into their stalls. "You'd best be heading back to the house," he said. "It'll be dark before long and Miss Sharon will be hunting y'all up for supper."

"You sound like a mother hen," Leslie Anne said jokingly. "Has my running away got even you worrying about me?"

Luther grinned. "I just know you ought not worry folks who love you."

"I agree, Luther." Leslie Anne patted him on the arm, then turned to Lucie. "Race you back to the house?"

"You honestly think you can outrun me?" Lucie asked.

"Let's find out."

"I never could resist a dare. Okay. Want me to give you a head start?"

"No way," Leslie Anne said. "I'm going to beat you fair and square."

Luther stayed out of the way as Leslie Anne and Lucie simultaneously counted down from three. Like a couple of whirlwinds, they ran out of the stables and up the path leading to the old mansion. Leslie Anne managed to keep pace with Lucie until nearly halfway to the house, then Lucie sprinted ahead, leaving Leslie Anne struggling to catch up.

"Leslie Anne?" a voice called from the woods.

You're imagining it, she told herself and kept running.

"Leslie Anne."

Don't listen. There's no one there.

Although she increased her pace, hoping to catch up with Lucie, Leslie Anne's gaze darted left and right, searching for the source of a voice she kept hoping wasn't real. And all the while, she waited to hear those three taunting words.

Who's your daddy?

WINDED AND PERSPIRING, Lucie reached the back porch of the old mansion. Stretching to relieve the tension in her body, she waited for Leslie Anne. After a couple of minutes, Lucie began to feel uneasy. Leslie Anne hadn't been that far behind her. Where the hell was she? After another couple of minutes passed, real fear tightened Lucie's stomach muscles.

As she ran back down the path, retracing her steps, she called out Leslie Anne's name and prayed nothing had happened to the girl who'd been left in her care.

CHAPTER SEVENTEEN

WHEN THEY RETURNED to the motel where they'd stayed the night before, Dante stopped at the door to Tessa's room, but as he started to unlock the door, she grasped his wrist.

"Come in and stay with me for a while," she said.

He looked into her eyes, those beautiful blue eyes the same color as Amy's, and all he wanted to do was grab her and hold on to her forever. But Tessa wasn't Amy, no matter how much she reminded him of her, no matter how much some heartbroken part of him wished she was. "I'm not fit company for anyone."

"I'm not looking for good company," she told him. "I just don't want to be alone, and I don't think you do, either."

He lifted his arm and skimmed her cheek with the back of his hand. "You shouldn't do this. And if you do, you'll regret it. It's not your responsibility to hold me together. And I'm warning you that I'm this close—" he indicated a quarter of an inch with his index finger and thumb "—to falling to pieces."

Admitting that he was on the verge of breaking down wasn't easy for him, but the last thing he wanted was for Tessa to see him fall apart. He was hurting more than he ever had, even more than the night Amy first disappeared. He'd been desperate then, but he'd kept hope alive for weeks and months afterward, always so sure he'd eventually find her alive.

And even later on, when he'd learned about Eddie Jay Nealy's killing spree and how Amy fit the profile for Nealy's victims, he had tried to convince himself that she hadn't been one of them. Even though eventually he had come to believe Amy was dead, that in all likelihood Nealy had killed her, a small kernel of hope had remained, buried deep in his heart.

Today, while he'd knelt in front of a pink marble headstone, that last fragment of hope had finally died.

Tessa grasped his hand. He curled his fingers over hers and held tightly. She dragged his hand slowly to her mouth and kissed his knuckles. He trembled inside. All his anguish suddenly combined with a purely human hunger for solace.

"You shouldn't be alone," she told him, still gazing into his eyes.

"I know you're a strong woman, Tessa, and God knows I need you, but—"

She pressed her fingers to his lips. "Come inside,

sit down and talk to me. Tell me about Amy. About how you met and fell in love."

A knot formed in his throat, threatening to choke him. Deep down inside, he was crying; and those tears were struggling for release. He wanted to refuse Tessa's offer, to tell her that there was no way in hell he was going to bare his soul to her. He couldn't talk about Amy, couldn't tell Tessa what it was like to love someone more than life itself. He'd never told anyone how deeply he mourned Amy, that with every breath he took he remembered her and missed her. The sweetness of her smile. The sound of her laughter. The smell of her neck when he'd nuzzled her playfully. The way she'd curled against him after they made love. Her voice whispering his name.

God, how many times had he heard her calling his name, pleading with him to find her, begging him to never stop loving her?

I still love you, Amy. I still love you.

"I can't," Dante told Tessa. "You don't want—"

Tessa took the key from him and unlocked her door, then reached out and clasped his hand. He looked at her and shook his head. Ignoring him, she tugged on his hand, urging him to enter her room. As if in a trance, he followed her and allowed her to lead him to the nearest of the two double beds. She grasped his shoulders and pushed him down on the edge of the bed, then sat beside him.

Tessa shrugged off her coat and tossed it into the

nearby chair, then she undid Dante's black leather jacket, eased it off him and whirled it through the air to land atop her coat.

He sat there, hurting, wanting to turn back the clock and change the past. But he could change nothing. He would never see Amy again, never hold her, kiss her, make love to her. He had lost her all over again. And this time it was forever.

For the past seventeen years, he'd been going through the motions, pretending he was alive, telling himself that if he could get through just one more day, everything would be all right. But he'd been kidding himself. Every morning he woke to a world without Amy.

Tessa took his hand, her touch gentle and loving. He could feel her warmth, could sense her sincere concern. He turned to her and for a millisecond, he didn't see Tessa Westbrook, a woman of thirty-five. He saw seventeen-year-old Amy Smith, her expression filled with love. Love for him.

"Amy?"

God, what had he been thinking? What had he said?

"I'm sorry, I—" He cupped her face between his hands.

Tears gathered in her eyes. "It's all right, Dante. It's all right."

"God, Tessa, don't let me hurt you. Don't let me—"

"Please, please…let me help you. Tell me about

your Amy. You've probably never talked to anyone about her, have you?"

Tears cascaded down Tessa's cheeks and fell on Dante's hands where they cradled her face.

"Don't cry, honey," Dante said. "It breaks my heart to see you crying for me."

"Then cry for yourself. Cry for you and Amy. Cry for what you can never have, for the life that can never be, for the love that's lost to you forever."

Her words cut into him like a razor-sharp blade, bringing his heart's blood to the surface, baring his soul for her to see. Only partially realizing what he was doing, he flung her away from him and shot up off the bed.

He made it halfway to the door before he heard her call to him. "You have to stop running sometime and it might as well be now. Amy's dead. She's been dead for seventeen years. But you're alive, Dante." He felt her presence even before she touched him on the back. "You are alive. Don't you know that Amy would want you to live, to love, to have a full and happy life? You owe it to her, to the love the two of you shared, not to crawl into that grave with her."

Dante whirled around, agony and rage white-hot within him. "Damn you!" he screamed at Tessa, then grabbed her and shook her. Shook her hard.

She wept uncontrollably, then when he released her, his breath ragged and hard, she came back to him, put her arms around him and said, "Cry for Amy. Cry for her and say goodbye."

He felt as if his heart was being ripped from his chest, as if he were dying by slow, torturous degrees. And then the first teardrop fell. Tessa stood on tiptoe and kissed the tear from his cheek.

"She'll always be a part of you and you can always love her," Tessa said, "but you have to let her go. You have to say goodbye."

A dam burst inside Dante. And seventeen years of grief and sorrow and guilt poured out of him. He wept as he'd never wept in his life, tears blinding him, the pain unbearable. Tessa held him as he trembled and cried. She kissed his cheek, his jaw, his neck and cooed to him. Comforting, loving sounds. He clung to her, holding on, trusting her, instinctively knowing that she and she alone could bring him through this soul-wrenching absolution and long overdue acceptance. Hopefully, with his sanity still intact.

"GOOD GRIEF, you scared the bejesus out of me." Leslie Anne swatted Charlie on the arm when he appeared out of nowhere. "Were you calling my name a couple of minutes ago?"

"Yes, I saw you and that Evans woman running and thought maybe something was wrong, so I called out to you."

"Oh, thank God it was you." Leslie Anne sighed with relief.

Charlie grasped her shoulders and squeezed gently. "How are you, dear girl? It's been a rough few days, hasn't it?"

"Yeah, it's been bad, but everything's going to work out."

"I love your spunk, you know. You remind me of your mama, the way she used to be before her accident."

Charlie sounded odd, as if something was bothering him. But maybe it was nothing more than the usual. Whenever he talked about how things had been with her mother and him before "the accident," he always got this funny look in his eyes and a catch in his voice. Poor old Charlie. He'd probably always be in love with her mother, even if he did eventually wind up marrying Celia someday.

"Are you all right?" Leslie Anne asked. "You seem kind of…I don't know, sad or something." She patted Charlie's left hand that still clasped her shoulder.

"I'm just worried sick about you." Charlie leaned over and kissed her forehead. "I sure am proud of the way you're handling things. You're a brave girl to not let this awful mess with the mystery caller telephoning your aunt Myrle and Olivia and God knows who else upset you. But you have to know it's all lies, that whoever is spreading the rumor that Tessa was raped by that serial killer, Eddie Jay Nealy, seventeen years ago, is out to hurt your family."

"Someone called Aunt Myrle…and Olivia? They…they told them that—" Leslie Anne felt as if she'd been hit in the belly by a hard fist and all the air had been knocked out of her.

"Oh, God, Leslie Anne, I thought you knew." Charlie's eyes widened in horror, his face went deathly pale. "I assumed they'd told you by now, to prepare you for when your friends start calling and…" He dropped his hands in front of him and wrung them together nervously. "I could cut out my tongue for telling you."

Feeling dazed and uncertain, Leslie Anne stared at Charlie for several seconds before the full impact of what he'd said hit her. The terrible secret her grandfather and mother had kept hidden from the world was no longer a secret. Someone had told Aunt Myrle and Olivia Sizemore.

It has to be the same person who sent me the newspaper clippings and that terrible note telling me that I was Eddie Jay Nealy's daughter!

"Oh, God, Charlie, this can't be happening." Tears filled her eyes and a hot, tingling sensation spread through her body.

"I know it's a lie, but lies can hurt," Charlie said. "We'll make sure everyone knows that there isn't a word of truth to it. We can't have people thinking—"

"But it is true," Leslie Anne said.

"What?" Charlie shook his head. "No. No, it can't be true."

"I didn't want to believe it, either, but…Mother and Granddaddy admitted to me that it's the truth. Oh, Charlie, I am that terrible man's child."

Leslie Anne threw herself at Charlie, who opened his arms to encompass her. She laid her head on his chest and wept while he patted her comfortingly on the back. She wished he'd say something so she would know he didn't hate her. She couldn't bear it if Charlie hated her.

Lifting her head and blinking the tears away, she looked up at him, but he was staring off into the distance. "Charlie?"

"Hmm?"

"Look at me."

He did.

"I'm still the same person I was before, aren't I? I mean, it doesn't make any difference that I'm—"

"No, of course it doesn't make any difference." Charlie reached down, grasped her shoulders again and pushed her at arm's length. "To those of us who love you, it won't matter, but to others, it might. You know how people can be."

"You think all my friends will hate me, don't you? And their parents won't let them have anything to do with me."

"You mustn't fret. Perhaps it's not too late to keep this under wraps. We can't be certain anyone other than Myrle and Olivia received a phone call."

"Leslie Anne! Leslie Anne!" Lucie's voice rang out loud and clear in the stillness of twilight.

"I'm here," Leslie Anne called. "Over here with Charlie."

Lucie came flying up the path and halted abruptly when she saw Charlie with his hands on Leslie Anne's shoulders. "Are you all right?" Lucie's right hand eased inside her jacket. Leslie Anne knew the Dundee agent was preparing to pull her gun if necessary. Earlier today, she'd seen the holster Lucie wore strapped to her left shoulder.

"No, I'm not all right." Leslie Anne pulled away from Charlie. "But you don't have to shoot the messenger."

"What are you talking about?" Lucie asked, a puzzled frown on her face.

"I'm afraid I did the unforgivable," Charlie said. "I've been so concerned about Leslie Anne since I heard the news that I rushed right over. And when Eustacia told me you two had gone riding, I couldn't wait to see if Leslie Anne was all right, so I came looking for her. I thought surely someone had already told her about the phone calls Myrle and Olivia—"

"You told her about those phone calls?" Lucie glared at Charlie. Her hand dropped away from her shoulder holster hidden beneath her jacket.

"I feel dreadful about it." Charlie hung his head. "Simply dreadful."

"It's not your fault, Charlie." Leslie Anne zeroed in on Lucie. "Why wasn't I told? You knew, of course. Did Granddaddy decide I wasn't to be told? Or—"

"Let's go back to the house and you can talk to

your grandfather," Lucie said. "And don't judge him too harshly. He's simply trying to protect you."

"I'm getting awfully tired of hearing that excuse every time somebody lies to me or doesn't tell me what's going on. I'm not a child, you know."

"Yes, you are a child," Lucie said. "And you're acting like one right now. If you want to be treated like an adult, then when we go back to the house and you speak with your grandfather, act like an adult and there's a good chance he'll treat you like one."

DANTE LAY on the bed beside her, his head resting on her breast, his arm draped over her waist. She had led him to the bed and held him while he cried, soothing him only with her touch. Words were superficial and inadequate at a time such as this. And time had no meaning. Tomorrow and yesterday blended into one, becoming only today, this hour, this moment. As she stroked his thick, black hair, she wondered if perhaps he'd fallen asleep. He was so quiet, so still.

"Tessa?"

Startled by the sound of his voice, a deep, soft murmur, she shivered. "Yes?"

"When I first met Amy, I thought she was the most beautiful girl I'd ever seen."

"Was it love at first sight for both of you?" Tessa asked, relief washing over her. Dante being able to talk about Amy was a good sign. A very good sign.

Dante sighed. "Nah, not for either of us. But it sure was lust at first sight for me. Man, did I want her."

"What about her?"

"She told me later that she was interested right away, but she'd heard the other girls talking about me. They'd warned her that I would break her heart."

"But you didn't, did you? You fell in love with her."

"Did I ever." Dante rolled over and sat up alongside Tessa, their backs resting against the pillows she had placed against the headboard. "I wish you could understand what it's like to love someone that much, the way I loved Amy. You know all those sappy things they say in love songs? Well, they're all true."

"What kind of engagement ring did you give her?" Tessa asked. "Women always want to know about things like that."

Dante lifted Tessa's hand. "No rings on your fingers."

She shook her head. "I had a lot of jewelry, several rings, even a beautiful ruby birthstone ring, but after the accident—" She huffed loudly. "I've used that word so many times to explain to the world what happened to me that I automatically use it."

Still holding her hand, he slipped his other arm around her shoulders. "I couldn't afford much of a ring for Amy, but I spent every dime I had on it. It was just a little half-carat diamond. Nothing fancy. But she loved it. You should have heard her squeal when I asked her to marry me and put the ring on her finger. You'd have thought it was the Hope Diamond or something."

"I'm sure to Amy it was the most beautiful, priceless ring in the world." If Dante gave her a rhinestone ring, she would treasure it, as long as his heart came with the ring.

Dante eased his arm from around her shoulders and held out his left hand. "She gave me this."

Tessa studied the handsome onyx ring with a small diamond in the center. If her guess was right, this was no cheap knock-off. "It's a very nice ring."

"The ring belonged to Amy's father. It was the only thing she had that belonged to him."

Tessa took Dante's hand. She ran her fingertip over the shiny black onyx setting. "You should wear this ring forever, in memory of Amy and the love you two shared."

Dante slid his big hand across the side of her face and down her neck. His thumb skimmed her lips as his fingers forked through her hair. Their gazes met and locked. Her heart stood still. His fingers worked through her hair, undoing the loose bun and setting her long, wavy hair free.

He lifted a strand of her hair and brought it to his nose, then closed his eyes and sighed. "You have such beautiful hair."

Did her hair remind him of Amy's? she wondered.

"Was your hair always this dark?" he asked.

"The older I get the darker the blond," she told

him. "When I was younger, it was a couple of shades lighter. I figure in a few years, I'll have enough gray hairs to warrant putting a color on it."

He opened his eyes and stared at her. "I know you're not Amy, if that's what's bothering you. I know she's dead. I know you're alive." His gaze bored into her. "And I know I want you."

"Are you sure it's me you want?"

"I'm sure."

CHAPTER EIGHTEEN

LUCIE HAD her hands full and needed help. She, Leslie Anne and Charles Sentell had returned to the house to find Sharon Westbrook trying to deal with pure bedlam. Every couple of minutes, the phone rang and a red-faced G.W. dared anyone to answer it. His sister was doing her best to soothe him, but with little success. Celia Poole kept snapping at everyone and demanding to know where Tessa was. Teetering nervously around the room, Myrle continuously wrung her hands and wept. Hal and Eustacia hovered in the background, a stunned expression on the butler's face and tears in the cook's eyes. Tad Sizemore watched the whole scene with bored indifference. Amazingly enough, it was Olivia Sizemore who calmly asked Lucie what she could do to help.

"Speak to Mr. Carpenter and have him man the telephones," Lucie said. "Please ask him to tell anyone who calls that the Westbrooks are aware of the rumor being spread and will issue a statement to the press sometime tomorrow."

Olivia nodded.

"Have Eustacia prepare coffee and serve it as soon as possible. It'll give her something to do. Besides, it wouldn't be wise to pour everyone a stiff drink, so coffee will have to suffice," Lucie said, then turned to Leslie Anne, who stood beside her, a glazed look in her eyes. Lucie grasped the girl's arm and shook her gently. "I'm going to need your help, honey. Can you help me?"

"What do you want me to do?" Leslie Anne asked.

"Go over there and see if you can do something to calm your grandfather. Your aunt doesn't seem to be having much luck."

When Leslie Anne only stared blankly at Lucie, she didn't mince words. "You don't want your grandfather to have a heart attack, do you?"

"No, of course not."

"Then get over there right now."

Before Leslie Anne took more than a couple of steps, Myrle saw her and screeched. "Oh, my poor child. My poor little Leslie Anne." Myrle came rushing toward her great-niece, her arms outstretched. "Thank the good Lord my sister never lived to see this day."

Lucie turned quickly to Charlie. "See if you can do something with Mrs. Poole. And get her daughter to help you. Ms. Poole's bitching isn't helping anyone, least of all her mother." Celia Poole was acting like a hateful bitch, which Lucie suspected the woman was.

Without a word, Charlie Sentell moved into action, effectively cutting Myrle off before she reached Leslie Anne. Lucie breathed a brief sigh of relief, then gave Leslie Anne a nudge.

"You want to be treated like an adult, now's your chance to act like one. Put your grandfather first. Think about what this is doing to him. You're his number one priority. Go over there and show him you can handle this, even if you have to fake it. Understand?"

"Mama should be here," Leslie Anne said. "Has anyone called her?"

"I'll take care of that, you just do what I told you to do. Okay?"

"Okay." Like a windup doll, Leslie Anne walked toward her grandfather.

Lucie ducked out of the room and into a secluded nook down the hallway. She dialed her cell phone. Dom Shea answered on the second ring.

"Dom, it's Lucie. Look, we've got big trouble here at the Leslie Plantation and I need backup."

"Vic and I will—"

"No, just send Vic. I want you to get in touch with Dante and Tessa Westbrook. When I call their cell phones, I keep getting voice mail. I don't know what's going on with them, but they need to get back here pronto. If necessary, go to Louisiana and bring them home."

"What's going on?"

"It seems somebody made more than a few phone

calls this afternoon," Lucie said. "This mystery person apparently informed all of the Westbrooks' family and friends that Tessa was raped seventeen years ago and that Leslie Anne is Eddie Jay Nealy's daughter."

"Good God!"

"Oh, that's not the half of it. I've got a houseful of weeping, half-hysterical family members here right now, the phone is ringing off the hook and it's only a matter of time before the local press will be beating down the front gates."

"Should we involve the sheriff?" Dom asked.

"Not yet. Just send Vic ASAP and then hunt down Dante and Tessa."

THE MOST exhilarating sensation swept through Tessa, as if she'd been waiting a lifetime for this moment. To be with this one man. Tessa's body tingled. Her nipples tightened. Her femininity moistened. Had she known this kind of sexual hunger when she'd been a teenager, before her life had been changed forever by the actions of a maniac? In the years since, she'd had sex on several occasions—to prove to herself that she hadn't been scarred for life by the rape—and she'd found those liaisons pleasant enough, but void of any real passion.

"Tessa, are you sure?" Dante asked, his black eyes raking over her with a hunger she recognized as identical to her own. "If you have any doubts—"

"I've never been more sure of anything in my

life." She held out her hand to him. "I want us to make love."

He took her hand, then pulled her into his arms and kissed her. First her chin, then her cheeks. His lips grazed her temples and forehead. Sweet and tender. Hesitant, but not uncertain. He caressed her neck and glided his fingertips over her shoulders and down her arms, his touch featherlight and unbearably sensual. It amazed her that such a large, powerful man could be so gentle. He handled her as if she were made of spun glass. As if she were the rarest treasure on earth.

His incredible gentleness was her undoing.

The stirring of passion within her intensified. She yearned for more than tenderness, wanting Dante's control to crumble. "I won't break, you know," she whispered in his ear just as his big hands hovered over her breasts.

He groaned, the sound animalistic. And he covered her breasts with his open palms, lifted them and rubbed his thumbs across her nipples. Even through the barriers of her silk blouse and lace bra, she felt the friction almost as if her breasts were bare. A yearning gasp escaped from her parted lips.

"I want to look at you," he said. "I want to touch you and taste you all over."

When he jerked the ends her blouse up and out of her slacks, she shivered with anticipation and when he undid the small pearl buttons, she studied his large dark hands. Long, broad fingers. A dusting of black hair. Amy's father's onyx and diamond ring shimmered on the third finger of Dante's left hand.

Don't think about Amy, Tessa told herself. *Don't let thoughts of another woman ruin this time with Dante.*

He removed her blouse, but when he reached to unhook the front closure on her bra, she pushed his hands aside and reached out to him. Their gazes collided. She smiled and undid one button on his shirt, and then another and another. And when she had his shirt completely undone, he yanked it out of his trousers and pulled it off.

His hard, muscular chest tempted her beyond reason. When she rubbed her fingertips over his tiny male nipples, he sucked in his breath. She delved her fingers through the thicket of dark, curly hair that spread out over his upper chest forming the top of a "T" while the lower half tapered off over his lean belly and inside his pants. While she savored the feel of him, his strength and pure masculinity, he unhooked her bra and spread it apart. She slid her hands down his sides and unbuckled his belt, her fingers trembling ever so slightly in her haste to undress him.

With both of them bare from the waist up, Dante pulled her against him, pressing her breasts into his chest as he kissed her. All gentleness was gone, replaced by raging hunger. This was what she wanted, what she needed. Tessa participated fully in the savage kiss, his fierce hunger feeding hers. Their tongues mated in a wild dance, their hands exploring, enticing, arousing.

They tore at each other's remaining clothing, flinging garments onto the floor and down toward the foot of the bed. When they were totally naked, Dante tossed Tessa onto her back, then straddled her hips. As he stared down at her, she gazed up at him. Perspiration dotted his forehead and upper lip. Lust shimmered in his eyes.

He hovered over her, big and dark and powerful. All man. His swollen sex jutted forward, just barely touching her mound.

Tessa's heartbeat thundered in her ears.

"God, honey, I don't have any condoms." Dante groaned. His shoulders sagged.

"I don't think I can wait for you to go out somewhere and buy a pack," she told him truthfully.

"Are you saying—"

She lifted herself up and reached for his penis, the actions simultaneous. She pressed on the small of his back as she guided him into her, then she bucked up just enough to take him completely inside her body. He moaned roughly and thrust into her deep and hard.

Nothing had ever felt so good, so right, as having Dante inside her. She clung to his shoulders, her nails biting into his flesh, clamping down on his rock-hard muscles. He slid his hands under her hips and lifted her up, taking her completely, filling her to the hilt. Whimpering gasps and sighs of pleasure escaped from her lips as he lunged and retreated repeatedly, building the tension inside her quickly. Her body joined his, setting an identical rhythm, moving together as if they'd made love countless times and knew one another the way only old lovers did.

Rapidly losing control, his movements frantically increasing in speed and roughness, Dante hammered into her. And she loved it. Her whole body came alive as it never had before, bursting with energy, expanding and contracting, milking him with feminine strength. Her climax hit her with earthshattering force. As she cried out and fell apart, Dante came, his orgasm intensifying her pleasure.

She held on to him as his body melted into hers, a heavy yet precious weight on top of her. When he rolled over and off her, he curled his arm around her and brought her close, then kissed her. She snuggled against him and sighed. The lingering scent of her perfume mingled with the faint scent of his aftershave. Both blended with the odor of perspiration and sex. A sweet contentment settled over Tessa and she refused to allow any doubts or uncertainties to rob her of this sweetness. She laid her hand over Dante's heart, loving the way touching him made her feel.

They rested there for endless moments, neither of them speaking, only holding each other. And then Dante broke the silence.

"Are you hungry?"

She laughed. "Now that you mention it…"

"Why don't we take a shower, then find a restaurant? I'm suddenly starving."

"Sounds like a plan." Reluctantly, she eased away from him and sat up in bed. "Do you want the bathroom first or—"

He shot up, grabbed her hand and pulled her out of bed with him when he got up. "Let's shower together," he told her. "It'll save time and—" he winked at her "—I'll even wash your hair for you." His gaze traveled down to the apex between her thighs.

Her cheeks flushed, but she wasn't really embarrassed. She loved the way Dante was looking at her, as if he wanted her again already. She threw her arms around his neck and rubbed herself against him. "In that case, I say one good turn deserves another."

Laughing, Dante swept her up into his arms and carried her into the bathroom.

ALL HELL HAS BROKEN LOOSE at the old Leslie Plantation, and it's completely my doing. I created this havoc by simply making a few telephone calls to certain people, beginning with Olivia and Myrle. But I didn't stop there, with G.W.'s girlfriend and sister-in-law. Oh, no. I knew that in order to stir things up enough to keep G.W. off balance and show Leslie Anne the nightmare her life would become, I had to reveal the ugly truth to enough people so that word would soon spread throughout Fairport. And it has.

Lucie Evans and Vic Noble were doing an admirable job of keeping the hounds at bay, so to speak. But they finally had to call in the sheriff to post deputies at the front gates to keep the press from scaling the walls. By morning, the story of Tessa Westbrook's rape seventeen year ago and Leslie Anne's true parentage will be front-page news. Even G.W. can't stop it. Not now.

I must concentrate on Leslie Anne, push her little by little, but not so much that anyone becomes suspicious. They'll be watching her like a hawk, so I'll have to be careful and strike when she's alone. I thought she would fall apart this evening, but she didn't. Instead of demanding attention by acting out, she conducted herself quite well, her greatest concern apparently for her grandfather. The girl is made of strong stuff, so pushing her over the edge might prove impossible. In that case, I'll move right along to Plan B. Whether she kills herself or I do it for her doesn't really matter. The end result will be the same. Leslie Anne will be dead. Tessa will be devastated and inconsolable. And I'll have rid myself of the two major obstacles standing between me and what I want.

DANTE CONCENTRATED completely on Tessa and for the first time since he'd been young and in love with Amy, he felt more than sexual desire for a woman. Maybe it wasn't love, but it sure as hell was something pretty powerful. Had Tessa stirred to life a long dormant emotion inside him solely because she reminded him so much of Amy? Or was it because she had suffered unbearably at the hands of the same monster who had killed Amy? He didn't know for sure. But one thing he did know was that he liked Tessa for herself and truly admired her. What strength and determination it must have taken for her to have survived Nealy's brutality. And not only survived, but recovered. She'd built a good life for herself and her child. How many women could love the child of the man who had raped and tortured her? But Tessa Westbrook was no ordinary woman. She was a rare breed.

When they entered the bathroom, he turned on the shower, stepped into the tub and held out his hand for Tessa. She took his hand and joined him. She looked so small and delicate standing there naked, her long hair hanging across one shoulder, the ends resting against the rise of her breast. He leaned down and licked the nipple. Sighing, she arched her back and threaded her fingers through his hair.

While the warm water sprayed down over them, Dante closed his eyes and kissed a path from Tessa's breast, over her belly and across the front of first one thigh and then the other. When he stood up and opened his eyes, she swayed toward him. He caught her with one hand, sliding it around her waist, then pulled her to him slowly, letting the passion between them continue to build.

"I'm going to bathe you." He nipped her earlobe. "Turn around and I'll start with your back."

While she pivoted around, he removed the small bar of soap from its wrapper, reached around Tessa and yanked a washcloth off the rack at the back of the tub enclosure. He lathered the cloth, then lifted his hand, anticipating not only the pleasure he would give her, but the pleasure he would receive in return. When he looked at her back, his hand paused mid-air. Tessa's body was smooth, sleek perfection, except for a series of thin white scars that crisscrossed her back and buttocks.

My God!

"They're very faint now," Tessa said. "Years ago they were hideous."

Dante dropped the washcloth. It hit the bottom of the tub with a squishy flop. "Oh, babe..." He wrapped his arms around her and hugged her fiercely. Protectively. Tears stung his eyes as he imagined how she'd gotten those numerous scars.

"The doctors said that he used a whip of some kind," she said unemotionally. "Judging from the injuries themselves, they believe he whipped me repeatedly."

"Tessa, my sweet Tessa." With his arms wrapped around her, he lowered his head and kissed her shoulder.

"Let's not waste our time talking about him or what happened. Please..." She turned in Dante's arms, stood on tiptoe and kissed him. "I know what happened to me because of what I've been told, but I have no memory of it. In a way, I'm very lucky that I can't remember. The way things are, I don't have to relive that time."

Dante kissed her. Devoured her. He'd never felt as protective and possessive about a woman. Not since Amy.

Before he realized what she intended to do, Tessa took charge. She kissed his chest, then his belly and as she eased down in front of him, she circled his penis and drew it toward her mouth. He hadn't known how much he wanted her to do this until she licked him from tip to root and then back up again. Groaning as he grew harder by the minute, he closed his eyes and allowed her free rein. Her mouth closed over him, sealing around him like a moist glove. After only a few minutes of her constant attention, he grabbed her head and held her tightly while he came. He felt as if the top of his head had exploded. She withdrew from him slowly and licked her lips. He reached down and dragged her up his body and held her off her feet until they were eye to eye. She wrapped her legs around his waist, leaned into him and kissed him passionately.

When she came up for air, he said, "Didn't you say earlier that one good turn deserves another?" He bent over and picked up the washcloth. "But first, I'm going to give you that bath I promised."

He moved the cloth over her with reverence, worshipping her body, striving to give her pleasure with each touch. She surrendered herself to his care and he took great pride in the fact that she trusted him so completely.

When they eventually stepped out of the tub, Dante dried her slowly, then himself quickly. With her hair only towel dried, he lifted her into his arms and carried her back to bed. When she lay before him, he spread her thighs apart and knelt between them. She tensed. He reached up and tweaked each nipple. She gasped.

"Relax, honey. Relax and enjoy."

She did relax, but only for a moment. When his tongue touched her intimately, she cried out and arched her back, lifting her hips. He took her actions as an invitation to finish what he'd started. He concentrated completely on one small area of her body.

She smelled clean and fresh. And tasted musky and sweet.

He made love to her with his mouth, using his tongue, his lips and his teeth. She writhed and whimpered and her feminine folds flooded with delicious moisture.

Within minutes, he felt the tension building rapidly inside her and sensed that she was on the edge. Increasing the speed and strength of his strokes, he brought her to a throbbing climax. Her body shook with release and all the while he continued the deep, penetrating lunges. She cried out and grabbed his head, her fingers digging through his hair. While she floated back down to earth, he lifted his head.

"You are so wonderful," he told her. "I love making love to you."

"Oh, Dante…Dante…"

Lowering his head again, he petted her with his tongue, running the tip around the outer perimeter of her mound. And that's when he noticed something peculiar, something he hadn't seen until that very moment. There in the crease where her left thigh joined her body, and barely noticeable, was a small, leaf-shaped birthmark, two shades darker than her natural skin tone. Dante froze. He lifted his head and stared at the birthmark.

It couldn't be. It just couldn't be. He shut his eyes, then reopened them and looked again. But there it was. He reached out and traced the outline of the oval, leaf-shaped birthmark.

Tessa giggled. "That tickles."

"You have a birthmark right there." He touched it with his fingertip.

"Yes, I know."

Amy Smith had a birthmark identical to the one on Tessa Westbrook.

"Dante, are you all right? Is something wrong?"

The motel telephone rang.

"Who the hell?" Dante kissed Tessa's birthmark, his heart beating ninety to nothing. "I'd better get that. It could be important. Although I don't know why whoever's calling wouldn't have used our cell phones."

"I turned them off after we got back here to the motel," Tessa told him. "We needed some time when the world couldn't reach us."

"Yes, we did." He tumbled across the bed and grabbed the phone off the hook. "Moran here."

"Dante, it's Dom. What the hell's going on? Lucie's been trying to call you and Tessa for several hours now. And you do realize you didn't inform us where you'd be staying. I had to track y'all down."

"What's going on? Is something wrong?"

"Yeah, something's wrong. The whole town of Fairport got let in on the big Westbrook secret this afternoon."

Dante sat straight up on the side of the bed and eased his feet onto the floor. "Who and how?"

Tessa crawled over and inched up beside him. "What is it?"

"Somebody made a bunch of phone calls," Dom continued over the phone. "Probably the same person who sent Leslie Anne Westbrook those newspaper clippings. Anyway, the mystery caller informed one and all that Tessa was raped seventeen years ago and impregnated by her rapist. And the caller didn't leave anything out, including the rapist's name."

Dante gritted his teeth, then reached over and put his arm around Tessa's waist. "We'll head home right away. Any chance we can commandeer a helicopter ride back to Fairport?"

"I've taken care of that. There's a helicopter waiting for y'all at the airport. Just get back here as fast as possible. Lucie says things are bad and getting worse by the minute."

Dante hung up the receiver and turned to Tessa. "We have to go back to Fairport immediately."

He hurriedly relayed the information Dom had given him. Tessa jumped up off the bed and began picking up their discarded clothing, her actions frantic and unsteady. Dante grabbed her and hauled her up against him. "Calm down, honey. Everything will be all right. I'm going to be right at your side, no matter what happens."

"I don't care about myself," she told him. "All that matters is Leslie Anne."

No, Leslie Anne wasn't all that mattered. Tessa mattered. To him, she mattered more than anything or anyone else, just as Amy had. Whatever suspicions he now had about Tessa couldn't be fully explored until later. Not until they took care of the current crisis. But once he reunited Tessa with her daughter, he was going to find out how it was possible that Tessa Westbrook had a birthmark not only in the exact same spot as Amy Smith, but that the leaf-shaped nevus was identical to one that had been in the crease of Amy's inner thigh.

CHAPTER NINETEEN

"SHE LOCKED HERSELF in her room and barricaded the door," Lucie told Dante and Tessa as they rushed up the hall toward Leslie Anne's suite. "I've been able to maintain a dialogue of sorts with her, but she's angry and confused. And it doesn't help any that we haven't been able to clear out that three-ring circus downstairs. I believe your aunt is making arrangements for the whole lot to spend the night."

On the flight in from Rayville, Dante had held Tessa's hand and assured her that she could count on him to help her through whatever she and Leslie Anne faced. And she had clung to Dante, not only in a physical sense, but emotionally, as well.

"When we spoke to Aunt Sharon downstairs, she told us she had called Dr. Lester and that Leslie Anne and Olivia managed to persuade Daddy to take the sedative the doctor prescribed," Tessa said. "I'm as concerned about my father's health as I am about what this is doing to Leslie Anne."

"Is Mr. Westbrook still lying down?" Lucie asked.

"Yes, and he's resting," Tessa said. "Olivia is sitting at his bedside. Aunt Sharon says that Olivia has actually been quite helpful."

"Much to my surprise, she has been," Lucie said. "And so has Leslie Anne. You would have been so proud of your daughter. Despite what she was going through herself, she managed to hold it together until she made sure her grandfather was all right."

"Leslie Anne did that?" Tessa swallowed her tears.

Lucie eyed Dante's arm clasped around Tessa's waist, then gave him a what's-going-on-here look. "Did y'all come up with any useful information in Louisiana? Any clues that might help us identify our mystery caller?"

"No, nothing that will help us figure out who's creating all these problems for the Westbrooks," Dante said.

Lucie nodded. "If you two want to take over here, I'll go down and give Vic and a Dom a hand." She looked at Dante. "Vic and Dom have a report for you, when you have time to sit down and go over it with them."

"Sure thing. Just as soon as we let Leslie Anne know we're here," Dante said. "Her welfare comes first, before anything else."

"Yes, of course." Lucie offered them a smile. "See y'all later."

"Later," Dante replied.

Tessa smiled at Dante, loving him for caring about

her daughter. Battling the tears threatening to choke her, she knocked softly on the bedroom door. "Leslie Anne, it's Mama. Dante and I are here. May we come in and talk to you?"

"Dante's here?" Leslie Anne asked, a pathetically hopeful note in her voice.

"Yeah, sweetheart, I'm here," Dante said.

"You know what's happened, don't you?" Leslie Anne spoke through the closed door. "Everybody in Fairport knows that Eddie Jay Nealy was my father."

"How about opening the door so we can talk face-to-face?" Dante tightened his hold around Tessa's waist.

Silence. Then they heard a bumping sound, followed by scraping and finally the click of the lock. The door swung open and a red-nosed, swollen-eyed Leslie Anne came barreling toward Dante and threw herself into his arms. Tessa moved aside when Dante enveloped her daughter in his big, strong arms. At that moment, Tessa closed her eyes and said a prayer of thanks that God had sent Dante Moran into their lives. He was a good man, with an understanding heart. A man capable of deep, abiding love.

As he stroked Leslie Anne's back comfortingly, Dante talked in a low, steady voice. "The whole town learning the truth is pretty bad, isn't it? All your friends and their parents know what happened to your mother seventeen years ago, and you're worried about what they'll think and how they'll feel about you."

Clinging to Dante, Leslie Anne gulped down a sob. "I knew you'd understand." She glanced up over Dante's shoulder at Tessa. "Mama, I know this isn't your fault."

"Of course it's not your mother's fault." Dante turned Leslie Anne in his arms, cupped her chin and lifted her face. "Look at me."

She did. He smiled at her. Tessa held her breath. And miracle of miracles, Leslie Anne smiled back at him.

"You have people who love you, people who will take care of you and protect you," Dante told her. "Your mother loves you more than anything. You know that. And so does your grandfather. And I care about you and I'm going to be sticking around to protect you. So, listen up, okay? It's not going to be easy facing the world, but you're going to do it. And you're going to hold your head high. You have nothing to be ashamed of."

"But I am ashamed of—"

Dante tapped her mouth with his index finger. "You're ashamed of nothing. You are Leslie Anne Westbrook. You're beautiful, intelligent and your mother's daughter."

"I wish everyone could see me as you do."

He caressed her cheek. "You're going to find out who your real friends are over the next few weeks. But remind yourself as often as necessary that if anyone cuts you out of their life, it'll be their loss, not yours."

"Oh, Dante. You sure do know all the right things to say, don't you?" Leslie Anne hugged him again, then turned to her mother. "I'm sorry your trip was cut short. How did it go?"

Tessa laughed, then reached out and pulled her daughter to her. "Why don't we let Dante go downstairs for his meeting with the other Dundee agents while you and I have a mother-daughter talk?"

Leslie Anne hugged Tessa, then looked at Dante. "You won't leave, will you? You are going to stick around like you promised."

"I'm not leaving," he told her. "I don't make promises unless I intend to keep them."

"I trust you," she said. "You trust him, too, don't you, Mama?"

"Yes, I trust him," Tessa replied. *I trust him with my life…with my heart.*

DANTE MANAGED to avoid the Westbrooks' guests, whom he'd been told by Hal Carpenter were in the parlor and waiting to be assigned bedrooms for the evening. Luckily the old mansion was enormous. He figured there might be as many as ten bedrooms divided among the center of the house and the two wings. When he entered the library, he found the other agents scattered about in various chairs throughout the room.

"Sorry to have kept y'all waiting," Dante said, then zeroed in on Lucie. "I'd like to speak to you privately, Lucie. I have a special assignment for you, concerning this case."

"Want us to step outside?" Vic asked.

"No, Lucie and I will step outside, then I'll be back to listen to what y'all have found out."

Alone in the hallway, Dante scanned left and right, as far as he could see, making sure there were no eavesdroppers nearby.

"This isn't about the Westbrook case, is it?" Lucie asked.

"Only indirectly." He condensed the story that Deanetta Knight had shared with him and Tessa, hitting the highlights, but giving Lucie the basic information about another young, blond girl's body being cremated and her ashes buried in Richland Parish.

"Oh, Dante, I'm so sorry," Lucie said. "You're pretty sure this other girl was Amy, aren't you?"

"I was until…" *Until I discovered a leaf-shaped birthmark on Tessa's body.*

"Until what?"

"You'll tell me I'm crazy, that I've lost my mind."

"Try me," Lucie said.

"I want you to find out something for me."

"You aren't going to tell me—"

"Tessa Westbrook has a birthmark identical to one that Amy Smith had and in the exact same spot."

Lucie stared at him, eyes wide, mouth open.

"Say something, Lucie."

"Holy shit!"

"What are the odds that—"

"Two young blondes were found tossed out on the side of Interstate 20 in Richland Parish, less than a week apart. One was dead and the other barely survived." Lucie took in a deep breath and blew it out on quickly. "But G.W. identified the one who was alive as his daughter and no one who knew her questioned who she was when he brought her back to Fairport."

"Correct."

"Tessa may have a birthmark like Amy, but she doesn't have her face. Tessa doesn't look like Amy," Lucie said.

"No, *she* doesn't, but her daughter does."

"Are you thinking plastic surgery? But why would she have needed plastic surgery?"

"Maybe she didn't need it," Dante said. "G.W. told everyone Tessa had been in a car wreck. That would be the perfect excuse to have plastic surgery performed."

"Are you saying you think G.W. purposefully identified the wrong girl and had her face altered to resemble his daughter? Is that what you want me to try to find out for you, whether or not Tessa had plastic surgery?"

Dante shook his head. "I intend to ask G.W. that question myself, as soon as he's rested and calm. What I want you to find out for me is Tessa's, G.W.'s and his late wife Anne's blood types. When I con-

front G.W., I want proof of some kind that Tessa—
or whoever she is—isn't G.W. and Anne Westbrook's
daughter."

I COULD WAIT until things settle down, but if I do
that, it could be too late. I need to act very soon, while
the household is in utter chaos. Although Leslie Anne
managed to conduct herself quite well this evening,
it was obvious to everyone that she's teetering on the
edge. And I helped add a little fuel to the fires of
speculation by making a few well-chosen comments
to the others, hinting that the poor child couldn't
help being unstable, all things considered. I even
suggested that she should be watched closely, just in
case... I didn't use the word suicide. I didn't need to.
Everyone knew what I meant.

   Now that Tessa and Moran have returned, there
will be two more people hovering over the pampered
princess. She'll be guarded more securely than Fort
Knox. That simply means I will have to find a way
to get her all to myself for just a few minutes. And
when I do, I know precisely how I'll dispose of her
in order to make it look like suicide. Of course, I shall
be devastated by the child's death, completely heartbroken. And there will be no reason for anyone to
suspect me of having lured Leslie Anne to her death.

"THE PACKAGE Leslie Anne received was posted here
in Fairport," Vic told Dante. "Regular U.S. mail. The

date and place are plainly visible on the envelope. Lucie checked the envelope, newspaper clippings and note for fingerprints before she handed the package over to you and found only one set of identifiable prints. We compared them to Leslie Anne's and as we suspected, they were hers. The other prints were smudged, but our guess is they belonged to various postal employees. Our mystery guy—or gal—would be too smart to leave fingerprints."

"Okay, so we know the package was posted locally," Dante said. "That doesn't mean the sender lives here in Fairport. He could have posted the package here hoping to make it appear he lives in the area."

"I'd say the odds are he does," Dom said. "And the odds are even greater that it's someone close to the family. He didn't try to blackmail G.W. or Tessa, so quick cash wasn't his objective. Whoever sent the package and made those phone calls wants to destroy the Westbrook family."

"Who has reason to hate the Westbrooks that much?" Dante asked.

"G.W. has made some business enemies," Vic said. "But we checked out everyone who's ever threatened G.W. personally and we came up with nothing suspicious. That leads me to believe we're dealing with someone who has a very personal reason to want to rip the family apart. Someone who'd profit in some way by wreaking havoc on the Westbrooks."

"G. W. Westbrook is a very wealthy man." Dom

Shea opened a briefcase lying atop the mahogany desk, removed a file folder and held it out to Dante. "And he has quite a few people financially dependent on him. We ran a check on those people and didn't come up with anything conclusive, but several of them have less than sterling reputations."

"Give me a brief rundown on each person," Dante said. "Not including Tessa and Leslie Anne, of course."

"Of course," Dom replied. "First you have Sharon Westbrook, G.W.'s only sister. She doesn't have a dime to her name. Her brother has supported her all her life by giving her a generous allowance."

"How generous?" Dante asked.

"A hundred and fifty thousand a year, plus a clothes allowance." Dom tapped the folder against his open palm. "Sharon is a free spirit, the type who joined the hippie movement in the sixties. You know—sex, drugs and rock 'n' roll. She changes men like she changes underwear. And word is she has a thing for younger guys. Tad Sizemore in particular."

Dante rolled his eyes. "Interesting, but it doesn't give her a motive. Besides, she seems genuinely fond of her family."

"Next, there's Myrle Poole. G.W. has the same allowance set up for his sister-in-law as he does for his sister. Mrs. Poole is widowed and her husband, who was a gambler, left her and her daughter penniless when he died twenty years ago. Myrle's high society here in Fairport because she was a Leslie. Her life seems to be comprised of social functions and little else."

"What about G.W.'s niece, Celia?"

"She's been married and divorced twice and gets alimony from hubby number two, but not a dime from her uncle."

"Hmm…" A lot of facts, Dante thought, but nothing that pointed a finger at anyone.

"Then we've got the godson," Vic said. "Charlie Sentell works for Westbrook, Inc. and makes two-hundred thousand a year. At least this guy actually works for his money, but word is that he's overpaid for what he does."

Dom laid the file folder back in the briefcase. "And there's the girlfriend, Olivia Sizemore. G.W. paid for her extremely nice riverfront home, gives her a five thousand dollar a month allowance and buys her jewelry and clothes. And mama takes care of her sonny boy, Tad, out of what she gets from G.W. But mama's not the only older lady providing him with TLC. Like we mentioned, it's rumored Tad's got this on-again-off-again thing with Sharon Westbrook, who is old enough to be his mother."

"All this information proves is that G.W. is a generous man and he's got a lot of deadbeats freeloading off him." Dante looked from Dom to Vic. "Is that all we've got?"

"That's it," Dom said.

"No proof of any kind against anyone." Dante grunted. "Any theories?"

"Maybe money has nothing to do with it," Vic suggested. "Maybe it's only personal. But either way, we've got nothing. I'm not even getting a gut reaction to point me in the right direction."

"What we need is to get a look at G.W.'s will," Dante said. "Money can be personal. Who, other than Tessa and Leslie Anne, are named in the will? It's possible this entire upheaval has been set up to give the old man a heart attack."

"Could be," Vic agreed. "At least you've got a theory. That's more than Dom and I came up with."

"The only way we'll know what's in Westbrook's will is if he tells us," Dom said.

A steady knocking at the closed library doors drew the attention of all three agents. Vic, the closest to the pocket doors, slid the doors open. There stood Lucie and Sharon Westbrook.

"Sorry to bother y'all," Lucie said, looking straight at Dante. "I made those phone calls and expect to hear back by morning."

Dante nodded.

"I ran into Ms. Westbrook in the hall and she wanted to find out if we all need rooms for the night and if anyone would like a late supper."

"You can go to the kitchen to eat or Eustacia can bring you a tray," Sharon said.

"We're fine." Dante glanced at the others. "We'll

all be staying the night, but we won't require four separate rooms since we'll be taking shifts so that two of us are on duty at all times."

"We'll certainly have a full house tonight," Sharon said. "I'll arrange for Eustacia to prepare a couple of guest rooms for y'all," Sharon said. "And if there is anything else any of you need, don't hesitate to ask. I'm very grateful that y'all have been here to handle this terrible situation."

When Sharon turned to leave, Lucie called to her, "Ms. Westbrook, may I ask you a question?"

"Yes, certainly."

Lucie stared at the portrait hanging over the fireplace in the library. "Who's the pretty young woman in that picture? I've been curious about it since I first saw it. Is that the late Mrs. Westbrook?"

"No, that's not Anne." Sharon gazed at the portrait, then sighed. "That was painted when Tessa was seventeen, before—" Sharon paused. "She's lovely now, of course, but she was a very pretty girl before the plastic surgery. She has Anne's coloring, but everyone thought she looked like me back then. She was a Westbrook through and through."

"Tessa had plastic surgery? When and why?"

Lucie asked the questions Dante wanted to ask, but he somehow hadn't managed to get the words out of his mouth.

"She had plastic surgery done to reconstruct her face," Sharon said. "You know she was brutalized by that awful man. Her back is covered with scars where he whipped her and her pretty face was beaten almost beyond recognition."

Rage boiled inside Dante. He clenched his fist. "Beating a woman in the face wasn't part of Eddie Jay Nealy's M.O. He beat, whipped and cut his victims' bodies, even cracked open their skulls, but he never touched their faces."

"Well, in Tessa's case, he did." Sharon glowered at Dante. "I remember the first time Anne and I saw her, after G.W. brought her back to Fairport. Her face was covered in bandages. She couldn't walk, could barely utter a word and she stared at us as if we were strangers." Tears trickled down Sharon's cheeks. "It was a terrible time for us, but we were so thankful Tessa was alive that nothing else mattered."

"Mrs. Westbrook had already been diagnosed with terminal cancer, hadn't she?"

Once again Lucie spoke for Dante. God, had he gone mute? He wished that damn roar in his head—caused from the rush of blood and the erratic racing of his pulse—would stop so that he could think straight.

"Yes, Anne was dying, but she fought to the very end to live because she didn't want to leave G.W. and Tessa. But I believe it was Leslie Anne who helped Anne survive as long as she did. She outlived the doctor's prognosis by nearly two years."

"Thank you," Lucie said.

Sharon looked at Lucie, obviously puzzled, but she simply nodded and left the room.

"You two take the first shift," Lucie said to Dom and Vic. "I think Dante needs to get some rest." She came over to him, slipped her arm through his and told him, "Come with me. We'll check on Tessa and Leslie Anne before we turn in."

As they walked down the hall toward the foyer, Dante finally managed to speak. "G.W. would have done anything to have prevented his wife having to see her daughter die before she did."

"Yes, he would have," Lucie agreed. "He might even have identified Amy Smith, who had amnesia, as his daughter, once he knew Tessa Westbrook was dead. And the only way to pull off the hoax was if plastic surgery was performed on Amy's face. The two women were about the same height, same size, same hair and eye color."

Dante halted, nausea churning in his stomach. "Either we're both crazy or there's a damn good chance that the woman upstairs with Leslie Anne right now isn't Tessa Westbrook."

"You're right," Lucie said. "And if she isn't Tessa, then there's an equally good chance that woman is Amy Smith."

CHAPTER TWENTY

LESLIE ANNE curled up against her mother where they sat together in the antique canopy bed. Some of the best memories of her life, especially her childhood, were moments like this, of her and her mother together. When she'd been much younger, Mama had read her a bedtime story every night and stayed with her until she'd fallen asleep. And anytime she'd had a bad dream, she either slept the rest of the night in her mother's bed or Mama slept with her. Lying here now, her head on her mother's shoulder and cocooned in her mother's arms, Leslie Anne felt so secure, so loved. And knowing Dante was downstairs, that he was going to stick around for a while, at least as long as they needed him, made her feel protected.

Odd how she'd never thought about those kind of things—being loved, being safe, secure and protected—until lately. Those things had been a given in her life, things she'd taken for granted. But that had been BTAT—before the awful truth—and now was ATAT.

In a way, nothing had really changed, and yet everything had changed. Mama and Granddaddy and Aunt Sharon still loved her. She was still the same person she'd always been. Same hair, eyes, nose and mouth. Her home was the same, her room just as it had always been. But nothing would ever be the way it had been before. She realized she could accept the fact that her mother and grandfather had lied to her and she understood their reasons for doing it. But how could she ever come to terms with one irrefutable fact—Eddie Jay Nealy was her biological father. And everyone in Fairport already knew or they'd soon know what had happened to Tessa Westbrook and exactly who Tessa's child was. No one would ever look at her the same. Not ever again.

Her life had changed in another way, too. Dante Moran. Her hero. She supposed that since she'd grown up without a father, subconsciously she'd always been looking for one. There had been a time when she'd thought her mother might marry Charlie. She'd been okay with the idea of Charlie for a stepfather, but that was before she'd understood that a woman shouldn't marry a man just to give her child a father. Thank goodness her mother hadn't settled for good old Charlie. Thank goodness she'd waited for a man like Dante to enter her life. Well, their lives actually. From the moment Dante had burst into the Bama Motel and rescued her, Leslie Anne had felt a weird sort of connection to him. Instant trust. Yeah, that had been a big part of it. Trusting him with her life. And she suspected that when they first met—only a few days ago?—Dante and her mother had felt something a lot more powerful than simply instant trust. At least Leslie Anne hoped so.

Am I wrong about Mama and Dante? Do I want there to be something romantic between them because I'd like nothing better than for Dante to be my dad? My stepdad.

Tessa kissed Leslie Anne's temple. "It's getting late, sweetie. You should try to get some sleep."

"Will you stay with me?" She glanced at her mother and noticed the oddest expression on her face. "Mama?"

Tessa sniffled, then laughed. "I'm all right, just concerned about you and your grandfather and—"

"We're going to be all right, all of us. You and me and Granddaddy," Leslie Anne said with a great deal more conviction than she felt. "I'm through with acting like a silly child. I promise. No more running away. No more temper tantrums. From now on, it's the Westbrooks against the world. Right?"

"Right." Tessa laughed in earnest then as she hugged Leslie Anne. "You've had to grow up really fast, haven't you? And I'm so sorry."

"It's okay. Really it is."

"No it's not, but it will be. There aren't going to be any more lies between us. Not ever. But you do know that Granddaddy and I did what we thought was best for you."

"I know. Heck, I'd have done the same thing if I'd been you two." She said it not only because that's what she knew her mother needed to hear, but because she was beginning to understand how true it was. They had lied to her to protect her, because they'd believed it better for her and everyone involved to not know about her mother's rape.

"Leslie Anne, baby girl, will you...will you see Dr. Barrett again?" Tessa asked.

Leslie Anne pulled away from Tessa and flopped over in the bed. After propping her elbow on a pillow and bracing her chin with her palm, she looked right at her mother. "Yes, I'll see him again. And I promise not to threaten to kill him."

"You did no such thing." Tessa's lips curved into an almost smile. "Not really."

"No, not actually, but I did imply that he should worry that I might. I figured he knew I was just acting out, which I won't do again. I swear." She crossed her heart.

"I believe you." Tessa's expression turned deadly serious. "Sweetie, I need to ask you something, something that Tad mentioned to—"

"Tad? God, Mama, who listens to that jerk?"

"It seems that from a conversation you had recently with Tad that he came away with the impression that thoughts of...well, that you were..." Tessa huffed in exasperation. "Tad thinks we should be concerned that you're having suicidal thoughts."

"What?" Leslie Anne sat straight up and glared at her mother. "You're kidding? Where did he get an idea… Oh, shit." Leslie Anne grabbed her mother's hands and held them as she looked straight into her eyes. "Yesterday morning—God was it only yesterday? Well, anyway, right after I ran away from Dr. Barrett, I was angry. Mad at the world. And yes, I did wonder if maybe I should just jump into the river. I ran into Tad right after that and I might have mentioned to him what I was thinking about."

"Oh, Leslie Anne."

She squeezed her mother's hands. "I'm not going to kill myself. I promise. It was just a passing thought. I swear. Eddie Jay Nealy did enough damage to this family and I'm not going to let the fact that he's my biological father hurt you or Granddaddy…or me!"

"That's my girl. Oh, sweetie, I'm so proud of you."

"Well, you know this doesn't mean I'm all right about everything—about your lying to me and about the fact that you were raped and got pregnant with me because of it. I know I'll need help coming to grips with everything, but right now, I just want us to find the person who sent me those newspaper clippings and told everybody in Fairport about Eddie Jay Nealy."

"That's what we all want, and I'm sure it's only a

matter of time before Dante and the Dundee agents discover his or her identity."

"I think I know who it is."

"What? How could you—"

"Mama, this morning I heard a strange voice calling my name and at first I thought it was a dream. But it wasn't. He said—and the voice was disguised, but I think it's a he—well, he called my name and then he said, 'Little girl, who's your daddy?' That voice woke me, but I couldn't find anybody in my room. But it was real. It wasn't a dream, because when Eustacia brought my breakfast tray, I found a note hidden in my napkin and the note said what he'd said. 'Little girl, who's your daddy?' He was in our house this morning and he's here tonight."

"My God! What did you do with the note?" Tessa asked.

"I tore it into a million pieces."

"Oh, honey, you shouldn't have." Tessa cupped Leslie Anne's chin. "You said you think you know who he is."

"I think it's Tad Sizemore. He's just enough of a weasel to do something that despicable."

"But why would Tad—?"

"I don't know. Maybe it's because you and I don't like him and his mother. I'm sure Olivia would like nothing better than make our lives miserable, plus show Granddaddy how loving and supportive she can be. She probably put Tad up to it. They want Granddaddy's money, don't they?"

Tessa patted Leslie Anne's cheek. "I'm not sure Tad and Olivia have a strong enough motive. Besides, how could Tad have found out about my past?"

"How could anybody have found out? Somebody told him. Actually Granddaddy probably told Olivia one night when they were in bed together and she told Tad."

"No, honey, your grandfather has never told anyone other than your Aunt Sharon."

Leslie Anne yawned. "I think I'm right about Tad and we should tell Dante."

"You're worn out and so am I," Tessa said. "Let's put on our pajamas and go to bed. We'll talk to Dante first thing in the morning and tell him what you suspect."

"But Dante promised he'd come back up here after his meeting. I want to wait up for him."

"All right, we'll wait up for him, but in the meantime, let's get ready for bed. And you can tell me every detail about the voice you heard and the note you received."

AT ELEVEN FORTY-FIVE, Dante made the rounds through the Leslie Plantation, checked in with Dom and Vic, then dropped by Leslie Anne's suite. When he found the door closed, he thought twice before he eased it open and went in. Walking quietly, he made his way into the bedroom, but paused when he saw

Tessa and Leslie Anne asleep in Leslie Anne's canopy bed. He stood there, several feet away, and looked at Tessa. She wore a pink floral, silk robe over a matching gown. Her long, wavy blond hair draped across her neck and rested against her chest. She was the most beautiful thing he'd ever seen.

Is it possible that she's Amy? More than anything he wanted to believe that she was.

How ironic that just when he'd finally given up all hope of Amy being alive and allowed another woman to become important to him, his hope had suddenly been renewed, rising like a phoenix from the ashes. But he couldn't—wouldn't—say anything to Tessa about his suspicions. Not until he had proof of some kind that she was not G.W. and Anne Westbrook's daughter. And even if it turned out that she wasn't the real Tessa Westbrook, that didn't automatically mean she was Amy Smith.

But what about the leaf-shaped birthmark?

Yeah, there was that. It wasn't scientific proof—no blood match, no fingerprint match, no DNA match. But what were the odds that two women with so many other physical similarities would have identical birthmarks in exactly the same spot?

Dante moved closer to the bed and studied Tessa's face in the soft glow from the bedside lamp. There was little of Amy in her features—except for the eyes. He'd noticed immediately, the first time he saw Tessa, that she had Amy's eyes. But Tessa's nose was smaller, her cheekbones a little higher, her chin rounder. Even her mouth was different. Not as full as Amy's had been. Images of Amy flashed through his mind. Amy at seventeen.

He thought about the portrait hanging over the fireplace in the library, the portrait of Tessa Westbrook—before the plastic surgery. The Tessa lying here now in bed with her daughter didn't look much like the old Tessa. As quickly as a snap of the fingers, Dante realized who the woman he knew as Tessa looked like—she looked like someone had taken Amy Smith and the original Tessa Westbrook and combined their features into one person.

His chest tight, his pulse racing, Dante reached out and lifted the sheet and blanket up and over the sleeping mother and daughter. His gaze drifted to Leslie Anne, who, lying there with her eyes closed, looked like the teenage Amy he'd loved and lost. She was such a beautiful child. Amy's child?

And there's your proof, he told himself. Leslie Anne was the living, breathing proof that Amy Smith was her mother.

Amy. My sweet, darling Amy. Tears clouded his vision. If only he could wake her and tell her who she really was. He had his Amy back, at long last. And yet not his Amy. She didn't remember him. Would never remember him, never remember the love they'd shared. Because of the brain trauma, her memory of the past was lost to her forever.

But this woman cares for me, he told himself, *maybe even loves me. We were drawn to each other without realizing why. Even if we didn't recognize each other, our souls made the connection.*

Leslie Anne moaned, then rolled over in her sleep and wrapped her arm around her mother. Dante's heart caught in his throat. This was Amy's little girl.

She should have been mine!

But she wasn't his, no matter how much he wished she was. If only he hadn't been such a conscientious teen, so careful to protect Amy every time they'd made love. But he'd loved and respected Amy too much to risk hurting her in any way. They had agreed that they would wait several years after they married before having children, so he'd always used a condom when they had sex. If only…if only…

Damn, don't do this! Yeah, condoms leaked sometimes. It happened. But hoping that it might have happened with Amy and him really was nothing more than wishful thinking. He was kidding himself big-time if he thought there was even the remotest chance Leslie Anne might be his. Wouldn't he have felt something special for the girl if she was his? Wouldn't some sort of paternal thing have kicked in?

Maybe it had. After all, he hadn't turned and walked away from her when he'd found out that she was Eddie Jay Nealy's biological offspring. By all rights, he should have despised the kid, but he hadn't. He didn't.

You're grasping at thin air. Be grateful Amy is alive. Don't dare ask for more. If accepting the fact that Leslie Anne is Nealy's daughter is the price you have to pay for receiving this miracle, then say "Thank You, God," and learn to love Amy's child as if she were your own.

Dante took one last look at the sleeping mother and daughter, then turned and walked out of the room. Tomorrow, he would confront G.W. And then he would tell Tessa that Amy Smith was still alive.

CHAPTER TWENTY-ONE

DANTE WOKE with a start when he heard someone knocking on his door. The last thing he remembered was taking off his shoes and lying down, fully dressed, across the bed. He sat straight up, rubbed his face, then got out of bed and headed for the door in his sock feet. Undoubtedly he'd slept in a crooked position because his shoulders and neck ached. As he opened the door with one hand, he rubbed the back of his neck with the other.

"Good morning, Sleeping Beauty." Lucie stood there smiling, a cup of coffee in her hand. "I come bearing gifts." She held out the white mug.

"What time is it?" Dante looked at his watch. Six-twenty. He reached out and took the coffee from Lucie, then motioned from her to come on in.

"Sleep well?" she asked as she entered the room.

Dante kicked the door shut. "Yeah, for a whole two hours." He sat on the edge of the bed and lifted the mug to his lips. After taking a couple of sips, he glanced at Lucie who had sat down beside him. "Anybody up and stirring?"

"Just us hired help," Lucie said. "Eustacia and Hal are in the kitchen. Dom's asleep and Vic's heading upstairs just as soon as you come down."

"No sign of Tessa this morning?"

Lucie shook her head. "Look, I didn't wake you up for nothing, you know. I have some information."

He took several more swigs of coffee, then gave her a questioning look.

"While I was enjoying my breakfast a few minutes ago, I received a phone call from Daisy. Our Ms. Efficiency always amazes me. She managed to get hold of some of the information you wanted. It seems Dundee often uses freelance computer experts who can take sneak peeks into things like blood bank databases. Lucky for us that G.W. and Tessa are both regular blood donors so getting their blood types was easy. Getting Anne Westbrook's blood type will take a little longer, but Daisy said she'd call as soon as she hears anything."

"What's Tessa's blood type?"

"B positive," Lucie said. "G.W.'s is A positive."

"Amy was B positive." He didn't need any more proof that Tessa was Amy Smith. One or two things could be coincidence, but there were too many exact matches between Tessa and Amy for them to be mere chance. Tessa and Amy were one and the same. They had to be. There was no other logical explanation.

"It's still not proof," Lucie said. "But until you

can get a DNA test run, you can't be a hundred percent sure."

"I'm sure. My gut instincts have been telling me all along that Tessa was Amy. I just wasn't listening because I'd stopped believing in miracles." Dante got up, finished off his coffee quickly, then handed Lucie the empty mug. "Make a point of talking to Myrle Poole as soon as she gets up this morning. Ask her what her sister's blood type was. Tell her whatever you need to tell her to get the info."

"What are you going to do now?"

"I'm going to wake up G.W. and have a little man-to-man talk with the old buzzard."

WHEN TESSA WOKE, she looked over in the bed beside her and found it empty. She snapped up and looked around, then heard someone moving around in the sitting room.

"Leslie Anne?"

"Come on in here, Mama," Leslie Anne said. "Aunt Sharon just brought us a breakfast tray and she's going to stay and have coffee while we eat."

Tessa got up, raked her fingers through her hair and tied her robe's silk belt around her waist. After putting on her house slippers, she stretched several times before walking into the sitting room.

"Good morning." Sharon held out a cup of coffee to Tessa. "Leslie Anne tells me that she slept well. Did you?"

Tessa accepted the coffee, took a sip and smiled at her aunt. "Yes, I did, oddly enough. I don't remember hearing the phone ring once all night long."

"That's because the Dundee agents disconnected the phone service," Sharon said. "We're to use only our cell phones for the time being."

"Who's up and about this morning?" Tessa glanced at the wall clock and noted it was one minute past seven. "Forget I asked. I didn't realize it was only seven o'clock."

"I asked her if she'd seen Dante this morning," Leslie Anne said. "But she hasn't."

"But I did get a glimpse of that gorgeous Vic Noble." Sharon grinned. "And Lucie Evans, of course. I believe Mr. Moran is still asleep."

Tessa wanted to see Dante first thing, before the household woke and prying eyes began watching her every move. She had to tell Dante about the taunting voice and the follow-up note that Leslie Anne had received. Even though she didn't really think the culprit was Tad Sizemore, she would tell Dante that Leslie Anne suspected Olivia's darling boy. But the first thing she wanted to do the moment she and Dante were alone was to kiss him and see if kissing him would affect her the same way this morning as it had last night.

She would let Dante sleep until seven-thirty, then she would go wake him. Maybe wake him with a kiss. "I'll just take coffee this morning. I want to grab a quick shower and get dressed as soon as possible. I need to speak to the Dundee agents before I check on Daddy." Tessa looked right at Sharon. "Olivia didn't stay the night in Daddy's room, did she?"

Sharon laughed. "No, she didn't. I walked her to her room myself. The last thing G.W. needed last night was that femme fatale sharing his bed. Although giving the devil her due, I don't think she'd willingly do anything to harm G.W. After all, she wouldn't want anything to happen to her money supply, would she?"

"I guess we'll be cooped up here all day, won't we?" Leslie Anne sighed. "I mean, with the reporters camped out down at the gates and everybody in town probably talking about us, we can't show our faces in Fairport any time soon."

"I think you two should pack your bags and fly off with me to somewhere warm and exotic. Why not our place in St. Thomas?" Sharon removed the cover from a plate of cinnamon toast and held it out to Leslie Anne.

"That might not be a bad idea." Leslie Anne turned to Tessa. "What do you think, Mama? Should we run away and hide, but this time do it as a family?"

"We'll see," Tessa replied. "But not until we deal with the situation and find out who created this havoc. Once that's done, then, yes, I think a family vacation is in order."

"In the meantime, why don't you and I get outside this morning," Sharon suggested. "We can putter in the garden or go horseback riding or just take a walk."

"Will that be okay?" Leslie Anne asked Tessa.

"Yes, of course. Just stay with Aunt Sharon and don't go off alone anywhere."

DANTE KNOCKED on the door of G.W.'s bedroom suite and when he got no response, he tried the door and found it unlocked. When he entered the sitting room, he heard rustling in the other room. Assuming it was G.W., Dante waited. *Stay calm and in control,* he reminded himself. *Don't lose your temper. Don't push the old man too far too fast.* He's not going to willingly admit what he did. He has a major investment in Tessa—in Amy—and her daughter. They are his family now. He'll fight to keep them. God knows G.W. had done a great deal more than lie to his granddaughter about her paternity.

"What the hell's going on?" G.W. stomped out of the bedroom, putting on his robe as he entered the sitting area. When he saw Dante, he stopped short. "What's wrong? Has something happened to—"

Dante held up his hand in a stop gesture and walked toward G.W. "Tessa and Leslie Anne are fine. They're still asleep."

G.W. let out a relieved breath. "All right. Want to tell me why you were beating my door down at seven in the morning? If it isn't something urgent, it could have waited until later."

"It's urgent," Dante said.

"You've found the person who sent—"

"No, not yet."

"Then what is it?"

"You might want to sit down, Mr. Westbrook."

G.W. eyed him suspiciously. "I take it that this is not good news."

"Not for you."

G.W. eased down on the settee and glared at Dante. "Well, spill it."

"While Tessa and I were in Rayville, we met a very interesting old woman who worked at the Maitland Funeral Home seventeen years ago." By the strained expression on G.W.'s face, Dante could tell he recognized the name of the funeral home.

"So? What has this old woman and that funeral home to do with me and my family or our present situation?"

"You paid for a young blond woman's body to be cremated and her ashes buried in an unmarked grave. The county coroner, Aaron Maitland, took care of the job for you through his position as the owner of the Maitland Funeral Home. Tell me, G.W., just how much did you pay him to hide the fact that two of Eddie Jay Nealy's victims had been found in Richland Parish, only a week apart?"

G.W. sat perfectly still, his face somber, his eyes

downcast. "There was another girl, one of Nealy's victims who died. She fit Tessa's description, so I was called in to identify the body, in case it was Tessa."

"And it wasn't your daughter?"

"No, of course it wasn't."

"Why did you cover up the truth about this girl being one of Nealy's victims? Why have her cremated? Why pay for an expensive pink marble headstone for her? You made sure any evidence of her existence was destroyed."

G.W. lifted his head and stared at Dante, but his eyes were glazed over with memories. "You know and understand why I covered up what had happened to Tessa. I didn't want her marked for life by what had happened to her. She'd been through enough. And when I found out that no one had claimed the other girl's body, that apparently she had no family who was searching for her, I—I made arrangements for her to be taken care of."

"Why cremation?"

"I don't know. Maybe the funeral director mentioned something about it being less expensive. I can't recall the exact reason."

"It wouldn't have been because you didn't want anyone ever digging up the body to identify it?"

"Moran, what's this all about? What difference does it make to you that there was another victim and that I paid for the funeral?"

Dante moved across the room, taking slow, deliberate steps, never once taking his eyes off G.W. The old man shifted nervously.

"Why did Tessa need plastic surgery?" Dante asked.

"What?"

"She hadn't been in a car wreck. That was just the story you told. So why did she need to have plastic surgery on her face?"

"Because Nealy had beaten her severely. He'd brutalized her. Her once-pretty face was a bloody mess."

"That's odd," Dante said. "I've made a study of each of Nealy's victims whose body was found. If he disfigured Tessa's face, she was the one and only woman he did that to. So, why her?"

"How should I know? The man was a maniac."

"He was a serial killer with a specific M.O.," Dante explained. "He did brutalize his victims. He beat them, cut them, whipped them, raped them repeatedly and probably tortured them for days. But he always left the woman's face untouched."

"Well, he didn't leave Tessa's face untouched."

"I believe he did. I believe that you had a plastic surgeon operate on Tessa's face for another reason."

"That's absurd. Why would I do something like that?"

"You identified the girl in the hospital as your daughter, you brought her back to Fairport and flew in a top-notch plastic surgeon to reconstruct her face, to make her look as much like Tessa Westbrook as he possibly could. But plastic surgery could do only so much."

G.W.'s face paled. He shook his head.

"You told everyone that she'd been in a car wreck, everyone except your sister. Did you tell her the truth, the whole truth?" Dante asked. "Does she know that the woman you've been passing off as Tessa West-brook for the past seventeen years is really a young girl from Texas named Amy Smith?"

"You're out of your mind, Moran." G.W. jumped to his feet. "I didn't pay the Dundee Agency to—"

"The lies stop now. You've been found out."

"You're out of your mind, Moran."

"Did you know that Leslie Anne looks just like Amy Smith?" Dante asked.

"That's not possible! Besides, how could you possibly know? Where did you get pictures of this Amy Smith?" G.W.'s voice rose louder and louder with each word he spoke.

"Did you know that Amy Smith had a leaf-shaped birthmark identical to Tessa's and in the exact same spot?"

"What the hell are you talking about? How would you know—"

The door to G.W.'s room flew open and Tessa stood there glaring back and forth from her father to Dante. "What's going on in here? We can hear you two all the way down the hall? And what was that you just said to my father about Amy Smith and I having identical birthmarks?"

"Tell her," Dante glowered at G.W. "Tell her or I will."

"Tell me what?" Tessa looked at her father.

"It's not true," G.W. said. "Don't believe a word he says."

Tessa entered the room and stood halfway between Dante and G.W. She looked right at Dante and asked, "Whatever it is, I want to know."

Dante swallowed. God, he'd thought this would be easier. But he suddenly realized that Tessa might not be as thrilled as he was to learn her true identity. It didn't matter. He'd gone too far to have second thoughts now.

"You're going to find this difficult to believe," Dante said. "But I have every reason to believe that you aren't Tessa Westbrook."

CHAPTER TWENTY-TWO

THERE WAS A CHILL in the air this morning, but that wasn't unusual for late October in Mississippi. Leslie Anne loved this time of year. Autumn was her favorite season when the world around her came alive with brilliant colors. She also loved spending time with Aunt Sharon because her great-aunt said and did the most outrageous things. And she didn't treat Leslie Anne as if she were a child. Hadn't it been Aunt Sharon who'd given her that first driving lesson when she was eleven and in Granddaddy's vintage Porsche no less? And who had answered her question about why little boys had wee-wees and little girls didn't, when she'd been in kindergarten and Jason Stuart pulled down his pants during playtime? As she'd grown older, she'd come to understand why Granddaddy often criticized his sister for her outrageous lifestyle. Aunt Sharon drank, smoked and cursed like an old sailor. She also had hordes of boyfriends, some young enough to be her son. But despite all her aunt's flaws, Leslie Anne adored the woman.

As they strolled through the garden, Aunt Sharon puffed on her cigarette, then paused and glanced at Leslie Anne. "Is it too cool out here for you? If it is, we can go back in."

"I'm fine, if you are. I'd rather be out here when everyone is getting up and things start buzzing in the house again. I don't see why the whole bunch had to spend the night. It's not like any of them can actually do a damn thing to help us."

"Young lady, did I hear the word damn come out of your mouth?" Aunt Sharon's tone was deadly serious, but she wasn't able to maintain the accompanying stern look. She kept her lips pressed together in an effort not to smile, but she couldn't repress a throaty chuckle.

"You do a pretty good imitation of Granddaddy," Leslie Anne said. "Except he never laughs when he's scolding me."

Sharon put her arm around Leslie Anne's shoulders and gave her a squeeze. "G.W. doesn't mean to be such a stick-in-the-mud. He just wants you to be a lady, like your mother and grandmother."

"I know."

Sharon nodded. "We could go down to the summerhouse and build a fire in the fireplace. What do you say?"

Before Leslie Anne could reply, Olivia came rushing toward them, all aflutter. It wasn't until Olivia reached them that Leslie Anne saw Tad standing on the patio, watching. A shiver of uneasiness rippled up her spine. She didn't like Tad. And she didn't trust him.

"Sharon, please come with me," Olivia said, then glanced at Leslie Anne. "It's nothing to concern you, dear. I—I have a slight emergency and need your aunt's assistance." Turning back to Sharon, she looked at her pleadingly. "Now, please. And do hurry."

"Olivia, what on earth's gotten into you? Is the house on fire?" Sharon asked.

The highly agitated way Olivia was acting sparked Leslie Anne's curiosity. "Must be something important. Why don't we just go back to the house with Olivia—"

"No!" Olivia cried, then took a deep breath. "I mean, there's no reason for you not to finish your morning walk. Tad will be glad to accompany you." She glanced over her shoulder and motioned to her son. "I wouldn't ask if it weren't important."

"Oh, all right." Sharon grimaced, then said to Leslie Anne, "Whatever this is, it shouldn't take long and then we'll have the whole morning together. Is that okay with you?"

"Sure, go ahead. I'll be fine." She'd be fine all right, but she had no intention of wandering off alone somewhere with Tad Sizemore.

After her aunt and Olivia headed back toward the house, she didn't wait for Tad to catch up with her before she hurried off toward the summerhouse. She'd build a fire there, then curl up in one of the rattan chairs and do her best to forget, for just a little while, that her life would never be the same again. Not now that everyone in Fairport knew the truth about her and her mother. And if Tad insisted on bothering her, she'd tell him straight out that she didn't want his company.

"Wait up, kid," Tad called. "I've been assigned to baby-sit you."

Not slowing down her fast gait, she called back to him, "I don't need a baby-sitter. Go away and leave me alone."

"Sorry. Afraid I can't do that."

There was something in the way he'd spoken that unnerved her. She paused momentarily, then quickly glanced over her shoulder. Her gut instincts warned her to run. But with Tad blocking the path, she couldn't run back to the house.

THAT'S IT, LITTLE GIRL. Run. Run as fast as you can. You're all alone. No one, not even you, realize how alone you really are. How vulnerable. What easy prey. Where are all those Dundee agents when you need them? Inside the house, waiting for instructions and listening to the hullabaloo going on upstairs. Whatever had G.W. so upset that you could hear his ranting and raving throughout the entire house will keep everyone occupied long enough for me to do what has to be done. How convenient that all the attention is focused on G.W. at the moment, that no one is keeping tabs on Leslie Anne.

That's it, little girl. Keep running. I'm right behind you.

From the direction in which she's heading, she must be going to the summerhouse. Good. That's not far from the river. If I can't persuade her to continue her morning stroll near the cliff overlooking the river, then I'll use force. After all, I'm bigger and stronger and if necessary, I can knock her out and carry her. I have to do away with Leslie Anne before anyone realizes she's all alone and missing. I'd be a fool not to take this golden opportunity. Another like it might not present itself anytime soon. I'll toss the little bitch off the cliff to her death; then while they're all searching for her, I'll sneak up to her suite and type the suicide note. Perfect timing is essential. I must take every precaution not to be caught. And there is no reason anyone would suspect me. Don't I love Leslie Anne? Haven't I loved her since the day she was born?

"YOU GODDAMN lying son of a bitch," G.W. bellowed at Dante. "Don't listen to him, Tessa. Don't listen to a word he says. He's crazy. I want him out of here." He glared menacingly at Dante. "You're fired! The whole lot of you."

"Daddy, will you please calm down?" Tessa felt

torn in two as she glanced back and forth from her father to Dante. She'd heard what Dante had said, but her brain hadn't been able to fully process the information. She stared at Dante. "What do you mean, I'm not really Tessa Westbrook?"

"Don't you say another word, Moran," G.W. warned. "So help me God, I'll kill you if you voice that damn lie again."

"It's not a lie and you know it," Dante said. "The girl you identified as your daughter seventeen years ago in that Richland Parish hospital wasn't really Tessa Westbrook and you know it. She was Amy Smith, a seventeen-year-old girl from Colby, Texas."

"Lies. All lies. The man is mad!" G.W. dived toward Dante, murder in his eyes.

Tessa jumped between her father and Dante, laid her hands on G.W.'s chest and held him off. "Look at me, Daddy. Look at me and tell me Dante is wrong, that he's mistaken."

G.W. inhaled and exhaled, then focused on Tessa's face. "He's mistaken. He's as wrong as wrong can be. You're Tessa. My Tessa. Anne's little girl. I brought you home to your mother badly damaged, but still alive. You have to understand that it would have killed Anne if she'd lost our only child. And she had such a short time to live as it was."

The truth hit Tessa like a sledgehammer right between the eyes, creating not only emotional anguish, but mental overload and physical pain. As she looked deeply into her father's brown eyes, she gasped and began shaking. Oh, God…oh, God! This couldn't be happening. This wasn't real. She was still asleep and having a nightmare.

"Daddy…" Her voice sounded strange, even to her.

"You're mine. My daughter. And Leslie Anne is my granddaughter. Nothing that man—" G.W. pointed to Dante "—says will change that fact. Please, Tessa, believe me. I love you and Leslie Anne more than anything in this world."

She saw her father crumble before her very eyes, like a sand castle destroyed by the incoming tide. Instinctively she wrapped her arms around him. "It's all right, Daddy. We'll work through this. And I know you love me and Leslie Anne. We love you, too, and nothing will ever change that. I promise you."

Tessa led G.W. over to a wing chair, urged him to sit, then knelt in front of him and held his hands. "Tell me the truth. Was the girl who was cremated and buried in Richland Parish Amy Smith or Tessa Westbrook?"

Looking down at their clasped hands, G.W. wept. Tears streamed down his cheeks. "The sheriff called me to come in and identify the body because the girl fit my missing daughter's description. I prayed that when I got there, it wouldn't be Tessa. I knew if Tessa was dead, Anne would die, too, that without her daughter, she'd lose the will to live." G.W. lifted his face and through tear-filled eyes, looked at Tessa. "The dead girl was our daughter."

Tessa felt as if a huge hand was squeezing the life out of her. She held on to G.W.'s hands tightly as she glanced over her shoulder at Dante. He came toward her, but when she shook her head, he paused several feet behind her. With her mind whirling crazily and a feeling of numbness creeping through her, Tessa concentrated on her father. *But he's not your father,* an inner voice reminded her. *Because you aren't really Tessa Westbrook.*

"Am I Amy Smith?" she asked G.W.

He shook his head. "Possibly. I never knew your name for sure, but Sheriff Wadkins told me that there was a girl from Texas who'd come up missing right after my Tessa had and there was a good chance you were a girl named Amy Smith. An orphan. A girl with no family to miss her or mourn her, so I made arrangements—financial arrangements—with the sheriff, his one deputy who knew the truth and with the coroner. I thought I'd buried the truth along with...with my daughter."

Tessa glanced back at Dante again. Their gazes collided. At that moment, she wasn't sure who she felt sorrier for—G.W. or Dante. And she was torn between the two men—the man she thought of as her father and the man who was her lover, who had been her first and only love when she had been Amy Smith.

Perhaps she'd been born Amy Smith and lived the

first seventeen years of her life as Amy Smith, but that wasn't who she was now. She was Tessa Westbrook. She didn't remember Dante as a teenager or anything about her former life in Texas.

And she never would remember.

Concentrating on her father—and G. W. Westbrook was her father, now and forever—Tessa reached out and wiped away his tears with her fingertips. Looking him square in the eyes, she smiled at him. "Daddy, I love you. Maybe what you did was wrong, but I believe you did it for all the right reasons."

"I swear to you that—" he gulped "—even though saving Anne from the heartache of losing her only child was my main consideration at the time, I thought I was doing something good for you, too. A poor little orphan girl. It was as if God sent you to me—to us."

"I believe He did. It was meant for me to help Mother through the last years of her life and to give y'all a grandchild."

G.W. cupped Tessa's face and pulled her to him for a kiss. "You are as much mine as if you'd been born to me. And God, you must know the sun rises and sets on Leslie Anne as far as I'm concerned."

A loud, thunderous knocking interrupted them, then the door to G.W.'s suite flew open.

"G.W., what the hell's going on? Olivia said something terrible was happening up here, that you were bellowing like a bull." Sharon stormed into the room, then paused and looked from one person to the other. "My God, what is it? All three of you are crying." She stared wide-eyed at Dante.

"G.W., darling." When Olivia started toward G.W., Sharon reached out and grabbed the woman's arm.

Not now! Not now! Tessa wanted to scream. *And not in front of Olivia.*

"Olivia, I appreciate your wanting to help," Sharon said. "But I believe this is a family matter. Would you please leave us alone?"

"G.W., is that what you want?" Olivia looked pitifully at G.W.

"Yes," G.W. said. "Sharon's right. This is a family matter."

Tossing her head back in a show of hurt feelings, Olivia turned and marched out of the room, but left the door open behind her. Dante walked over and closed the door.

Sharon stared at him. "Family doesn't include you, Mr. Moran."

"Dante stays," Tessa said in no uncertain terms as she rose to her feet.

Sharon grunted. "I want to know what the hell has happened."

"Tessa knows," G.W. said.

"Of course she knows," Sharon replied. "The whole frigging state of Mississippi probably knows by now."

Suddenly Tessa realized that if Aunt Sharon was

here, then she wasn't with Leslie Anne. Surely Sharon hadn't left her alone, not after Tessa had specifically told her not to.

"Where's Leslie Anne?" Tessa asked.

"What? Oh, she's with Tad," Sharon said. "When Olivia came rushing to find me, Tad was with her and he volunteered to stay with Leslie Anne."

"No," Tessa said. "God, no!"

"What's wrong?" Dante asked.

"Tad is the last person on earth Leslie Anne should be with," Tessa said. "She's convinced that he's the person who sent her the newspaper clippings. And yesterday morning, this strange voice woke her, saying 'Leslie Anne, who's your daddy?' and then she found a note with the same message hidden in her napkin on her breakfast tray. She told me late last night that she thinks Tad is behind everything that's happened recently."

"Why would she think Tad was—" Sharon looked at Tessa.

"Damn, I wouldn't put it past that good-for-nothing boy." G.W. shot out of the chair. "We've got to find her." G.W. looked at Dante. "I'll deal with you later. But for now, you're rehired. Get out there and find my granddaughter before that stupid boy fills her head with a lot of other nonsense."

"I'm sorry," Sharon said. "I had no idea. If I'd known…"

Tessa and Dante rushed out of the bedroom suite

together and made a mad dash down the hall. When they reached the top of the stairs, Tessa paused long enough to say, "Leslie Anne is my first priority, but as soon as I know she's safe, you and I will talk."

He nodded. "Let's go find your daughter."

Thankful to have Dante at her side, Tessa hurried downstairs, protecting her daughter Tessa's only thought.

"NEED HELP building that fire?"

Leslie Anne jumped around, then smiled when she saw who the intruder was. "I've just about got it, but thanks."

"How are you this morning?"

"I'm okay."

"Are you sure? You know you can always talk to me. I realize you've got your mother and G.W., but since they were involved in the cover-up, you might not want to talk to them."

Leslie Anne sighed. "I was pretty angry with them when I first found out and I acted like an idiot by running away, but now I'm determined to act like a grown-up. Lucie Evans told me that if I wanted to be treated like an adult, I should start acting like one."

"Are you saying that an adult wouldn't be upset if she found out her biological father was a serial killer who had impregnated her mother when he raped her?"

Leslie Anne gasped. "Does the fact that Eddie Jay

Nealy is my biological father make you think less of me?" Realization suddenly dawned. "You—you already knew, didn't you? You knew the truth about what happened to my mother. You knew there was no John Allen. How long have you known?"

"For quite some time. And does that knowledge make me feel differently about you, think less of you? Of course it does. I've always been rather fond of you because you were Tessa's child, but once I learned the truth—that you were that monster's daughter—I hated you almost as much as I hated him for what he'd done to Tessa."

Leslie Anne backed away, fear clutching at her heart. She had thought the worst thing she had to fear was the knowledge that Eddie Jay Nealy had fathered her. But looking into a set of cold gray eyes, she knew it wasn't. Leslie Anne realized she should fear for her life.

CHAPTER TWENTY-THREE

DANTE HAD Lucie wake Dom and alert him and Vic of the problem. Their objective was to find Leslie Anne Westbrook. Everything else had to wait, at least temporarily. He had no choice but to put aside his personal feelings and concentrate solely on finding Tessa's child. *Amy's child.* God only knew how he'd put his feelings on hold, even for a few minutes, let alone however long it would take to track down Leslie Anne, not when she could well be anywhere on the vast Leslie plantation? He could and would do it for Tessa's sake because he loved her. He'd loved her as Amy Smith seventeen years ago and now he loved her as Tessa Westbrook. What difference did her name make to him? None. Absolutely none. She was the girl he'd loved, the woman he loved. And he felt certain that she loved him, too.

But she will never remember her life as Amy. She'll never remember what the two of you shared.

"Look, there's Tad," Tessa cried. "He's coming out of the summerhouse. But I don't see Leslie Anne."

"You stay here," Dante said. "Let me talk to him."

"If he's said something to upset Leslie Anne, I'll—"

"Morning," Tad called to them and threw up his hand. "Is everything all right with G.W.? We could hear him hollering through the whole house, and Mother was terribly worried."

Dante rushed ahead of Tessa and met Tad coming up the path. He grasped the guy by the lapels of his fancy suede jacket and glared at him. "Where's Leslie Anne?"

Tad gulped. "I—I don't know. She ran off and left me. I've been looking all over for her." He glanced down at where Dante gripped his jacket. "Would you mind not wrinkling the material. This jacket cost a small fortune."

Dante loosened his hold, but didn't release Tad. "Sharon Westbrook said she left Leslie Anne with you. What did you say to her to make her run off?"

An incredulous expression formed on Tad's face. "I didn't say boo to the kid. She told me to get lost, that she wanted to be alone. What the hell's the matter with y'all anyway?"

Dante let go of Tad's lapels. "If you're the one who sent Leslie Anne those newspaper clippings and have been harassing her, I'll—"

"You think I—" Tad gulped several times. "I didn't do it. I swear. How could I have possibly known what happened to Tessa all those years ago?

Hell, man, seventeen years ago, I was only twelve. Besides, that information was top secret, wasn't it? You'd do better trying to find somebody who would have had a way of finding out and a reason to want to upset the applecart."

Tessa came up beside Dante. "Tad, swear to me that you didn't—"

"I swear." He crossed his heart. "I didn't know. Not until everybody else found out. And even if I had known, I wouldn't have told Leslie Anne. My father was a real piece of work, too, so I understand how it is. I wish I'd never known who my father was."

Tessa placed her hand on Dante's arm. "I believe him," she said.

"Yeah, I do, too. Which means—"

Tessa sighed. "She's out there somewhere alone, and we still don't know who sent her those newspaper clippings or who sneaked into her room and taunted her while she was sleeping and left a note on her breakfast tray yesterday morning."

Dante had a bad feeling in the pit of his stomach. A really bad feeling. Instinct warned him that something more was going on here than someone revealing an ugly truth about Tessa having been raped and Leslie Anne being the rapist's child. Someone hadn't hesitated to emotionally harm Leslie Anne. What if that person intended to harm her physically? But the real question was why and who? When a man as wealthy as G. W. Westbrook was involved, Dante's guess was that the motive somehow revolved around money. G.W.'s millions.

Dante hitched his thumb toward the house. "You're free to go," he told Tad.

As soon as Tad was out of earshot, he turned to Tessa. "We'll find her soon. She can't have gone far." He wanted to allay Tessa's fears, but he needed information from her that might shed some light on who would benefit if Leslie Anne was out of the way. "I have to ask you something, but I don't want you to go reading anything sinister into what I ask."

"What is it? Tell me." Panic laced Tessa's voice.

Dante grasped her shoulders. "Don't go nuts on me, honey. Okay?"

"Okay."

"Have you seen your father's—G.W.'s—will?"

"I'm not sure what you're asking."

"Are you and Leslie Anne his beneficiaries?"

"Yes, we're the major beneficiaries," Tessa replied. "He's provided generously for Aunt Sharon and Aunt Myrle, too. And he left stock in Westbrook, Inc. to Celia and Charlie."

"On G.W.'s death, you inherit Westbrook, Inc., right? And the bulk of G.W.'s money, too, then in turn Leslie Anne is your sole beneficiary."

"Yes, that's right, but—" Tessa sucked in deep breaths. "Why are you asking me about Daddy's will? Dante, please, you can't think someone—"

"If Leslie Anne isn't in the picture and for some

reason you can't run Westbrook, Inc., who takes charge? Who runs the company and oversees G.W.'s vast fortune? Who is the next in line? Your aunt Sharon? Or someone else?"

Tessa cried out as she held up her hands in a stop gesture. "You're wrong about this. Tell me you're wrong. He'd never harm Leslie Anne in any way. He loves her. He was willing to marry me and adopt her."

Dante shook Tessa gently to gain her full attention. "Are you saying that Charlie Sentell is—"

"If for any reason I can't act as the executor of Daddy's will, then that task falls to Charlie. Or at least it did. Only a few weeks ago, Daddy told me he planned to change his will and name Walker Benson, a Westbrook, Inc. vice president, as the backup executor because he'd come to realize what a poor businessman Charlie is."

"Did Sentell know your father intended to—?"

"Yes, of course. I was there when Daddy told Charlie, but Daddy assured Charlie that his inheritance hadn't changed, that he would still receive a—"

"Has the will been changed?"

"Not yet."

"How did Sentell react when G.W. told him what he intended to do?"

"At first he was upset, but then he calmed down rather quickly. Perhaps too quickly." Tessa laid her hands on Dante's chest. "I'm telling you that it can't be Charlie. He doesn't have it in him to harm anyone, least of all Leslie Anne. Charlie loves me—he loved Tessa Westbrook—and he loves Leslie Anne."

"Are you willing to bet your daughter's life on it?"

CHARLIE GRUNTED as he walked along the unkempt path leading to the cliff overlooking the river. He'd taken a seldom used route, just in case anyone was looking for Leslie Anne. Slowing his pace, he shifted Leslie Anne in his arms. She was deadweight. The girl was heavier than she looked.

It had been so easy to pick up one of the small logs in the bucket beside the fireplace and tap her on the head with it. After all, once he tossed her over the cliff, she'd go rolling and tumbling, hitting her head and bruising her body on the way down. Later on, who would be able to say she'd received a blow to her head before she jumped to her death?

REGAINING CONSCIOUSNESS, Leslie Anne felt totally disoriented. And her head hurt like hell. She opened her eyes a fraction and realized someone was carrying her. *Charlie? Think, Leslie Anne, think,* she told herself. *What happened to you?* The last thing she remembered was bending over the fireplace at the summerhouse. Something hit her in the head. What?

Charlie had been there. He'd know. She started to ask him, but a gut reaction stopped her, warning her to remain quiet. Why was Charlie carrying her? Was he rushing her back to the house? Or was he—?

Grunting, Charlie shifted her weight in his arms. She closed her eyes and kept them closed as she tried to think.

"How can such a little thing be so damn heavy?" Charlie said aloud. "Just hang in there. It's not much farther."

What wasn't much farther? Leslie Anne wondered. The house? Help? What?

Why couldn't she think straight? Maybe it was because her head kept pounding as if a giant hammer was beating on it. And she felt sick to her stomach and terribly dizzy.

Suddenly Charlie stopped. He heaved a deep sigh. Leslie Anne opened her eyes a fraction and glanced around. They were nowhere near the house. Actually they were on the cliff overlooking the river. Why had Charlie brought her here?

Before she realized his intentions, Charlie lifted her out over the edge of the cliff and let go of her. Realization hit her suddenly. She screamed and grasped for Charlie, barely managing to grab hold of his jacket.

"Damn, I thought I'd knocked you out cold."

What was he saying? He really did intend to throw her over the cliff, didn't he?

As she held on for dear life, she looked up at him and said, "Why are you doing this?"

He grabbed her wrists and jerked her hands off his jacket, then her held tightly, dangling her over the edge. Her feet swayed in the air as she thrashed about, trying to find her footing.

"If Tessa had married me, she could have saved you and herself. If she'd married me, it could have all been mine. That was G.W.'s plan—for Tessa and me to marry. And even when she kept refusing me, I thought that eventually she'd give in. So did G.W. That's why he made me the executor of his will, if for any reason Tessa couldn't be. But he finally gave up and so did I."

"I'm confused, Charlie. How is killing me going to change anything?"

"You'll be dead and Tessa will have a nervous breakdown," Charlie said. "And all this will happen before G.W. changes his will that leaves me in charge of his fortune."

"Please, don't do this." She thrashed around like mad, trying to get her feet to touch the ground.

"Stop wiggling around," he told her. "I'll drop you if you don't be still."

He laughed, the sound frighteningly maniacal.

Leslie Anne caught a glimpse of someone coming up behind Charlie. Since her vision was slightly blurred, she couldn't make out who it was. But it had to be someone who'd help her. If she could just manage to keep Charlie from tossing her over the cliff for another minute or two, there might be a chance she wouldn't die.

"How did you find out about Eddie Jay Nealy

being my father?" she asked. *Keep him talking. Buy yourself some time.* "Have you always known? Did Granddaddy tell you?"

"Inquisitive little bitch, aren't you? But don't think you can say or do anything that will stop me."

"Please, just tell me before you…"

"Your aunt Sharon let it slip one night when she was as high as a kite and we were in bed together. The next morning she didn't even remember I'd screwed her, let alone that she'd told me the family's deep dark secret."

"Please, Charlie, don't do this. Please." She felt him loosening his grip, releasing her wrists. He was going to drop her. She'd fall off and down the cliff and hit either the water or the bank below. Either way, she'd be dead.

"Help me!" Leslie Anne screamed as Charlie released her and let her fall free.

CHAPTER TWENTY-FOUR

DANTE SHOVED Charlie Sentell aside as he reached out for Leslie Anne, praying with everything in him that he could save Tessa's child, a child who, under different circumstances might have been his. With one foot planted firmly on the edge of the cliff and the other skidding precariously over the ledge, he grabbed Leslie Anne around the waist, then yanked her toward him and into his arms. His foot slipped. Dirt and grass oozed up around his shoes as he dropped to his knees, all the while hanging onto the priceless bundle in his arms. He fell backward, onto the solid earth. He heard rather than saw the struggle between Tessa and Charlie. The man screeched incoherently as Tessa kept asking him why.

Dante rolled over and laid Leslie Anne on the grass. Their gazes met. He reached over and caressed her cheek. "You're safe, honey. Stay put."

She nodded. He came up on his knees, then stood. Tessa pounded her fists all over Charlie's head and chest as he tried to duck and at the same time grab her. Just as Dante moved in to grasp Charlie, the man managed to circle Tessa's waist and whirl her around so that her back was to his chest. Before Dante could do anything except watch helplessly, Tessa gave Charlie a backward shove and the two of them went plummeting over the edge of the cliff. Dante cried out and grasped for Tessa, but their hands missed by a hairbreadth. He rushed to the ledge and watched as Tessa grabbed hold of a thick tree root protruding out of the side of the jagged cliff. Charlie hung on to Tessa, refusing to release her. Dante held his breath and prayed.

This couldn't be happening. He couldn't lose Amy a second time. The first time had nearly destroyed him.

"Tessa!" He lowered himself to his belly and extended his reach as far down the side of the embankment as he could, but his grasp didn't extend quite far enough to reach her. "Let her go, you son of a bitch," Dante called to Charlie.

"Never." Charlie Sentell smiled.

Damn the bastard.

Tessa wriggled, trying to free herself from Charlie's tenacious grip. Suddenly his hold about her waist began to loosen. His hands slid down her hips. She wriggled again as she hung on to the tree root with every ounce of her strength. Dante tried again to reach her, leaning over the edge as he dug the toes of his shoes into the earth.

Charlie's death grip eased down Tessa's thighs.

"I can't hold on much longer," Tessa cried to Dante. "He's pulling me as hard as he can."

"Hold on, Tessa. Please, honey, hold on."

Suddenly two big hands circled Dante's ankles from behind. He glanced over first one shoulder and then the other. Dom Shea held his right ankle, Vic Noble the left.

Thank you, God!

With Dom and Vic holding him, Dante inched farther down the rocky embankment until his fingertips grazed Tessa's. Holding her around the calves, Charlie gave Tessa one final jerk. Simultaneously, Dante grabbed onto Tessa's hands and pulled while Charlie Sentell lost his hold on her and fell through the air. Dante tugged Tessa up, as Charlie fell.

Dante was too busy holding Tessa in his arms to see Charlie hit the river below, but in the back of his mind he thought that no one could survive such a fall.

"Oh, Dante." Tessa melted against him, holding him with all her might.

"He's our hero, Mama. He saved me again. And he saved you."

Leslie Anne pulled away from Lucie, who'd been holding her back, and came running toward her mother and Dante. Tessa eased out of Dante's embrace and opened her arms for her daughter. The moment she engulfed Leslie Anne, Dante wrapped his arms protectively around both of them.

"Lucie, why don't you help Dante get Ms. Westbrook and Leslie Anne back to the house?" Dom said. "Vic and I will call the sheriff and then go down to the river and see if we can locate Sentell's body."

SEVERAL HOURS LATER, after Sheriff Coburn had come and gone, after Charlie's body had been retrieved from the river and after G.W. had issued a command for everyone—Celia, Myrle, Olivia and Tad—to go home, Tessa pulled Dante out of Leslie Anne's room.

"Are you sure you're ready to leave her alone?" Dante asked.

"She's not alone. Aunt Sharon and Daddy are with her and will stay with her so you and I have a few minutes to talk."

"Do you think we can hash everything out in a few minutes?"

"We can't hash out *everything*—" she emphasized the word "—if we live to be a hundred. But I think there are a few things we can settle pretty quickly."

"Such as?"

"Let's go downstairs," she said. "We need complete privacy."

Dante followed her down the stairs and into the library. She closed and locked the door, then turned to him. All he could see was Amy's blue eyes looking at him.

"I might have once been a girl named Amy Smith, but I have no memory of being her. For all intents and purposes I'm Tessa Westbrook. Can you accept me for who I am *now?*"

"What do you mean? Can I love you the way I once did now that you go by a different name? Of course I can. I do. I think on some purely instinctive level I sensed all along that you were Amy."

She groaned. "That's just it. I'm not Amy. I can never be Amy again. No matter how much either of us wish I could remember the past, remember what we meant to each other, I can't remember. I never will. The doctors explained that any memories I had are lost to me forever."

"I know that." His mind knew what she was saying was true, but his heart was having a difficult time accepting the fact. This beautiful woman—the only woman he had ever loved—wasn't Amy Smith any longer.

When he reached for her, she sidestepped him. "You were attracted to me when you didn't know I was Amy, so do you think you can learn to love Tessa Westbrook?"

"I do love you, no matter what your name is. You and I were made for each other. We were destined to be together," he told her. "God has given us a second chance, the kind of second chance most people only dream of—having a lost love return from the dead."

"I believe you could be right about that." She smiled at him, all the while tears gathered in her eyes.

Amy's eyes.

"Even when we didn't recognize each other, our

hearts—maybe even our souls—knew who the other was," Dante said.

"Things won't be the same, you know. I'm not Amy Smith. And you're not that crazy-in-love nine-teen-year-old boy."

He walked toward her, determined to hold her. To hold Amy in his arms once again.

She didn't hesitate, didn't put up an argument of any kind when he embraced her. She wrapped her arms around his waist and lifted her face for his kiss.

The sweetest kiss he'd ever known.

And then they simply held each other. And cried.

TIME STOOD STILL. Lost all significance as Dante held her. She didn't remember loving him when she'd been Amy Smith, but she loved him now as Tessa Westbrook. Whether or not her heart remembered him, she didn't know. But there wasn't a doubt in her mind that her soul recognized his, that their souls were united now and for all eternity.

"Dante?"

"Hmm…?"

"Were we lovers?" she asked. "I mean were you and Amy lovers?"

He cupped her chin and lifted her face. "Yes, we were lovers. I told you, didn't I, that she—that you wouldn't even let me kiss you for a couple of months after we first started dating."

Her heart had come up with this incredible notion

and she had to voice it, had to find out if what she hoped for could possibly be true. "Dante, did we make love anytime close to the night I was…that Eddie Jay Nealy kidnapped me?"

He kissed her forehead, then looked directly at her. "The night before you disappeared, we made love in my car. We pulled off into an alley there in town and made love before I took you home."

She grasped Dante's hand. "If we made love right before I was kidnapped, then isn't it possible that I got pregnant that night? Don't you think there's a chance that Leslie Anne could be yours?"

He pulled away from her. "You don't know how I wish that was true. I'd give anything if I was Leslie Anne's father."

"But you don't think you are, do you? Is it impossible?"

He shook his head. "No, it's not impossible, just highly improbable. You see, Amy and I—you and I used protection. I never made love to you without using a condom."

Hope died within her. But not quite all hope. "Condoms aren't foolproof."

"No, they're not."

"I think we should make certain that she isn't yours," Tessa said.

"When we have the DNA test run on you to confirm that you are Amy Smith, we'll have one run on Leslie Anne to see if she's mine."

Tessa held out her hands to him. "And if she's not? If she really is Eddie Jay Nealy's?"

Dante took her hands in his and pulled her to him. "I love you…Tessa. I want to spend the rest of my life with you, if you'll have me. And I'd like to be a father to Leslie Anne, whether she's biologically my child or not."

"Oh, Dante, do you mean that? Do you love me…love my daughter and me so much that it doesn't matter?"

"Lady, the only thing on earth that matters to me is that you're alive and in my arms and that you're mine. Now and forever."

"I love you, Dante Moran. I'm sure I loved you when I was Amy Smith, but I can't believe I loved you then half as much as I do now."

"You're going to marry me one of these days, aren't you?" He nuzzled her neck.

"You bet I am. But maybe you and I should get to know each other. After all, you're a stranger to me and despite your having known me as Amy Smith, you really don't know Tessa Westbrook all that well."

"How long a courtship do you have in mind?" he asked. "I'm a patient man, honey. I've waited seventeen years to find you, so I can wait a little while longer to make you my wife. But not too long."

"How does six months sound to you?"

Groaning, he frowned at her. "During that six months, we don't have to be celibate, do we?"

She laughed. "God, I hope not. Now that I've discovered how fabulous sex can be, I'll probably be jumping you every chance I get."

"I like the sound of that."

Tessa took his hand. "I should be getting back to Leslie Anne."

"I'll go with you. It's time I got to know my new daughter."

"Oh, Dante." Emotion caught in her throat. If only…dear Lord, if only… "I don't want Leslie Anne to know that there's a chance you might be her father. Not until we get back the DNA results. I'm not going to build up her hopes only for her to find out that you're not her father."

"I agree," he said. "But between now and then, I'm going to prove to Leslie Anne what a great dad I can be."

Together, hand in hand, Tessa and Dante left the library, walked up the stairs and to Leslie Anne's room. Tessa would cherish that fragile kernel of hope in her heart. If there was any true justice in this world, Dante would be her daughter's father. But whether he was or not, she knew that the three of them could be a family, just as she and Leslie Anne and G.W. and Sharon were a family. Love and commitment made a family, not just the bonds of blood.

The minute Dante opened the door to Leslie Anne's sitting room, she came rushing toward him. "Aunt Sharon and Granddaddy told me all about how mother was once a girl named Amy Smith and that you two were in love and…oh, Mama…Dante…it's all so wonderful, isn't it?"

"Yes, sweetheart." Tessa wrapped her arms around her daughter. "It's all so very wonderful."

EPILOGUE

TESSA LAY in the hammock on the porch of their vacation house on St. Thomas, her hands resting protectively over her protruding belly. She and Dante were expecting their second child in two months. The ultrasound had confirmed that this squirming little bundle of joy was a boy. They'd already chosen a name. George Wesley Moran, named for his grandfather G.W. They would call him Wes. Leslie Anne had insisted. And being the big sister gave her certain privileges.

Looking out toward the ocean, Tessa watched Leslie Anne and Dante swim to shore, both of them laughing. Tessa sighed with contentment. Her life was perfect. Absolutely perfect. Even if she would never remember being Amy Smith, she had the very best of Amy's life. She had Dante. The man she loved. The man who loved her. Loved her as both Amy Smith and as Tessa Westbrook.

He loved her so much that he'd given up his job at Dundee and gone to work for her father at Westbrook, Inc. And to G.W.'s surprise, he was turning out to have quite a head for business.

"Decaf iced tea?" G.W. held out a tall, frosty glass to Tessa.

"Thanks, Daddy." She accepted the glass and took a sip.

"Look at those two, would you?" G.W. watched Leslie Anne and Dante horsing around on the beach. "They're so close and love each other so much, you'd never realize he hadn't raised her from an infant."

Tessa reached up and grasped her father's hand. "A lot like you and me, Daddy."

G.W. smiled, a wistful look in his eyes. "You're the child of my heart, even if you're not my biological daughter." As Dante and Leslie Anne came running toward the beach house, G.W. squeezed Tessa's hand. "Thank God, Dante turned out to be Leslie Anne's real father. I know he's the kind of man who would have loved her regardless, but for her sake—and yours—I'm so very thankful."

"We all are," Tessa said, remembering the day the DNA tests had confirmed that not only was she Amy Smith, but that Leslie Anne was Dante Moran's daughter. She'd never forget the pure joy on Leslie Anne's face when they'd told her.

As soon as she came up on the porch, Leslie Anne gave her grandfather a peck on the cheek. "Where's my iced tea?"

"Coming right up," Aunt Sharon said as she brought a tray of iced tea glasses out on the porch.

Dante squatted beside Tessa and laid his hand over her stomach. "How's my boy doing? Still using mommy as a punching bag?" As if on cue, their son began squirming. Dante rose up and over Tessa, then leaned down and kissed her belly.

"Would you two like to be alone?" Leslie Anne asked jokingly. "I can take the old folks into town to do some shopping."

Sharon set the tray on the wicker table, then swatted Leslie Anne's behind. "Old folks indeed. I'll have you know that I have a date tonight with a darling young man not a day over thirty. And he's bringing his mama along for G.W."

Everyone laughed. Aunt Sharon would never change and they loved her just the way she was.

"Does he have a younger brother?" Leslie Anne asked.

"If he does, he has to pass inspection," Dante said. "You know the rules. No boy dates my daughter without my approval."

Leslie Anne groaned. "Daddy, you've scared off every boy in Fairport. Can't you leave the boys here on the island alone?"

"Not on your life," Dante told her.

Tessa reached up and dragged Dante into the hammock with her. "You three go shopping. And don't rush back. Stay all afternoon. Dante and I can amuse ourselves."

"I believe that's our cue to leave." Sharon motioned to the others, then turned around and went back inside the beach house. As soon as Leslie Anne and G.W. followed her, Dante cuddled close to Tessa. She turned so that they lay face-to-face, then she kissed him.

"I love you, Mr. Moran," she said.

"And I love you, Mrs. Moran." He patted her belly. "And I love this baby and our daughter and G.W. and Aunt Sharon. Heck, I love the whole damn world."

As they lay there in the hammock, a tropical breeze caressing them, they held each other. Not one day went by that they didn't thank God for their good fortune. They were blessed. Truly blessed. They'd been handed not one, but two miracles. A love that had been lost to them had been reborn, stronger than ever. And a child had found her true father.

Life is good, Tessa thought. Oh, yes, life is good.